BY MATTHEW NORMAN

Domestic Violets
We're All Damaged
Last Couple Standing
All Together Now

All Together Now

er Now

orMan

2021]
ebook) |
21102 (ebook)
7626 (ebook) |

OOKS

Copyright © 2021 by Matthew Norman

Published in the United States by Ballantine Books,
an imprint of Random House, a division of
Penguin Random House LLC, New York.

BALLANTINE and the HOUSE colophon are
registered trademarks of Penguin Random House LLC

Library of Congress Cataloging-in-Publication Data

Names: Norman, Matthew, author.
Title: All together now : a novel / Matthew Norman
Description: First edition. | New York : Ballantine Books,
Identifiers: LCCN 2020052210 (print) | LCCN 2020052211
ISBN 9781984821096 (hardcover ; acid-free paper) | ISBN 9781984
Classification: LCC PS3614.O7626 A78 2021 (print) | LCC PS3614.
DDC 813/.6—dc23
LC record available at lccn.loc.gov/2020052210
LC ebook record available at lccn.loc.gov/202005221

Printed in Canada on acid-free paper

randomhousebooks.com

2 4 6 8 9 7 5 3 1

First Edition

Book Design by Diane Hobbing

For Ryan Hermsen, my oldest friend

All Together Now

"I wish I had better news for you, Robbie. I really do."

Dr. Osborne laces his fingers together atop his desk as he says this, and smiles. It's a nice smile—warm and kind—but world-weary, too.

Robbie lets out a long breath. "That's a shame," he says. "You were my Hail Mary."

"I know," says Dr. Osborne. "Often when people come to see me, they're hoping everyone before me was wrong. That's not the case today, unfortunately. I'm sorry."

A fluttering V of birds passes outside.

It's sunny out—beautiful, actually—because weather doesn't care about context, it just does what it's going to do, and Robbie is surprised by a rush of sadness. After all, this was *always* what Dr. Osborne was going to say. Earlier, as he lay perfectly still during the humming CT scan, Robbie doubted that he'd feel anything. But now here he is, feeling. "This must be the worst part of your job," he says.

"What's that?" asks Dr. Osborne.

"The part where you have to tell people that there's no hope."

A kid's crayon drawing hangs on the wall behind Dr. Osborne, yellowed with age. World's #1 Dad. "You know, I don't like to think in those terms," he says. "Hope means different things to different people."

Looking through the window again, Robbie sees a small bird, alone against the clear sky, rushing to catch up to its flock. Even from a thousand feet away, Robbie can see how desperate it is, flapping and flapping.

"But as I was saying. I'm afraid I agree with your other doctors. With their diagnoses. The severity, in particular. The timeline, too. All of it."

Robbie has an idea that if he continues talking—if the two of them keep chatting here in this cluttered office overlooking a vast Minnesota parking lot—the clock won't start ticking down just yet. But all he can think to say is "Shit."

"Agreed," says Dr. Osborne. "Sometimes that's the best word we've got."

"So that's it, then?" asks Robbie.

"No, not at all. Sure, it's the end of *one* thing. But, in a way, it's the beginning of something else. With our diagnosis set, we can focus on what comes next. We can think about things like your comfort. About the quality of your life. Most importantly, we can think about helping you make the time you have as full and fulfilling as we can."

Robbie nods, taking all of this in. "Yeah, but that's . . . *it, though,* right?"

Dr. Osborne tilts his head and lifts his shoulders just slightly— the world's most sophisticated shrug.

"All right," says Robbie. "But that last thing you said, the full and fulfilling part?"

Dr. Osborne shifts in his chair. "You've lived an extraordinary life, Robbie. That's all well-documented. The work you've done. The things you've accomplished. I can't imagine fulfillment being an issue, if you don't mind me saying."

"That's nice of you to say, Dr. Osborne. But as far as what, exactly, I'm supposed to do when I leave here, I find myself at a loss."

Dr. Osborne leans forward now. Robbie does, too, and for a

silent moment they're like two men about to share a secret. "Take stock," he says.

"Take stock?"

"Yes. Of everything. Make a list of the most important people in your life. The ones who really, *truly* matter. Then, spend as much time with them as you can."

Robbie expected more. Something medical—a last-ditch effort or maybe an experimental treatment. This is better, though, because this is real. "I'll think about that," he says. "In the meantime, about your diagnosis."

"Yes?" says Dr. Osborne.

Robbie looks out the window again. No birds this time, just blue. He does some quick math in his head, because math is the most comforting thing he knows. "Would it change things at all if I offered you ten million dollars?"

Dr. Osborne's face goes still. But then, that smile again—warm and kind. The kid's drawing is of a stick man holding a baseball mitt. A pink heart floats next to a smiling sun.

"Fine," says Robbie. "I can go as high as fifteen."

Dr. Osborne's smile becomes a hopeful little laugh, because, apparently, that's his thing: hope. Who knows? Maybe he really is the World's #1 Dad. "If only it were that easy, Robbie."

He's right. If only.

Dear Baltimore Prep Rejects:

"You know, we <u>really</u> need to get together."

How many times have we said these words to each other over the last few years? Too many, right? That's why I'm writing this letter. I've decided to throw us a Memorial Day party on Fenwick Island, and you're all invited.

Travel and accommodations will be taken care of. Cat, the plane will come get you in L.A. Wade and Blair, I'll send cars to New York and D.C. to get you both. Blair, please bring Martin and the twins with you. I'd love to finally meet them.

Look for an e-mail soon with details, like addresses and a complete itinerary. But, in short: I've planned everything. All you have to do is show up. It'll be just like old times.

I know this is late notice, and you may already have plans. But I miss you guys. And, frankly, I really need to see you.

Your Friend,

Robbie

Friday

Chapter 1

Blair Harden is sitting in the sort of traffic you usually associate with movies about the end of the world. The cars are stacked in tight rows on U.S. Route 50 East. Occasionally, there'll be a brief stretch of open road—like a prison break—but then everyone slams on their brakes again.

Blair looks up through the windshield and imagines a meteor approaching. It enters the atmosphere through the clouds, cuts across the sky, and then blows everything up. Boom.

"Just go," Martin whispers from the driver's seat.

He's not addressing anyone in particular, Blair knows. This is just what her husband does: he talks to traffic.

"The gas pedal," he says. "The one on the right. Just push it."

"We should've left earlier," Blair whispers. This couldn't be less helpful, but she says it anyway, because, well, marriage. Martin squeezes the steering wheel in response.

They've opted to drive themselves to Fenwick Island instead of accepting Robbie's offer of a car. This made sense at the time, but it'd be nice now, Blair thinks, to be cradled in whatever luxurious thing Robbie would've sent for them. They've been on the road for nearly an hour now, but they're barely out of D.C., and the minivan smells like Goldfish crackers and melted crayons.

Martin taps the dashboard screen, flipping from '90s on 9 to

'80s on 8. It's an entirely symbolic gesture. The volume is so low that neither of them can hear it, because five-year-old Kenny is passed out in his car seat, and everyone in the vehicle knows that waking him for anything short of a car fire would be a catastrophic mistake.

They inch forward. Martin brakes. They inch forward some more.

There's another minivan in front of them. It's maroon, and it has a bumper sticker that says I USED TO BE COOL. It's the same model as the minivan Blair and Martin are driving: a Honda Odyssey. Their Odyssey is Lunar Silver Metallic, which is just a fancy way of saying gray. Buying a minivan was another thing that made sense at the time, but now Blair hates the Odyssey more than any other single object in her life.

"Mommy," whispers Michelle, Kenny's twin, younger by eleven agonizing minutes. She's wearing ladybug earbuds. "Can we listen to Taylor Swift?"

Blair holds her finger to her lips, and Michelle frowns.

THE BALTIMORE PREP REJECTS WERE best friends.

Correction: the Baltimore Prep Rejects *are* best friends. Tense is tricky when you're in your thirties and you're talking about people from high school, but ask any one of them who their best friends are and they'll list one another, despite the fact that they're scattered all over the country now and haven't all been in the same room in six years.

Blair McKenzie, Cat Miller, Robbie Malcolm, and Wade Stephens earned their nickname the first week of June in their senior year at Baltimore Catholic Preparatory High School. One week before graduation, three of them were expelled, one of them dropped out in solidarity, and the Baltimore Prep Rejects were born.

Blair looks back now at the twins. Michelle is focused on her iPad, and Kenny is sleeping so hard that his head looks like it's on sideways. Blair takes out her phone and scrolls back through the group's text chain from two weeks ago.

SHE WAS STANDING IN THE kitchen wearing yoga gear when Robbie's invitation arrived. It was hand delivered and expensive looking, with gold foil on fancy card stock. The Malcolm Capital logo had been pressed into a red wax seal on the envelope, like on a bottle of fancy scotch. Blair read it and immediately texted Cat.

Hey. Did you get this thing from Robbie?

It took two hours for Cat to reply, which was typical. Cat lives in L.A., so she's always dropping in and out of text chains at weird hours, like she's beaming in from a different dimension.

Just got it. You going?

Blair replied that she didn't know yet. Then she asked, You?

Ten seconds later, Cat replied, What has two thumbs and likes free beach vacations? She included two thumb emojis for emphasis.

I'll talk to Martin about it, wrote Blair.

Cat replied, Lame! Then she wrote, That's why I don't have a husband. I like being totally in charge.

Blair wrote back, Wait, THAT'S why you don't have a husband? She smiled when she saw Cat's reply, which was two dancing girl emojis, a unicorn, and a rainbow. Blair couldn't remember if Cat was seeing anyone. She didn't want to ask, though, because it would've highlighted that they hadn't spoken in a while, so, instead, she replied, Miss you, to which Cat sent a little cartoon heart.

A few hours later, after Blair had picked up the twins from school, she texted Cat again. Do you think Wade will go?

Cat wrote back, I don't see why not. Wade likes a free party as much as this girl.

Maybe we should text him, Blair wrote, going for casual.

Cat, however, saw right through it and replied with an eye-roll emoji. You mean, maybe I should text him?

Blair didn't respond. She didn't know what to say. A few minutes later, though, Cat texted again, and this time she included Wade.

Wade? Fenwick? You in?

For a while, nothing. Blair kept glancing at her phone to see if she'd missed a text. She cut carrots for the twins. She helped them with their reading flash cards. She pulled a piece of carrot out of Kenny's nose. Wade's reply came as she was loading the dishwasher.

It's bullshit that Cat gets a plane. I want a plane.

Cat chimed in immediately. So that's a yes?

I guess, wrote Wade. Should I be embarrassed that my calendar is so open?

This was rhetorical. At least that's how Cat took it, because she wrote, Wade and I are in. What say you, Blair Bear?

Blair could've asked Martin. She could've called him at his office and explained the situation. They could've discussed it, like healthy married couples are supposed to do. Instead, she wrote, We're in!

Cat sent a gif of a cat wearing a bikini, and it was settled. The Rejects were headed back to Fenwick Island.

BLAIR LOOKS BACK AGAIN. SUCH an odd instinct of motherhood: this need to constantly check on your kids, like she'll suddenly find them chugging wine coolers and smoking unfiltered cigarettes.

The trip started with a mini Taylor Swift marathon. Michelle and Kenny are on a huge Tay-Tay kick at the moment, particularly the song "Shake It Off," which they played on repeat nine times after Martin pulled out of the driveway. Nine times. Thirty-three minutes of "Shake It Off." It was a strategic move to allow it, though. Whenever the chorus played, Kenny threw himself from side to side against his car seat restraints. By the seventh time through, he'd danced himself to unconsciousness.

Martin changes lanes and shifts in his seat. This lane isn't going any faster than the one they just left. "You're *sure* you want me there this weekend, right? Like, *sure* sure?"

Martin has asked her this at least five times in the last two weeks, most recently an hour ago as they loaded Peppa Pig floaties into the Odyssey. "Yes," she says. "I am."

Brake lights reflect off his sunglasses.

"They're my best friends," she says. "They've never even met you. The twins either."

"I know," he says. "But the kids'n I, we could've stayed home, given you some adult time. I wouldn't have minded."

Blair sighs and checks Michelle and Kenny again. This time, she sees Taylor Swift, all lanky and annoyed, sitting in the wayback, shaking her head. Blair has been doing this lately: she's been imagining that Taylor Swift hangs out with them, because when you listen to the same song over and over, you lose some of your mind. Imaginary Taylor Swift shoves Michelle's pink duffel. *He doesn't get it, Blair. He just doesn't.*

Imaginary Taylor Swift is right; Martin *doesn't* get it. Which is why Blair nearly asks him, "Did you ever stop to think, Martin, that maybe this will be good for us? For our marriage?" Instead, she reminds him that he and the twins were specifically invited. "It'd be rude for you not to come," she says.

His hand moves to the display screen again, like he's going to adjust the volume, but he thinks better of it. "Do you think I'm going to feel old, though?" he asks. They pass a fender bender— two SUVs on the shoulder, flashers flashing.

"You brought your walker, right?" Blair asks. "You know how your hip acts up in this humidity."

"Ha-ha," he says. "It's just . . . you're all a lot younger than me."

"Martin, you're fifty," she says. "Fifty is the new—"

"Late forties?"

"Exactly," she says. "You could pass for, like, forty-eight, easy."

Some more distance passes, a few miles, maybe. It's hard to tell how far you've gone when you're not really moving.

"I still can't believe you went to high school with Robbie Malcolm, though," he says. "Do you have any idea what that guy's worth?"

Blair thinks about this. She *does* know, in a vague way, although once the number entered the billions she stopped trying to wrap her head around it. A few months ago, she was at Starbucks stirring Splenda into her flat white when her eyes fell on a coffee-stained *Wall Street Journal,* folded open to a random spot somewhere in the middle. The headline read:

"Robbie Malcolm Knows Everything"

"When we were sophomores, he opened an E★TRADE account for his mom," Blair says. "She put an addition on their house when we were seniors."

Martin whistles quietly through his teeth, and then they come to a full stop. Another fender bender. People keep crashing slowly into each other. "What's he like? You know, in person?"

Blair calls up an image of Robbie in her mind, her billionaire friend who looks like a perfectly normal person. "Sort of quiet," she says. "Shy at first. Mathematical. He's a very precise person."

"Makes sense," says Martin. "This is good. Let's go over Cat and Wade again. I hardly know anything about them."

"Okay, well," she says, "Cat's smart. Funny, too. She's a producer on a morning talk show in L.A. Gay. Blond. And she's short. Did I mention that? Like, fit-in-your-pocket short."

"No," says Martin. "You *didn't*. See? This is good. How about Wade? I looked up his book on Amazon. Twenty-seven reviews. It came out years ago, right?"

"Six," she says. "Six years ago." Blair aims one of the AC vents at herself. "It wasn't very successful. It's a really good book, though."

"I've never met a writer before," Martin says. "Is he . . . writery?"

"Writery?"

"You know. Does he recite poetry and wear an ascot?"

Kenny kicks the back of her seat in his sleep. "Do you know Eeyore, from Winnie-the-Pooh?" she asks.

"Eeyore?" he says. "The sad donkey-looking thing?"

"Yeah," she says. "That's Wade. He's a sad donkey. But more high functioning. He's like a tall, human version of Eeyore. And he loves the Beatles. Don't get him started on the Beatles. I'm serious. He won't shut up."

Martin is looking at her now, smiling.

"What?" she asks.

"Hon, what's up with Wade? Whenever you talk about him, you get fidgety."

"No, I don't," she says, fidgeting. She switches from the whispering '80s back to the whispering '90s, which feels like a power move.

"Might as well just tell me." He gestures to the postapocalyptic traffic. "We've got time."

"Fine," Blair says. "Wade used to be in love with me."

Martin nods, accepting this without expression or comment.

"Cat was in love with me, too, actually," she adds. "At least for a little while. That was me. I was the girl who everyone loved."

"What about Robbie?" Martin asks. "Did he love you, too?"

He's teasing her, Blair knows, and she wonders if this is so unbelievable to him: people being in love with her. "No," she says. "Robbie was always in love with Cat. He never admitted it, but he was."

Martin laughs quietly.

"What?" she asks.

He lowers his sunglasses to the tip of his nose. "This should be quite a weekend."

Chapter 2

Wade Stephens hasn't left New York yet. He's in his apartment, and he's on the phone with his literary agent, Brandon. They're forty-five seconds into their conversation, and Brandon has already sighed twice, which is never good. "Okay," Wade says. "I'm ready. What've you got for me?"

Brandon doesn't say anything. Or maybe he's hung up.

"Brandon? You there?"

"Um, like I said in my email, Wade, I don't have much."

Just then, there's a knock at Wade's apartment door. "Oh shit," he whispers.

"What?" asks Brandon.

"Someone's knocking at my door."

"Okay. Why are you whispering? Are you about to get murdered?"

"No," says Wade. "I'm pretty sure I'm about to get evicted."

Wade again wonders if Brandon has hung up on him. It would make sense, actually. As far as literary agents go, Brandon is a pretty big deal.

"You're not just trying to make me feel guilty, are you?" asks Brandon.

Another knock—a tap—as if Wade is being visited by a polite, medium-size bird. "Turns out my landlord has this crazy policy about tenants paying rent every month."

"Well, that's bullshit," says Brandon. "Get out of there. Go hide in another room or something."

"I live in a studio, Brandon. There *is* no other room. This is all the rooms."

"Go hide in your terrible little bathroom then," says Brandon. "Also, can we stop it with the whispering? I feel like we're having phone sex."

"Wade? Waaaaaaade!" It's his building manager, Mrs. Suzuki, out in the hallway. She's a sweet, very friendly little woman who sometimes brings him ginger cookies, but today she is Wade's enemy.

BRANDON IS RIGHT. WADE'S BATHROOM *is* pretty terrible.

It's about the size of a restroom on an airplane, and, for some unknown reason, it's always damp. Wade closes the door and sits on the toilet-seat lid. "Okay, I'm safe. What were you saying? *No news? Nothing?*"

Brandon sighs again—his third. The health of agent-writer relationships can be measured by this one metric: SPC, sighs per call.

"All right," says Brandon. "I'm just gonna tear off the Band-Aid here, Wade. We've gotten a few more passes. Five of them. No, wait, actually, shit, six."

"Six? You've gotten six more rejections? I talked to you, like, three days ago."

"I know," Brandon says. "It's not ideal."

"Not ideal? No kidding. You said we'd have better luck with smaller publishers."

"I know. I thought we would. I may have been wrong. This isn't a science, Wade."

"Well, what'd they say?" Wade hears typing. "Are you emailing right now?"

"I'm multitasking," says Brandon. "They said the same thing everyone has said. In a rare show of unity, the indies, the mid-tiers, and the Big Five publishers are all in agreement about not wanting to buy your second novel. It's like they're stonewalling you."

"Motherfucker," says Wade.

"I know," says Brandon.

"Shit," says Wade.

"Definitely," says Brandon.

Wade wonders if Mrs. Suzuki is still outside. He also wonders if it's possible to drown yourself in a New York City shower. "What about my first book?" he asks. "Does that count for nothing? It did well, right?"

"I don't know if you want me to tear off *all* the Band-Aids, Wade, but *Feedback* did well-*ish*. At best. Plus, that was six years ago. You have any idea how many novels James Patterson has put out in the last six years?"

"No," says Wade.

"Neither do I, actually," says Brandon. "Let's just assume it's an assload. Listen, though. Six years aside, this was *always* a tough sell. I told you that when you pitched it to me. I told you that after the first draft. I told you that *again* after the seventh—"

"I get it," Wade says.

"Sorry," says Brandon. "I'm not good at the bad-news part of this job. It's like I'm disappointed *for* you, but then I project that disappointment *onto* you. I'm working on it."

Wade looks up at his bathroom ceiling, at the water stains and flaking plaster like dirty snow. "I just don't get why nobody likes it," he says.

Brandon doesn't sigh this time, it's more of a low-level moan. "Dude," he says. "A collection of loosely linked short stories based on Beatles lyrics isn't exactly something the world's clamoring for right now. It's niche. Like, *niche* niche."

"Come on," says Wade. "They're the biggest band ever."

Wade takes this moment to notice himself in the bathroom mirror. As far as timing goes, it's not great, what with him looking all dejected and sitting on a toilet. He happens to be wearing one of his Beatles T-shirts. The screen print is from the Fab days, bowl cuts and fresh faces.

"I'm familiar with the Beatles," says Brandon. "They broke up half a century ago. Two of them are dead. And nobody buys short-story collections anyway. That's just a business fact. Even if they did, I'm not sure you can even legally publish this thing. Who owns the rights to all those lyrics you borrowed? If it's Yoko Ono, you're fucked. I saw her at the Met Gala a few years ago. She looked terrifying. Crap. I'm sorry. I'm being awful again."

Wade pokes at his shower curtain. "So, what now?"

"It's still out with one editor," says Brandon. "Some tiny imprint in the Village. They've done some goofy music-inspired stuff, like your book. I found an editor over there. Maybe he'll like it. Or maybe he doesn't actually exist. I might be getting catfished."

Wade hunches forward, elbows onto knees. "Well, that sounds promising," he says.

"Normally I'm not a fan of your naked cynicism, Wade," says Brandon, "but I think it's good here. It's important to manage our expectations. Self-care. Shit, what time is it?"

Wade looks at his watch, but he's not sure if Brandon expects an actual answer.

"I gotta go, Wade. There's this thing uptown. Blaine and I are visiting preschools for Duncan. Not sure if you've heard, but kids are expensive. So, maybe you can think about ditching karaoke lit and writing Daddy something I can actually sell?"

Since Brandon and his husband adopted their son, Brandon likes to casually refer to himself as Daddy. Under normal circumstances, Wade finds it charming. "Yeah, gladly," he says. "But what sells? I'm genuinely curious. I don't even know anymore."

"A kids' book, maybe?" says Brandon. "People buy the shit out of those things."

"Can you say *fuck* in kids' books?" asks Wade.

"I don't know. Maybe in Europe. Duncan's favorite book is about a chicken who won't eat vegetables. Seriously, though, figure it out. Write something marketable, I'll sell it, Duncan can go to school with Alec Baldwin's kids, and you can stop getting tossed out of studio apartments."

Wade used to daydream about literary awards. He imagined multibook deals, film options. Now he mostly just wishes he had health insurance and a structurally sound bathroom ceiling. "When do you think you'll hear from this guy?" he asks. "The editor?"

"Soon," says Brandon. "Any day now."

"Really?" asks Wade. "That fast?"

"You're goddamn right. Come on, Wade. Remember, I'm Brandon fucking Ross."

BY SHEER FORCE OF HABIT, Wade washes his hands after hanging up.

He leaves the bathroom, tiptoes to the peephole, and finds that Mrs. Suzuki is gone. He leans on the door and looks at his apartment, already feeling pangs of nostalgia as he pulls a flannel over his Beatles T-shirt. When his phone rings, the caller ID reads Luxury Transport—which makes sense, because Wade is clearly a man accustomed to the finer things.

"Hello?" he says.

"Is this Mr. Wade?" The voice is male, formal sounding. "I am Khalid. I am taking you to Delaware today, sir. I will be there in three minutes and fifty seconds."

When Wade steps out into the hallway, he discovers two things. First, one of the wheels of his roller bag has broken off, which, metaphorically speaking, is pretty right on. Second, there's a sticker stuck crookedly to his apartment door: NOTICE OF EVICTION. Mrs. Suzuki has added "Sorry Wade!" in glittery purple pen.

And, because she really *is* a sweet lady, she's included a frowny face.

"All right, then." Wade's voice echoes in the empty hallway. "Let's hit the beach."

DOWN AT THE CURB, WITH a minute and a half to spare, Wade takes out his phone and goes to his first novel on Amazon. He has no idea why; no good ever comes of this.

Feedback is the story of a fictional rock band from Baltimore that hits it big and stumbles face-first into the trappings of success. It's currently ranked #942,007 in books, and the last reader review, two stars, posted three months ago, reads: "Came 2 days late. Amazon Prime my @ss!!"

A horn blasts, and a black Cadillac Escalade pulls to the curb. It's so fancy that people on the street stop and look, like he's a Jonas Brother or Céline Dion. The driver's side window powers down, and there's Khalid, who sounded older on the phone.

"Mr. Wade?" he says.

"You can just call me regular Wade," says Wade.

Khalid smiles, sly. "As you wish, Mr. Regular Wade. Hop in."

Wade looks over at the bodega across the street. "I was gonna maybe grab some snacks for the ride, if that's cool."

"Of course," says Khalid. "You are in charge."

"You want anything? I'm buying."

Khalid says no thank you. He rolls the window up, but then immediately rolls it back down. "Actually, if they have gummy bears . . ."

Wade nods. "Good choice." And then he tosses his busted roller bag into the hundred-thousand-dollar Escalade and jogs across the street.

Chapter 3

Being friends with Robbie Malcolm can be weird sometimes.

For one thing, getting ahold of him is tough. For security reasons, his phone number and email addresses change constantly, and his whereabouts at any given moment could be one of at least eight locations, from New York to Baltimore, San Francisco to London, and so on. It's more than just logistics, though.

The fact is, Robbie just isn't a normal person. He never was, even when they were teenagers. He speaks quietly and hyper-articulately, but he does so with very little inflection, like an actor playing a lifelike robot. He often seems aloof, and he avoids eye contact, but when he shifts his attention directly onto you, the intensity of it is disarming.

He'll go months without being in touch. There's nothing unusual about that per se, because old friends often go long stretches without speaking. But when he does resurface, he does so suddenly, and usually with some grand gesture attached, like hand-delivered invitations to free beach weekends.

One evening last year, Blair's phone rang just before dinner. It was Robbie, calling from a number she didn't recognize. There were traffic noises and a weird, European-sounding police siren in the background.

"I have a meeting with Congress next week," he told her,

matter-of-factly, like he was telling her about an upcoming dentist appointment.

"Congress?" Blair laughed. "Like, all of them?"

Robbie paused. "Good question. I should look into that. A sub-committee, I think. I was wondering if you'd like to get coffee after. I'll have fifty minutes. An hour, maybe."

Even with all that in mind—the oddities of Robbie Malcolm's friendship—something about his invitation has been worrying Blair over the last two weeks. One line in particular, toward the end—"I really need to see you." She mentioned this to Cat and Wade when they were texting back and forth.

You don't think there's anything wrong, do you?

What do you mean? Cat wrote back.

Blair didn't know exactly what she meant. Doesn't it seem kind of weird?

Because why would Robbie *need* to see them? She got that he might *want* to see them. That it might be *fun* to see them. Need, though? But then Wade texted, I'm sure it's fine. It's Robbie, right? And then Cat piled on with He probably wants to tell us he's buying a WNBA team or funding a moon landing.

Blair had tried to convince herself that she was just worrying for the sake of worrying. Cat and Wade don't have kids like she does. Parenthood has a way of turning your brain into a dread-seeking machine. This is the fundamental difference between Blair and her friends. They're all adults, of course, technically, but Blair is a parent and therefore a different kind of adult. It's why none of them have met Martin and the twins yet.

She became friends with Cat, Robbie, and Wade when she was a teenager. Their friendship was grounded in collective youth, back when she was Young Blair. In the handful of times she's seen them since the twins were born, she's preferred to continue playing that role.

Now, though, still driving through traffic with her husband and kids, she's aware that she's not certain which version of herself she's supposed to be when they arrive. This dilemma—Young

Blair vs. Adult Blair—manifested itself perfectly last week. Her swimsuits had gotten ratty and misshapen over the last few summers. As she browsed for a new one in bed on her laptop while Martin slept beside her, she found that she couldn't make a decision.

Young Blair wore string bikinis. Young Blair charged into waves. She hopped fences and broke into hotel swimming pools and made out with whomever she pleased and snuck beer into Diet Coke cans to fool lifeguards. She stole weed from surfers and hitched rides in Jeeps. Young Blair didn't give a shit. What kind of swimsuit does Adult Blair wear?

MARTIN CLEARS HIS THROAT. "EVEN if I don't feel old, I'm definitely gonna feel boring." He says this apropos of nothing, which is how conversations go on road trips. They're through the worst of the traffic now. Kenny's starting to stir. He'll be awake soon, demand things, like Pirate's Booty and string cheese and their full attention.

"You're not *that* boring," Blair says.

"I don't know," he says. "It's a dynamic group. A self-made billionaire, a TV producer, a novelist, and *you* . . . an artist."

Blair's chest tightens. Why do husbands do this? Why do they say the one thing you repeatedly ask them *not* to say? "You have to make art to be an artist," she says, a practiced line, because, in fact, Blair is a *former* artist. She's a freelance graphic designer now who specializes in laying out beautiful direct mail catalogs.

They drive on. The Odyssey is like an ugly boat, bobbing and floating. She looks over at Martin as he drives. He's in a light-blue polo and khaki shorts. Gray has settled in above his ears and close-cropped beard. He's summer casual and accomplished and handsome, and she imagines him from her friends' perspectives. Then she thinks about him from her own perspective.

She read an article last month about making marriages last. The writer, a woman, wrote that you should make an effort to remember the specific things you loved about your spouse early on, when everything was new, because those are the things you so quickly get used to. Blair focuses on his hands. Martin's hands are beautiful. They're big without being weirdly big, perfectly proportioned. She noticed them before he'd even asked her out, at the ad agency where they both worked. She didn't know if she liked him yet, but she knew it'd be nice to be touched by hands like his.

He cracks a knuckle now, breaking her concentration, and Blair wonders if she and Martin will get to spend any time alone this weekend. Which is an odd phenomenon of marriage: one moment you can want to murder your husband—legitimately kill him for calling you something you no longer are—and then the next moment you're driving by an outlet mall listening to Wilson Phillips and hoping you can reconnect.

You think he even knows, Blair? It's Imaginary Taylor Swift again. She's wearing sunglasses now, big and elaborate. *You think he knows how much is riding on this weekend?*

Chapter 4

As Blair, Martin, the twins, and Wade approach Fenwick Island from the ground, Cat Miller sits above it all aboard Robbie's jet. Her phone is on an armrest next to a crystal cup full of trail mix, which she hasn't yet touched.

Generally speaking, if you were to ask Cat whether or not it's possible to be miserable on a private plane, she'd say no. But here she is, freezing her ass off and trying not to cry. She takes a sip of rosé. This cup is crystal, too, heavy in her hand. "Rosé all day, bitches," she says quietly to herself as she looks down on a checkerboard of greens and browns.

Cat is wearing jean shorts, a T-shirt, and flip-flops. She was in a daze that morning when she got dressed, back in L.A. She didn't think anything of her outfit, because a plane ride is just a plane ride, right? Well, no. The second she stepped aboard this futuristic-looking thing, with its flat-screens and blasting AC vents and Malcolm Capital logos stenciled into mahogany, she felt like a rube. That's her big takeaway today: when you're on a private jet, dress like someone who looks like they should be on a private jet.

She eats an M&M out of her trail mix. A tiny airplane icon on one of the flat-screens draws a line across the length of the United States, showing how far she's flown. She imagines a similar graphic, but for herself, a little Cat icon crawling across a map of her life, going nowhere in particular.

Cat lets her flip-flops fall to the floor and tucks her feet under her legs.

There's a flight attendant aboard. Her name is Bianca, and she's as beautiful and scary-looking as a European eyewear model. "Ms. Miller," Bianca says. "We'll be landing soon. Can I get you more rosé?"

Cat looks at the empty crystal. "I think that'd be a bad idea, Bianca," she says. "But thanks." Then she considers asking Bianca some follow-up questions.

Bianca, do I come off to you as someone who is fundamentally unlovable? I know we've just met, but do you think I'd make a good mother? And finally, Bianca, do you think there's anything worse than when you see the three little texting dots on your goddamn iPhone, but then they go away and never come back? Like, what the fuck is that, right?

Cat doesn't ask these questions, because she's not insane, so Bianca smiles and goes back to her seat near the pilots. The plane flies through clouds, shuddering gently.

Don't ever break up with someone over text message. That's the day's second takeaway. However, this raises an important question. Does it count as a breakup if you were never technically together? If your entire yearlong relationship was . . . complicated?

Earlier, Cat and Gabrielle were texting back and forth through the plane's Wi-Fi. Cat sent her last text twenty-seven minutes ago: We're never really going to be together, are we? She's been waiting for a reply ever since.

That's her name, Gabrielle. As in Gab. As in the star and host of *The Morning Gab,* which is the show on which Cat is an associate producer. She doesn't call her Gabrielle or Gab, though. When they're alone, Cat calls her Gabby. She's wanted to ask Gabby that question for months—"We're never really going to be together, are we?"—but now that she has, she wishes she hadn't. There should be an unsend feature on iPhones, like time travel.

Cat eats some trail mix. When her phone finally vibrates, she stops chewing.

You know it's not that simple.

Did it really take Gabby twenty-nine minutes to come up with *that*? She looks out the window and sees trees—sand and water, too. She takes a deep breath and holds it. She bites her lip and types with her thumbs.

I deserve to be with someone who actually wants to be with me.

No half-hour gap this time. Gabby's response is instant.

Then you should go out and find her.

Cat sinks into her seat as the wheels touch down on the Delaware runway. She squeezes the bridge of her nose. "Dude," she whispers. "Fuck."

The thing about normal planes: they taxi forever after landing. They roll unendingly toward some distant Jetway across from a Chili's Express or whatever. This isn't a normal plane, though, so thirty seconds later, the engines shut off.

"All right, Mi— Oh, Miss Miller?" Bianca touches Cat's arm. "Are you okay?"

To be clear, Cat *isn't* crying, thank God, because crying in a pair of jorts on a private jet would be an indignity she simply couldn't handle. But, judging from Bianca's expression, Cat must look like she's about to. This makes sense, because Cat has just imagined a scenario in which forty-something years from now her body is discovered by a landlord after she's died alone in her apartment while eating a Hungry-Man frozen dinner.

The concern on Bianca's face creases the makeup between her eyebrows.

"Did you not enjoy the flight?" she asks.

"Oh, no," says Cat. "It was lovely."

"Good. Mr. Malcolm will be pleased to hear that." Then Bianca holds out a bag of trail mix and smiles. "I've taken the liberty of preparing a snack for your drive into Fenwick." This simple act of sisterly kindness is nearly too much, and Cat has to look out the window to keep herself from falling completely apart.

Chapter 5

Wade can't get over how ridiculous the Escalade is, like he's riding in a chariot. The big engine hums. The cool black leather interior is so soft he has to stop himself from rubbing his face against it.

He opens Instagram, and his phone knows exactly what he's up to. He only has to type *B* and Blair Harden appears. Her new last name is still jarring, even though it's not *new* at all. Wade still has her saved as Blair McKenzie.

In her latest picture, Blair is eating ice cream with her kids. Wade scrolls. Her husband, Martin, appears in maybe every tenth post, smiling, always, because he's the luckiest son of a bitch on earth. Wade stops at a selfie of Blair at a swimming pool. This is the image that most often stops him. The cover-up she's wearing has little pink turtles on it, the tip of her nose is sunburned, and her hair is pulled up. Her kids are a blur behind her, about to crash into water. Wade maximizes the picture until it's just her, and he thinks of a teenage Blair cannonballing into a hotel pool in her underwear.

Admittedly, this isn't what Wade should be doing right now. What he *should* be doing is calling his parents, which he's been putting off for months.

It's been a busy couple of weeks for Wade. Mrs. Suzuki's eviction sticker wasn't exactly a shock—what with her three official warnings—so he's had time to prepare. Since getting Robbie's invitation, he's cleared his apartment of everything that matters, fielded rejection emails from Brandon, and quit both of his jobs.

His main job, writing and editing onboarding materials for employees of the City of New York, was a gig he did mostly at home. When the Web portal asked if he was sure he wanted to discontinue employment, Wade couldn't help but detect a tone. He quit his other job, as a barista at Elephant Java, in person, which made his boss, Nan, laugh.

"Employees usually just kinda ghost on me," she said. "I appreciate the face-to-face."

"I figured I owed it to you," Wade told her. "You know, since you gave me all those free cranberry-orange muffins."

Nan wiped her palm on her apron and shook his hand. "Don't let the bastards grind you down, okay, Wade?" she said, which was a poignant thing to hear as he stood, espresso in hand, on the verge of personal ruin. She gave him one last muffin, for old times' sake.

He closes Instagram now, because enough already. A sign ahead reads WELCOME TO DELAWARE: ENDLESS DISCOVERIES.

HIS MOM ANSWERS ON THE first ring. "Hey, Wade. Any book news?"

Which isn't the start he'd hoped for. "Hey, Mom. Not yet."

"Well, these things take time," she says. "I was at the library yesterday in Roland Park. *Feedback* was checked out. Cool, right? Every reader counts."

"Indeed," says Wade. "So, listen, I wanted to talk to you. Is Dad there, too?"

"He's downstairs on his Internet bike," she says. "Want me to get him? He says it's a good workout, but I think he just has the hots for his instructor. You should see the outfits this woman wears. It's just boobs. Right in your face."

"Well, in that case," he says, "just us is fine. How is he, good?"

Wade's dad had a heart attack and nearly died when Wade was in high school. It was a long time ago, and he's transformed his life since with diet and exercise, but Wade always asks, like a nervous tic.

"He's fine," she says. "If that instructor keeps showing up in her sports bra, he'll be fit enough to ride in the Tour de France. Are you in a taxi? Sounds like you're driving."

"Kind of, yeah. So, I was thinking about maybe coming home for a while."

There's a pause—three seconds of weighted silence. "To Baltimore?"

"Yeah."

"For a visit?"

"I was thinking an extended visit."

"Is everything okay?"

"No, yeah," says Wade. "It's just, you know, Manhattan. I don't think I'm into it anymore." He hadn't planned on making New York City this particular story's antagonist, but here we are. "I miss Baltimore. Might be nice to get back and recharge."

She may not understand the complexities of book royalties—specifically that you don't get them from library checkouts—but she knows the tone of his voice and what it means. "Well, great!" she says. "I'll set up the basement for you. We'll move your dad's Internet bike to the garage. When should we expect you?"

"Next week. I'm going on a little trip first, actually. I'm meeting Blair, Cat, and Robbie down in Fenwick."

"Sounds like fun!" she says. "Oh, that reminds me. Your father wanted me to ask you. Is it true that Robbie rescued a cow from a slaughterhouse in Iowa?"

It's one of those non sequiturs so random you need a moment to recover, like you've been slapped out of a nap. "What?"

"Your dad saw it online. A cow escaped from a meatpacking plant. The article said the workers had to chase it across an interstate to get it back. Apparently, Robbie heard about it and bought it, so it wouldn't be slaughtered. The article said he named it

Helen. Sounds like something he'd do. You know, all that charity stuff."

Like a lot of people from Baltimore, Wade's parents are fascinated with Robbie. They catch stray bits of news and take it as hard fact. Last time they spoke, his mom asked if Robbie was dating Natalie Portman.

"I tell you what," says Wade. "I'll definitely ask him."

"Okay. Give my love to Blair and Cat. I miss those girls." She tells Wade that she can't wait to see him—that it'll be nice to have him home again. Tone reading is a two-way street with mothers and their sons, though, so he knows her cheer is mixed with worry. Wade isn't coming to Baltimore to recharge; he isn't some globe-trotting adventurer taking a break. Thirty-five-year-old Wade Stephens is moving home because he's broke.

When Wade hangs up, Khalid eats a handful of gummy bears and does Wade the courtesy of pretending he didn't hear any of that.

Chapter 6

"How much more minutes? Dad? Daddy? Daddy!"

Kenny is awake now. Martin corrects the boy's grammar and checks the nav. "Forty minutes, bud," he says. "Almost there."

They pass crab shacks and liquor stores, giant industrial sprinkler systems and billboards advertising God. Blair doodles a stern-looking bird on a Subway napkin from lunch, and Martin bobs his head to the '90s. She finds her phone and goes to Instagram to look at Cat's, Robbie's, and Wade's pages.

Robbie's social media presence is clearly run by a PR department, so it's full-on corporate. Cat's latest image is a sweaty selfie after a charity run. "It's Miller Time, Suckas!" And two weeks ago, Wade posted a manuscript-size pile of papers. "Book 2 is finally in the books. More to come. (I hope.)" There are zero comments and seven sad little likes. Blair hits the heart symbol, and now butterflies flutter in her stomach as she opens her email.

The first few are nothing: spam, a layout with markups from the client. The message that she was hoping to see sits beneath an email from Target. It's from the twins' art teacher, Mr. McGee, and those butterflies become something stronger, like roiling water, like adrenaline and danger. She angles the phone away from her husband.

The subject line reads Lower School Art Volunteer Hours, because Mr. McGee's subject lines are always innocuous.

She taps his message. `Pickup won't be the same today without you.`

Blair is careful to hide her smile in her hand. She doesn't reply, because she never replies right away. Instead, she thinks about the pickup line from yesterday.

The staff take turns working dismissal. Five teachers at a time stand outside helping the kids get into cars. The teacher you get is random, but when Mr. McGee is at the curb, Blair knows how to angle for him without making it look too obvious. Yesterday, when she opened the Odyssey's automatic sliding door, she took off her sunglasses. She'd just applied makeup in the Starbucks parking lot ten minutes earlier.

"Afternoon, Mrs. Harden," Mr. McGee said. "Beautiful day today. *Hot,* actually."

Blair felt herself flush, but she held his gaze. "Summer's almost here."

As she pulled away, she watched him in the rearview as he watched the back of her minivan.

And now, almost exactly twenty-four hours later, her kids are arguing over which one of them gets to claim the word *butt* in the alphabet game.

"I said it first!"

"But it's my butt!"

"Kids," she says, and they briefly hush. For *C,* they go with *cap* and *cow.* At *D,* Kenny points to his fly and shouts, "Ding-dong!" Martin drums his fingers on the steering wheel, and Blair thinks of the two swimsuits in her bag—a bikini and a one-piece. She'll decide which one to wear when they get there.

"Mommy?" Michelle points out the window. "What's that word? Sal-something."

It's the most ominous billboard yet, bold black letters against white. GOT SALVATION?

"Yeesh," says Martin. "I'll let you handle that one."

"Something you don't have to worry about, sweetie," Blair says.

Chapter 7

For Robbie Malcolm, it's the smell that gets him. It's sudden, like a flash of pleasant memory. From the back seat of a customized black Range Rover, he powers the windows down so he can get a full whiff of it.

"You smell that, D?" he asks.

The driver, a young man named Dash Walker, nods in the rearview mirror. "I do," he says. "What is it, exactly?"

"It's a combination of things," Robbie says. "The beach. The bay. Sunscreen. Boat fumes. Salt. Crab parts. The smell of my youth, basically."

"I like it," says Dash. "It's earthy."

Dash is Robbie's director of transportation and personal security, and the largest human being Robbie has ever met. They're on Route 404, approaching Fenwick Island from the north. Three computer monitors face the back seat, along with a retractable desk. The screens, which are muted, are tuned to different twenty-four-hour news channels.

As blurs of green fly by, lush and wild, Robbie makes a note to drive with the windows down more often. He thinks of smiling dogs sticking their heads out of cars, tongues flapping. "I wanted to get your thoughts on the house," he says.

Their eyes meet in the rearview mirror.

"Is it nice enough, do you think?"

Dash laughs. "Oh, sorry. You're being serious. I can never tell with you."

"I just really want everything to be perfect," says Robbie.

Dash looks at the road ahead, then back at Robbie. They pass cyclists in candy-colored shirts. "They're gonna love it, boss," he says. "It's the nicest house I've ever seen."

Robbie turns the monitors off one by one, because that's what people do on vacation. They unplug. Ten days ago, an anchor from the network on the middle screen mentioned Robbie on air. More specifically, he mentioned the absence of Robbie.

"Normally, in times like these, we turn to the prognosticators, right?" the anchor said. "We see what folks like Robbie Malcolm are up to. Not this time. The funny thing about Mr. Malcolm: nobody seems to know where he is. A little R and R? Something more strategic? Your guess is as good as ours."

The graphic on the screen asked, *Where in the World is Robbie Malcolm?*

"You have the files, right?" Robbie asks.

"I do. I'm keeping them close, like you asked." Dash reaches into a messenger bag on the passenger seat and shows Robbie three big envelopes. There are names written on them, one for each of his friends: Blair, Cat, and Wade.

"Good. And they're up to date?"

"Absolutely."

With the screens dark now, Robbie sees himself from three slightly different angles. He rolls up the windows, easing the roar. "Can I ask you something, Dash?"

"Yeah, shoot."

"This whole thing. This weekend. I'm not just being a rich asshole, am I?"

Dash holds the steering wheel at ten and two, like a kid taking a driver's test.

"You can tell me, you know. In fact, starting today, no more saying what I want to hear. Speak freely. Good or bad. And you can call me any name you want."

"I'll think about it," says Dash.

Robbie is aware that Dash hasn't answered his question.

Closer to the shore, traffic clusters and slows. They pass fruit stands and occasional bursts of wildflowers, and Robbie gets that familiar jittery rush that comes when he's *almost* to Fenwick Island. He's been coming here since he was a kid; they all have. This is where Baltimore kids come in the summer: the beaches of Maryland and Delaware. He thinks of Cat's grandma's old beach house, the Rejects' unofficial headquarters.

The Range Rover moves along a bend in the highway. A clearing in the trees up ahead reveals a smattering of modest homes at the edge of the two-lane road. A for-sale sign catches his eye. "Dash, pull over for a second."

"What? Here?"

"Yeah. Right here."

The Range Rover skids on loose gravel, and they come to a messy stop on the shoulder. Dash whips around in his seat. "You okay? Should we call someone?"

Robbie makes a triangle with his hands and slowly nods. "I'm fine. Blue house. Check out that car." There's a small single-story home in the middle of an overgrown lawn. A convertible sits in the driveway. "It's for sale," he says.

"The teal thing?" asks Dash. "You made me almost crash for *that*?"

"I'd says it's more turquoise than teal," Robbie says.

"Okay. Be that as it may."

Maybe Dash has a point. It's not a very nice car. It's old, but not in a classic way, just an old way. The paint is faded and one of the tires looks low. "You know what kind of car it is?"

Dash shields his eyes. "A Chrysler. A LeBaron, I think. A Chrysler LeBaron." The Range Rover idles; the AC hums. A few SUVs speed by, shaking the ground, and Dash draws a cautious sigh. "It's got a cracked headlight."

"So do I," Robbie says. "Come on, let's check it out."

Chapter 8

"Can I interest you in a little champagne?"

Joe, the driver, an older guy dressed in black, smiles over his shoulder, and Cat understands immediately that champagne would be a terrible, terrible idea. But then he says, "After all, you're on vacation, right?"

Cat has been staring at her phone, waiting for a breakup retraction from Gabrielle, something definitive and heartfelt. Nothing, though, not even text dots. She's just played out a fantasy in her mind in which she drops her stupid iPhone out the window and watches wrecked pieces of it skitter across the pavement. "Champagne?" she asks.

"See that cabinet? Enough liquor in there to float a Jet Ski."

She opens the little door at her feet and discovers beers, wine, some mini vodkas and bourbons, and a small bottle of Dom Pérignon. "I've never had Dom before," she says.

"Neither have I," says Joe. "How about you pop it open and let me know if it lives up to the hype."

She manages to open the bottle without shooting either of their eyes out. She takes a bubbly sip, which makes her burpy and light-headed. It tastes pretty much like any other champagne she's ever had. This clearly isn't what Joe wants to hear, though.

"How is it? Good as they say?"

"Even better."

A moment later, she's surprised to find herself pouring another glass. Outside her window, Fenwick Island is crowded with cars and pedestrians and people on beach bikes. It all looks smaller than she remembers. The glimmering expanse to her left is called Little Assawoman Bay, which always made the Rejects laugh when they were young. "My kinda bay," she must've said a hundred times. "I'm a bit of an Assawoman myself." Her friends would crack up, and Wade would give her a high five. They were her allies before allies were even a thing.

They turn onto Coastal Highway as her second glass of champagne disappears. She holds the bottle up. "You're sure you don't want any, Joe?"

"All yours," he says. "Promised the wife I'd stay outta jail this weekend."

"Ugh, wives," she says, which is the precise moment Cat realizes she's drunk.

They pass beach stores, a bike shop, some bars, and a Dairy Queen, all of which she recognizes. Normally, guzzling champagne in a decked-out Escalade would seem excessive, but two quick hits of alcohol mixed with the rosé already in her system have changed her perspective. Maybe champagne is actually perfect. You drink champagne at weddings and on New Year's Eve. At birthday parties and couples' showers. You drink champagne when you're toasting to what comes next. Right?

Cat reads Gabrielle's last text: Then you should go out and find her. It's like a motivational poster for gay girls. "Dude, fuck it," she whispers, typing as fast as she can, and then she hits Send. OK then. I guess I will. She steadies herself, because what she's about to text next isn't as simple. But, again, fuck it. New futures. Uncharted territories. All that crap. Also, I quit.

"Okey dokey," says Joe. "Here we are."

The Escalade stops. They're sitting in a gravel driveway. Cat hears waves crashing and birds calling. She sets her phone down. "Holy shit," she says.

Joe laughs. "My sentiments exactly. That right there is one helluva house."

Chapter 9

The doorbell doesn't work, so Robbie knocks.

Dash is looming beside him. "You said you wanted me to be honest, right?" he says. "Well, I'm thinking we can do better than this in the convertible department." He has his phone out. "Lemme check some dealerships."

Robbie shakes his head. "I'd like to avoid paperwork at the moment," he says. "Nobody knows where I am, remember?"

"Right." Dash looks back at the LeBaron. "Just guessing on the year, but Kelley Blue Book says seventeen hundred. Seems generous."

The door swings open, and a little girl appears. She's wearing bedazzled jean shorts and a one-piece bathing suit with a princess on the chest. "Hello," she says. Her head tilts up and her eyes get big. "Wow, how tall are you?"

"Um, six foot six," Dash says.

"That's a lot more than me. I'm three foot nine."

"Don't worry about him," says Robbie. "This is Dash. He's mostly harmless."

"It's true," Dash says. "High five?"

The girl tentatively touches her palm to Dash's big paw of a hand, and Robbie asks her if the car parked out front belongs to her. "No, it's my daddy's. We put the for-sale sign on it this morning. The wind kept blowing it out into the yard, so we had to use tape."

"Good thinking," says Robbie. "Is he here? Your daddy?"

The screen door smacks shut, and she vanishes into the house.

"I bet he'd do fifteen, straight up," whispers Dash.

Footsteps approach. "You're probably right," says Robbie. "I have this, though. Maybe just hang back. Try not to look so imposing."

The girl's dad appears. He's about Robbie's age, midthirties. He's wearing a Delaware Fightin' Blue Hens T-shirt. Like his daughter before him, he's startled by the size of Dash. The fact that Dash has a snake tattoo on his neck probably doesn't help. "What can I do for you guys?" he asks.

The girl pushes passed them. "He's six-six, Daddy," she says, retrieving a tipped-over bicycle from the driveway.

"Hello," says Robbie. "I'm in the market for a convertible." Robbie can tell right away that the guy doesn't recognize him. This makes sense. Robbie is a very particular kind of celebrity, one who's famous to only a specific type of person. The guy does, however, recognize that there's a Range Rover parked at the side of the road. The sun is hitting it just right, so the chrome around the headlights literally glimmers. "You are, huh?"

"Yeah," says Robbie. "That's my work car. I need something for the beach."

THEY WALK AROUND THE TURQUOISE convertible while the girl circles them on her bike. She rings the bell on her handlebars, which sounds like birds chirping.

"Still handles real well," the guy says. "Shocks are good. Transmission's tight, too. Never really had any problems. No accidents. It was my dad's car before it was mine. He loved it. Top goes up and down real smooth. Some old tapes in the glove. Yours if you want them. They aren't really my taste."

Dash toes at the partially deflated front tire, and Robbie wonders what kind of questions you're supposed to ask someone when you want to buy their car.

It takes gasoline, I assume. And the steering wheel, you turn it and such, right and left?

"I get to sit in the front seat when we go to the beach," the girl says from her bike.

"Can I ask why you're selling it?" Dash asks.

The guy touches the cracked headlight. "Oh, you know. Could use a little cash, I guess." He nods at his daughter. "Kids and all. You know how it is."

Dash gives the door handle a tug and looks inside.

"How much are you asking?" asks Robbie. "There isn't a price on the sign."

The guy flushes and looks away. Robbie's noticed this about people: they rarely look at you when they tell you what they want. "Could probably let her go for . . . maybe fifteen?"

Robbie looks back at the house. There's a plastic playset by the front stoop—some toys scattered in the yard. "I don't know," Robbie says.

"Well, I can work with you some. Price is flexible."

Robbie remembers a trip to Fenwick Island years ago, between their junior and senior years. The four of them—Blair, Cat, Robbie, and Wade—were traipsing along Coastal Highway lugging beach chairs and a cooler. It was hot as hell out. "You know what we need?" Cat asked. She was balancing a beach chair on her head. Her shorts were slung low on her hips, too big for her. "A convertible. How nice would that be?" They were tan and gritty from the sand and impossibly young. They had their whole lives ahead of them.

Robbie leans against the Chrysler's fender now. He's familiar with this dynamic: people waiting for him to speak, to calmly tell them what's going to happen. "You've got a vintage ride here," he says. "No rust that I can see. It's in solid shape, like you said. It's a good car. I see why your dad liked it so much."

"Yeah?" The man is clearly confused.

"I guess what I'm saying—" Robbie touches a scratch in the paint, like a scar, an imperfection made worse by time. "I think we can do a little better than fifteen hundred."

Chapter 10

Cat searches her inbox. There was an email a few days ago about logistics from a dude with a weird name—Rush, Blaze?—that listed the front-door code. The email referred to the house as "the Beach House," which, obviously, is bullshit. Beach houses are small and cramped with leaky outdoor showers and fish-shaped mailboxes and nicknames like "Sea & Sea Relaxing Factory." This isn't a beach house. This is a goddamn beach mansion.

"Think anyone's home?" Joe calls. He's back in the Escalade after insisting on carrying Cat's small roller bag to the door.

She imagines shooting a flaming arrow over the roof. But then, there it is, an email from Dash Walker. When she punches the numbers into the keypad, the lock disengages like a bank vault. "In there like swimwear," Cat says.

Joe chuckles toward the ocean. "Well, welcome to Fenwick." He cranes his neck, looking up at the house, like he's not quite ready to leave. "I was hoping I'd get to meet him, actually. You know, the man himself."

It takes Cat a moment to figure out that Joe is talking about Robbie, and she's not sure what to say. Robbie used to help her with her trigonometry homework in study hall, and now, well . . . all this.

Joe honks twice as he pulls away, and now Cat stands alone eating a handful of trail mix. She hiccups loudly. There's a corgi across the street: white, brown, and black. It's watching her through the railing of a neighbor's deck, clearly suspicious.

"I just quit my job," Cat calls, which feels strange to say aloud, even if just to a dog. The corgi yawns. "Also, I'm single now. So, if you know anyone."

HER FLIP-FLOPS ECHO THROUGH A spectacular, cavernous entryway.

"Hello?" she says, and that echoes, too. She climbs a flight of stairs to the kitchen, which is all steel and travertine. A wall of windows behind a long wood table delivers a panoramic view of a swimming pool and the ocean. "Goddamn," she says.

She opens the brushed-metal fridge, because it's impossible *not* to open fridges in strange houses. It's stocked with food and drinks, so she grabs a hard seltzer. Beyond the kitchen, there's a lounging room with some sort of videoconferencing equipment, complete with a wall-mounted monitor, a computer docking station, and a built-in camera. A giant pelican carved from driftwood stands nearby, because why not?

Upstairs, the bedroom doors have plaques with their names, and Cat's room is ridiculous, with a king-size bed that makes her feel even smaller than she normally feels. She parks her roller bag and walks out onto a private balcony. The house is maybe fifty steps from the beach. People lounge, run, laugh, fly kites, and throw Frisbees. She sees kids, because she sees kids everywhere lately. Plastic beach toys and waterlogged swim diapers.

"Do you ever think about babies?"

Cat asked Gabrielle this a couple of months ago. They were at a restaurant in Burbank, just the two of them. It was an official brainstorming session, but Gabrielle's foot rested on Cat's foot, hidden by a long tablecloth. An elderly couple had just stopped by to tell Gabrielle how much they love her show.

"Every woman over thirty thinks about babies," Gabrielle replied. She sipped her water with two limes and looked around the restaurant.

"What if I told you I think I might want one?"

Gabrielle bit her pen. They'd been jotting down ideas—potential segments and guests. "I bet you'd create a beautiful baby."

Cat leaned in and whispered, "*We'd* create a beautiful baby. Together."

Gabrielle laughed. "Who taught you science?"

Now, standing in the sunshine thousands of miles away in Delaware, the air raw and salty, she realizes what's been going on all this time. Cat has been talking about babies. Cat has been making plans. Cat has been telling herself that if she has a baby maybe Gabrielle will finally love her. She's been telling herself this for so long she's started to believe it.

Two dumb birds swoop, and Cat rubs her eyes. "You're such an idiot," she whispers. And that's when Blair and Wade arrive.

Her balcony is on the side of the house, so Cat has a view of the beach and the white-gravel driveway. Blair and her family pull up first, in a minivan, of all things. A black Escalade like the one that brought Cat from the airport drives up behind them. Blair steps out of the minivan and stretches, and, good lord, she's gorgeous. The van's side door slides open and the twins hop out. The boy is trying to wrestle his shirt off. Cat notices Wade then. He's standing in the driveway watching Blair and her family—Blair, specifically, Cat knows. Wade looks pale and out of place, like he might burst suddenly into flames. His roller bag tips over onto its side.

"Come on, Wade," Cat whispers. "Don't make this weird."

By the time she makes it downstairs and outside, Wade and Blair's husband are shaking hands.

"Nice to meet you, Wade. I'm Martin."

"Hey, Martin."

Cat stands on the front steps. No one's noticed her yet. She watches as Blair and Wade hug. "Do they not have sun in New York?" Blair asks him.

"Sun?" he says. "Is that what that thing is?"

"Kenny, put your shirt back on, please," says Martin.

The boy throws it on the ground. "I hate shirts!" he says. "Ooh, look, a dog!"

Martin spots the corgi across the street. "Oh yeah," he says. "Hey, doggie."

"Its ears!" says the girl. "They stick up."

Finally, Cat clears her throat. "Bad news, you guys," she says. "The rental house is a real dump."

Everyone looks up at the beach mansion. Blair and Wade pretend to be unimpressed. "Honestly," says Blair. "I expected bigger."

"It doesn't even have a decent place to land a helicopter," says Wade, deadpan.

"Is this *one* house or a lot of houses?" asks Blair's daughter.

Cat hugs Wade. Tall and skinny, like hugging a tree. "Flannel at the beach, huh?"

"I'm here representing the people of Manhattan." He takes the drink out of her hand. "What's this thing?"

"It's called a Truly," she says. "All the rage among suburban alcoholics."

Wade grimaces after a sip. "Are there more of them?"

"Does this look like a house that lacks things?" She turns to Blair now. "Come here, you hideous monster," she says, and Blair laughs. They kiss each other's cheeks. Blair smells wonderful, the way beautiful women smell, like they've been dipped in something extravagant.

Martin holds his hand out. "You must be Cat. Hi, I'm Martin." This man who has only existed on Instagram until now is very handsome. The Escalade that brought Wade pulls away— "Goodbye, Mr. Regular Wade!"—and everyone watches it go.

"So, here we are," says Wade.

"Blair," says Cat, "is that a minivan? Have you gone full mom on us?"

"It is," says Blair. They assess the vehicle in silence. "And apparently I have."

"The kids love it," says Martin.

"It has a little vacuum," Blair's daughter says. "A grilled cheese got stuck in the tube thingy once."

Wade raps the minivan with his knuckles. "It's the size of my apartment," he says.

"You're really short." The boy says this, shirtless still, hands on bony hips.

"Aaaaaand this is Kenny," says Blair. "Michelle, Kenny, say hi to my best friends."

Kenny slaps his bare stomach like a bongo and Michelle smiles shyly from behind Blair's hip.

"You're right, Kenny," says Cat. "I *am* short. But I'm also full of rage."

Across the street, the corgi yelps. Two cars approach: one a Range Rover, the other a blueish-greenish convertible.

"Is that Robbie?" asks Wade.

"Is that Bon Jovi?" asks Blair.

They're both right. Robbie's driving the convertible, and he's blaring "Living on a Prayer." He pulls in next to the minivan and cuts the engine, which also cuts Jon Bon Jovi. "You made it," he says. "All of you."

He gets out and hugs everyone. When it's Cat's turn, she holds him by the shoulders. "Dude, look at your skinny ass. You're like everyone in L.A. Are you off carbs or something?"

"I started working with a new trainer," he says.

When a gigantic man with a neck tattoo climbs out of the Range Rover, Cat says, "Oh my God," because day drinking affects her inner monologue.

"Guys, this is Dash," says Robbie.

The man—the giant—gives them a wave. He's wearing a tight

white polo, black pants, and tactical boots. His arm muscles are the kind with veins, like an action figure.

"Dash is my bodyguard."

"You have a bodyguard now?" asks Wade.

Before Cat can ask about ten follow-up questions, Wade keeps talking. "Okay, the house is all right, I guess, but is this your car? Blair's got a minivan, and Robbie's driving a Chrysler?"

Robbie doesn't smile very much, but he does now as he touches the car. Cat notices that he seems at ease. He looks happy. "It's a '92," he says. "I bought it for us."

The Rejects look down on their gift, which has more bird poop on it than you'd expect for a present. Kenny is standing before the Range Rover, flexing at his own reflection in its black paint. "Can I have this one?" he asks.

"We'll see," says Robbie. He points back at the LeBaron. "There're some cassettes in the glove compartment. I found the first half of the White Album. All yours if you want it, Wade."

"Hey, boss," Dash says. "Four o'clock on the dot. Check it out."

"Right," says Robbie. He and Dash look up, and now they're all staring at the sky.

"Are we supposed to be seeing something?" asks Wade.

Robbie holds up a finger. "Just a sec. Dash, you hear that?"

Dash points out over the beach at a dot in the sky. "There it is."

Looking up makes Cat dizzy, but she *does* see it, a small plane, approaching slowly, sputtering as it crawls across the sky.

"It's pulling a sign!" says Michelle.

"It's a banner plane," says Wade.

He's right. Small, noisy planes pulling advertisements behind them are a constant on the beaches here, like seagulls and clouds. This one's different, though, Cat sees. The sign it's carrying isn't announcing lobster rolls or bottomless Bloody Marys. Instead, it's a message just for them. "No way," she says.

CAT, BLAIR, WADE, MARTIN, MICHELLE & KENNY: WELCOME TO THE BEACH!

Robbie waves at the plane, and a tiny hand waves back.

"That's so sweet, Robbie," says Blair.

They watch as the plane drifts away, getting smaller and smaller.

"Bye-bye, plane," says Kenny.

"Hey, you guys should get a picture," says Martin. "Right? A reunion shot."

They all look at one another.

"That's a good idea, Martin," says Robbie. "Dash, do you mind?"

The first few shots include the whole group, and they're all disasters. The kids look in every direction except at the camera, Wade keeps blinking, and Cat seems all squinty and short. Then Dash takes a few of just Blair, Cat, Robbie, and Wade, and these shots manage to be quite good. Cat looks at the best one now, on Dash's iPhone, and you can hardly tell that she's been drinking all day and has nearly cried twice. Wade is standing up straight for a change, and his eyes are open. Blair is so beautiful she's practically glowing, and Robbie is still smiling. He doesn't just look happy, Cat thinks, he looks as happy as she's ever seen him.

Goddamn, Cat thinks. *I've missed these assholes.*

Chapter 11

"Shit, though, you guys, how long *has* it been?"

Cat asks this, and everyone goes quiet. It's just the four of them in the kitchen. Martin is with the twins downstairs in the game room. Blair can hear them over the sounds of pinball.

"Robbie, I saw you when you were in L.A. for that . . . I wanna say endangered species thing?" says Cat. "Wade, we were both in Baltimore at Thanksgiving."

Robbie points at Wade. "Orioles-Yankees at Yankee Stadium. Last season."

"Michael Bloomberg waved at you," Wade says. "He's very short."

"Blair," says Cat, "you made me meet you for yoga last summer when I was in D.C., even though I was hungover. When's the last time we were all together, though? Like, *together* together?"

Blair knows the answer to this. She's pretty sure Robbie and Wade do, too, because they've both gone quiet. She doesn't want to be the one to say it, though, so she lets the question hang until it becomes a rhetorical statement about the cruel passage of time.

"Well, we look good, at least," says Cat. "Wade, seriously, though, you need some sun. And who taught you how to cut limes? Those are too small."

Wade, who looks thoroughly abused, holds a paring knife. "I've missed you, Cat. You're a tiny burst of sunshine."

Cat and Wade are at the wet bar making drinks, and Blair and Robbie are leaning on the kitchen island. There wasn't a house tour, exactly, nothing formal. Instead, when they all came inside, everyone dropped their bags and ran around saying things like "Wow" and "Holy crap."

"You want a drink, Blair Bear?" Cat asks.

Blair very much does. She's been thinking about alcohol since Subway a couple of hours ago when Kenny dropped his turkey sandwich on the floor and yelled at everyone in the restaurant because he couldn't put his Kids' Pak toy together.

"What exactly are we making here, Cat?" asks Wade.

"Don't know yet. I'm creating our signature cocktail for the weekend. Something stiff and fruity."

"Hey now," says Wade, snickering. He looks up at Blair but then quickly looks away. It's the closest he's come to making eye contact with her since he arrived.

"I like your family, by the way," Cat says. "I dig Martin's vibe. I could see myself going for the silver fox thing if I were into dudes. Like a Papa-don't-preach kinda thing."

Blair tries another glance at Wade, but he's studying his limes like a surgeon, and she wonders if it's going to be like this all weekend between them.

The air conditioner ticks on, and Wade says, "At some point, I'm gonna jump off the roof into that pool, by the way."

"Oh, me too," says Cat. "Then I can sue Robbie. How much are you worth now, anyway? I should know, for the lawsuit."

They're blunt about Robbie's money, the Rejects; they have been since the beginning. It's a kind of bluntness that bleeds into other aspects of their dynamic, which is probably why Robbie clears his throat and says, "It was Wade's book launch, by the way."

"Huh?" says Cat.

Blair looks at Wade again. He's stopped cutting mid-lime, frozen.

"New York," says Robbie. "Last time we were together. Wade's reading, six years ago."

"Shit," says Cat. "That's right. Blair and Wade, you guys had sex."

Blair puts her hands over her eyes, mortified. "Cat!"

"Jesus," says Wade. "What's the matter with you?"

"What?" Cat says. "It's not like we don't all know."

Blair shushes everyone. "Stop it. Not *all* of us know."

"Ohhhh," says Cat. "Martin doesn't know? The kids don't know either, I assume."

"No," says Blair. "They're five. I was thinking I'd wait until they were at least seven before telling them about everyone I've had sex with."

Wade appears to be in pain, like he's shivved himself with the paring knife, and Blair considers that maybe her husband was right. Should she have come here alone? If she looks out the window right now, will Imaginary Taylor Swift be sitting on a deck chair and shaking her head?

"There should be, like, a PSA," Cat says. "A cautionary video everyone has to watch. Don't sleep with your best friends."

"I take it back, actually," Wade says. "I haven't missed you at all."

Cat spits lime rinds into the garbage and pantomimes zipping her mouth. "I got it, though. Mum's the word. Ixnay on the sexay."

"I've just realized something," Robbie says. "Cat, you're drunk."

"What? I am not."

Blair looks into her eyes, which are blue and glassy. "Yep, that explains it. How long have you been here? You want some water? We need to keep you hydrated."

Cat laughs. "I'm fine, *Mother*. I'm on vacation. And it's basically five o'clock, right?"

Martin steps into the kitchen now, and Blair feels the four of them go collectively tense. The twins are still shouting downstairs.

"We have to buy a pinball machine now," he says. "The kids're hooked on that thing."

"Yo, Don Draper," says Cat. "I'm making drinks."

"Great," he says. "This place is amazing, Robbie."

"Glad you like it," says Robbie. "I thought the kids might like their own little entertainment room. We researched the most popular games for kids five and up."

"That sounds like something you'd do," says Wade.

"Well, it's a hit," says Martin. "Oh, and Wade, I ordered your book. Blair won't let me read the copy on our shelf, because you signed it. She's afraid I'll ruin it."

Collectively, they go even more tense now, exchanging a quick four-way look of silent trepidation. Blair thinks of her copy of *Feedback* in their living room back in D.C. *To Blair, my very good friend.*

"Thanks." Wade shuffles—shy about his writing, like he always is. "I should've just brought you a copy and saved you the trouble."

"Nah." Martin puts his arm over Blair's shoulder, and she knows what's coming. She could type it out verbatim and pin it to the fridge. "It's important to support artists," he says.

"All right, here we go, team," says Cat. She pours something greenish into five glasses, then adds Wade's little limes. Everyone takes one. "It's vodka," Cat says. "And I added lots of squirts from those fancy little bottles, because I'm an elegant lady."

They clink their glasses.

"To the Rejects," says Robbie. "I'm really glad you're all here."

The drinks are so strong everyone doubles over. Wade clutches the countertop. "Goddammit. Cat, are you mad at us for something?"

"It's like paint thinner," says Blair.

Cat holds her glass up to the light. "When did you all turn into such little bitches?"

"Mommy? Daddy?"

Blair hears Michelle coming up the stairs. "Up here, sweetie," she says.

Michelle is in her swimsuit; a pair of goggles hang around her neck. "Can we go in the pool?" she asks. Before Blair can answer, Kenny enters. He's wearing his swimsuit, too, but it's on backward and his goggles are wrapped upside down around his forehead. "We gotta go in the pool!"

"At least somebody came to party," says Cat.

Martin takes a theatrical sip of his awful drink. "I'm on it," he says. "Hon, hang with your friends. Michelle, Kenny, it's cannon-ball time."

Michelle and Kenny cheer. And here's another odd phenomenon of marriage: sometimes what appears to be a sweet, selfless gesture is actually a symptom of an ongoing problem. Martin leaves to change into his suit while Cat throws grapes in the air from a giant fruit bowl for the twins to try to catch in their mouths.

"That's kind of a choking hazard, Cat," says Blair. "Oh, honey, don't eat floor grapes."

"Is your mommy always like this?" Cat asks the twins. She throws a grape up for herself, and it bounces off her nose.

"Like what?" asks Kenny.

"Such a *mom*?"

WHEN MARTIN RETURNS, HE'S WEARING navy-blue trunks. Michelle and Kenny scurry outside after him, and for a while, the Rejects watch through the glass as Martin flings the twins across the pool.

"Is it weird that I kinda want him to throw me, too?" asks Cat.

Blair sees Wade slouched in his Wade way, his lips pressed into a line.

"I also wanna bite your kids' faces off," says Cat. "Is that weird, too?"

"Maybe a little."

"Bad optics, probably," says Cat. "Drunken lesbian arrested on Fenwick Island for biting children."

Outside, Michelle screams as she flies through the air.

"Seriously, though," says Cat. "You've made a nice family for yourself, Blair." This is sweet to hear, and Blair wishes everything was as nice as it looks, framed in this enormous window.

"But enough about you," Cat says. "What's up, Hemingway? How's the next book coming? I need something to read."

Blair braces herself for Wade to say something sad and self-deprecating. But then he smiles. "I just sold it, actually," he says. "So I guess it's going pretty well."

Chapter 12

Wade didn't plan on lying. He wasn't sitting in the Escalade with Khalid for all those hours eating candy and concocting this utter, utter bullshit. But suddenly here he is, standing in a kitchen straight out of *MTV Cribs,* watching the handsome man who has stolen his life splashing around in a swimming pool, and it just springs forth, like a bullshit geyser.

He regrets it before the words fully leave his mouth. The mark of a truly stupid lie is one you tell knowing full well it'll be quickly and thoroughly debunked.

"Wait, what?" says Blair. She smiles. "Really?"

"Are you serious?" asks Cat. "Like, *sold it* sold it?"

The geyser is a force of nature now. "Not officially. I'm waiting to hear from my agent. Could be anytime. He's negotiating. A couple of offers came in this week."

"*This* week?" asks Robbie.

Wade is thrown, briefly, by his friend's tone. Blair and Cat are happy, but Robbie seems confused.

"It's kind of a blur. I was working at the coffee shop, then my phone blew up."

Cat punches Wade in the arm. "You're not fucking with us?"

"Is it *that* shocking?"

"Well, yeah, a little," she says. "No offense, but your whole vibe is pretty depressed-writer. You show up in a flannel, all mopey-looking and pale. I was scared you were gonna fill your shorts with rocks and wade out into the ocean."

Blair laughs.

"Nice reference," he says. "Very literary."

"English electives, yo," says Cat. "Give me a hug. I'm proud of you."

Wade stoops, and she squeezes him tight, standing on her toes.

Blair hugs him now, too. They did an almost-hug in the driveway earlier—one of those silly one-armed things that happen when you've got luggage. Now, though, her body presses to his, and by sheer physical geometry, the nape of her neck is inches from his face, and he closes his eyes.

"You said multiple offers?" asks Robbie.

"My agent thinks it'll go to auction," Wade says. "That's when a bunch of publishers want a book, so you let them all show up with their best offers."

"Cage-match style," says Cat. "Nice."

"Major publishers?" Robbie presses.

Wade wonders if Robbie is just being Robbie. Is he gathering info and running numbers, or is he onto him? "Three are," Wade says. "Two are more midtier. My movie agent thinks it's cinematic, so there's a chance for a film or TV option. TV, hopefully. Movies are mostly about *Transformers* and The Rock now." Wade should definitely stop talking, but he can't. "The streaming services are buying tons of content right now."

What is he even talking about?

"Why aren't we guzzling shots and taking our shirts off?" asks Cat.

"It hasn't sold *yet,*" he says. "The business moves slowly. A lot of back-and-forth."

"Nope." Cat heads back to the bar. "We're going to Shot Town."

Blair squeezes his arm. "I didn't know you had a movie agent."

There's a distinct possibility that Wade is a bad person. He's morally bankrupt, dishonest to his core. However, it's been a long time since anyone has been excited for him, and, right or wrong, it feels nice.

"Congratulations, Wade," says Robbie. "That's . . . really something."

He doesn't have time to assess the tone of Robbie's voice, because Cat is handing out shots.

"Maybe just do a small one, Cat," says Blair.

"Would you stop it? Our melancholy writer friend is gonna be a huge literary star. This is big. Cheers, bitches."

The shots, which are Amaretto, go down smoother than Cat's signature cocktail, which tasted like liquid bees. They set their little glasses down in a row, like they used to, back when shots were something they regularly did.

"On that note," says Robbie. "I'm heading up. Gonna rest a bit. Get situated."

"Boo!" says Cat.

Robbie smiles. "You guys have fun. Dinner's at seven. You'll like it, I promise. Congrats again, Wade." He stops at the stairs. "Oh, and Blair. Upstairs, on the third floor, next to my room. Come check it out later. We set something up for you."

When Robbie is gone, Blair says, "Does he look tired?"

"A little," says Cat. "He was traveling. I'm tired, too."

"Did he travel, though?" asks Blair. "Wasn't he here already?"

They all look at each other. None of them know. Either way, Wade likes the theory that Robbie is tired instead of suspicious. Kenny screams, airborne again, and they watch the boy crash into the water. Michelle paddles in circles in the deep end.

"I think I'll go swimming, too," Cat says.

"Yeah?" says Blair.

Cat chews ice and looks at them. "And this is what's gonna happen," she says. "Blair, I'm gonna swim in that ridiculous pool with your adorable kids and your hot husband. And while I'm doing that, you two are gonna work your shit out. Because this awkwardness, I don't like it."

Wade feels his face go hot.

Cat opens the sliding glass. "Also, I should probably tell you, I'm ninety percent sure I'm ovulating, so apologies in advance if I do anything crazy." Then, in one fluid motion, Cat steps out onto the deck, takes her jean shorts off, pulls her T-shirt over her head, and dives into the water.

"Well, Cat seems to be doing well," Wade says.

"We should keep an eye on her," Blair says.

As she watches Cat splash around, Wade looks at Blair, taking her in. How has it been six years since he's seen this real-life version of her? She's changed, but only subtly. Her eyes have narrowed, her face turned keener, as if motherhood has added a layer of watchfulness. He thinks of swans in Central Park circling their dopey-looking babies. "I'm glad she had a swimsuit on, at least," he says.

"I thought she was about to flash my children."

From the pool, Cat makes a cup with her palms and squirts Kenny.

"Is she happy, do you think?" asks Blair. "Or is she doing that thing where she's just pretending to be happy?"

Isn't that what everyone does? he thinks. Instead, he says, "I wasn't being *that* awkward, was I? I actually thought I was being stoic and dignified."

"Cat exaggerates," says Blair. "I was being awkward, too."

Wade thinks of the last time he saw her. She was leaving his apartment carrying her heels and a signed copy of his book. *Bye, Wade. I'll see you, okay?*

"You've been avoiding me," she says.

Wade goes to the fridge and grabs one of the Truly things that Cat was drinking, and Blair follows him. He hands her one, too, and together they walk out onto yet another deck. From this side of the house, they look down at people on their way to and from the beach.

"I haven't been *actively* avoiding you," he says.

"Mm-hmm." Blair's eyes are a color that shouldn't be: not quite blue, but not quite brown or green either. They blend into the scenery now, like trees against a partly cloudy sky.

"Your kids really are great," he says. "The girl one, I mean. The boy is clearly a monster."

Blair laughs. "Thanks. You're not wrong."

"Martin, too. He's . . . he's nice." Wade leaves out the handsome part. He also leaves out his theory that any man over forty who looks good shirtless should have to pay an annual fee, like a carbon emissions tax.

Dash, Robbie's bodyguard, appears down on the beach. He walks a few paces, then looks up at the house. He checks his phone and then gives them both a nod.

"Do all billionaires have bodyguards?" Blair asks.

"All the ones I know," he says.

Another banner plane passes, so they have an excuse not to talk for a moment.

"Can you believe I have a minivan now?" Blair says.

They can see it from the deck, parked next to Robbie's LeBaron.

"Those rims are pretty sick, at least," he says.

It's warmer on this side of the house, so he hangs his flannel over the railing. Blair looks at his Beatles T-shirt. "Still have your finger on the pulse of modern-day culture, huh?"

"What can I say? I'm an old soul."

"If Martin and I had had a wedding—like, an *actual* wedding—would you have come?"

The question throws him, blunt and out of nowhere. Five years ago, she sent them all an email explaining that she and Martin were going to the courthouse. Martin had been married before, so a big, showy thing seemed inappropriate. Cat emailed back that Blair was robbing her of an Instagrammable moment. Wade, though, was so relieved that he nearly dropped his phone on the street. "Of course," he lies.

"Good," she says. "And you did bring sunscreen, right?"

His heart swells for her. "You really have gone full mom, haven't you?"

"I'll give you a ride to soccer practice in my minivan if you want," she says.

They sip their Trulys, and she tells him that he deserves all this. "You've worked so hard, Wade."

He nearly asks her what she's talking about, but then he remembers the book bullshit. Nearly everyone who passes below looks up at the house and at them. Wade can tell the beachgoers are wondering who the hell he and Blair are to be in a house like this, and more specifically, who the hell Wade is to be standing next to a woman like her. "I'm not in love with you anymore," he says, because once you start lying you might as well keep going, like running downhill.

Her smile falls. "You're not?"

"So if you're worried about this weekend, about seeing me, don't be. I'm good. And you're good. We're both . . . good."

"That's a lot of goods."

"Talking is hard," he says, and then he holds out his drink. "Friends?"

She touches her can to his. It's a nice moment: just the two of them, at ease with each other, in the sunshine. Later, it'll be among the last moments he remembers before everything changed forever. "Friends," she says. "Now let's go back and make sure Cat doesn't drown."

Chapter 13

*W*e set something up for you.

Blair nearly forgot. Robbie had said it in passing. *Upstairs, on the third floor, next to my room*. She's sitting on her bedroom floor sketching cartoon animals for the twins, which is something they do often: Blair draws, and they color. They've requested squirrels this time. Michelle's has pretty eyelashes; Kenny's is wearing a football jersey.

"I need to run upstairs," she tells them. Martin is showering in the bathroom. "If you need anything, Daddy's just right there."

She stops at a window that looks down on the pool. Cat is still swimming, and Wade is reading in a deck chair. Blair wonders if he really doesn't love her anymore. Can that particular kind of love just be turned off?

Wade professed his feelings for her the summer before he went to college. Blair was staying local, at the Maryland Institute College of Art (MICA) in Baltimore, but the others were scattering: Robbie to Harvard, Cat to UCLA, and Wade to Hunter College in New York. "You know, don't you?" he asked her. His tone was somber, like a soldier being shipped to war. When she asked him what, he said, "That I'm in love with you."

Of course she knew. Everyone knew. Their classmates, their teachers, their parents. The skinny writer kid, Wade Stephens, was hopelessly in love with pretty, artistic Blair McKenzie. She laughed and told him to stop it. "You're drunk, dummy." They were at a party at a classmate's parents' place in Annapolis. Wade *wasn't* drunk, but he'd been drinking, so drunkenness was plausible. He never used the *L* word again until an hour ago.

And now Blair has questions. *Why, exactly, don't you love me anymore? Is it because I'm a mom now? Is it because I look different? Is it the lines here and here, or the fact that I'm eight pounds heavier than I want to be? Is it the minivan? Is that what finally did it?* Because, even though Blair doesn't love Wade and never has, it's always been nice to know he loves her.

They spot her now, spying on them. Wade drapes his flannel over his head and waves, and Cat blows her a kiss.

THERE'S A DOOR NEXT TO Robbie's bedroom, as advertised. Blair opens it, and, after a quick blast of AC, she sees an easel and an empty canvas at the center of the room. She notices two things next. First, the light bursting through the windows is wonderful, and second, she's looking at a brand-new, fully stocked art studio.

There's every painting supply imaginable: watercolors and oils, brushes hung on hooks, a crate of extra canvases. Razor-sharp pencils, both lead and charcoal. Sketchbooks. A drying station. A hinged drafting table in the corner, its vintage wood nicked but polished to a sheen. "Oh, Robbie," she whispers.

The room is whiteout stark, which is why her eyes go right to the frame on the wall. She immediately recognizes what's behind the glass. It's from the Style section of *The Baltimore Sun*.

"Controversial Painting Earns MICA Scholarship for Expelled Baltimore Prep Student"

Blair looks at her smiling eighteen-year-old self in the article, standing beside her prizewinning canvas. The painting is of two girls kissing in downtown Baltimore. One of them is short and blond, the other taller with dark hair, and they're both wearing

Catholic school uniforms. The *Sun*'s newsprint never quite did it justice, and it doesn't now, even mounted and hung in an expensive frame. The actual canvas, Blair's crowning artistic achievement, is stunning.

She goes to the easel at the center of the room and sits on the new stool. When she was young, there was nothing more inspiring than the promise of a fresh canvas. This one just looks blank. Her iPhone in her pocket digs into her backside. She means to set it next to a box of charcoal pencils, but then she taps her email, revealing another message from Mr. McGee. Their emails have always adhered to a certain cadence, a careful, flirty back-and-forth. This, though, makes two in a row, and there's that roiling in her stomach again.

I was right. Pickup without you really was terrible. I kept looking for you, like maybe you'd show up, even though I know you're out of town. How silly is that? Anyway. I'm feeling uninspired lately. I think you should send me something beautiful to paint.

LOOKING BACK, IT'S EMBARRASSING HOW quickly Blair confided in him. She gets why she did, though. There's this term in corporate America that she hates: "reaching out." But wasn't that exactly what she'd done? Reached out?

It was last September at parent-teacher night. Martin was traveling—a pitch in Chicago or maybe Dallas—so Blair was alone. Mr. McGee stood at the front of his paint-splattered classroom with his tie loose and his sleeves rolled to his elbows.

"So many schools in this country are cutting back on art," he said. He kept touching his glasses. "But *here* we still believe that boys and girls need creative outlets. After all, they've got their whole lives to do math, right?"

As the rest of the parents shuffled to the next stop on the

classroom-to-classroom walking tour, Blair lingered at a kid's painting: a smiling giraffe with giant ears.

"Cute, right?" said Mr. McGee. "We added gloss to make the eyes look damp."

"It's lovely." Blair surprised herself then by saying, "I paint a little, too."

Mr. McGee's demeanor changed—a palpable shift from polite interest to *real* interest. "Really?"

"Well, *painted*, I guess." She touched one of the giraffe's eyes. "I'm on an artistic hiatus. I'm . . . being a mom now."

It was clear enough, the story of modern American motherhood, of sacrifices and back burners and delayed gratification. She'd left Wagner, Givens & McClain after the twins were born to start freelancing, with the hope that it'd give her more time for her own work. It didn't, though, and she hadn't painted anything decent since.

Mr. McGee took a tentative step toward her. "I'd love to see your work sometime."

Which was how their emailing started: harmless, but not *really* harmless, because there's no such thing as harmless after a certain age. Her marriage to Martin had become one of *those* marriages, like a partnership. They were like co-CEOs of some child-rearing organization. Everyone says marriage is work, especially when kids come. She was shocked by just how right everyone was, especially with twins. Blair and Martin's sex life waned, as sex lives do when you're tired and working and pulled in every direction. Blair cut their relationship some slack at first. They even joked about it. They'd be lying side by side, both thoroughly wrecked after wrangling the twins to sleep, and one of them would reach for the other. "We're going to have so much sex one of these days," he'd say. She'd reply, eyes already beginning to close, "I can hardly wait."

They never quite recovered, though. The energy Martin once directed to her funneled to the kids—to parenting and providing. Martin sometimes slept with Michelle and Kenny in forts they'd built under the ping-pong table in the basement or in a pop-up tent in the backyard. Lying alone, reading or watching late-night hosts give monologues, Blair would wonder, *Is this just how it's going to be?*

When she eventually got up the courage to go down to the basement and take pictures of her old canvases and email them to Mr. McGee, he replied within minutes.

`Wow. You're a very, very talented woman.`

SHE HOLDS A CHARCOAL PENCIL now, medium thickness. She starts at the top of the canvas and lets her hand glide downward, drawing a curve and then another curve. In her anatomy drawing class in art school, she learned that a single wavering line can become a naked female hip.

"There you are, sneaky."

It's Cat, wet in a cover-up, standing at the door with Robbie and Wade. "Damn. Look at this room." They gather at Blair's shoulder to look at her canvas. "Have I been drinking all day," asks Cat, "or do I have a crush on that line?"

"Yes," says Wade. "And yes."

Cat goes to the *Sun* article and touches the glass. "Look at us, Blair Bear. My mom still blames you for turning me gay, by the way. She says she's cool with it now, but I don't think she's ever forgiven you."

Blair puts her phone on the table, facedown. "Tell her I'm not sorry. You still have the original, right?"

"Duh," says Cat. "It's hanging right by my front door in L.A."

"This room is crazy, Robbie," says Wade.

"You built this for me?" Blair asks him.

Robbie toes at the new slate floor. "You like it? It gets the best light up here, don't you think?"

"It's beautiful. But I'm here for three days. And I design catalogs now. I don't even know if I'm an artist anymore."

Robbie runs his hand along the drafting table. "Of course, you are."

"Yeah," says Cat. She straightens the article on the wall. Blair hadn't noticed that it was crooked before, but now it's perfect. "You're *our* artist."

When Martin says things like this, it feels like pandering. When Cat says it, though, Blair has to bite her lower lip to tamp down a tremor of emotion. "Thank you, Robbie," she says. "I love it."

Robbie nods and looks at his watch. "It's three minutes past seven," he says. "We're late for dinner."

Chapter 14

Robbie imagined dinner going differently. Something calmer, more somber, somehow. Certainly quieter. He's built his career on predicting things. It all comes down to math, really. Most things in life do, he's found—numbers and patterns. In this case, though, as he sits quietly holding a piece of garlic bread, he realizes he's misread the numbers.

They're gathered around the table, and it feels like a raucous Thanksgiving dinner. Dash arranged for an Italian place to cater. It was their favorite restaurant when they were young, because it was a block from Cat's grandma's place and pizza was half price just before close.

The meal began as predicted, with a white tablecloth and gentle music on the wireless sound system. But then Michelle and Kenny smeared tomato sauce all over everything, and Wade hacked into the stereo through Bluetooth. Now he's DJing off his phone while they eat. Kenny is shirtless, which Blair called "a preventative measure," and Cat is straight-up hammered.

"It'd be easier if I could just unhinge my jaw!" She tilts her head; a slice of pepperoni pizza dangles from her hand. "Kenny, help me jam this thing into my mouth!"

Blair slides a glass of water in front of her. "Cat, seriously, please drink this."

To its credit, the sun is cooperating nicely. The sky over the ocean is lit with swirls of pinks and oranges. Robbie takes a breath and says, "So, you guys—" but he's immediately interrupted by Cat, who asks, "What are we listening to?"

"Literally the greatest album in the history of music," says Wade.

Blair rolls her eyes. "Oh brother."

"Ah," says Cat. "Abb-Blah Road."

"That's not how you say it," says Wade.

"If it helps, I agree," says Martin. "The medley at the end still gives me chills."

"*Thank you,* Martin," says Wade. "See? *Some*body here gets me."

"Ha!" says Cat. "Old dudes love the Beatles."

Martin smiles. "Ouch."

"Sorry," says Cat. "Beatles burn. Whatever, though. It doesn't count as old if you're still good-looking. Those're the rules. Look at me. I'm almost thirty-six, but I'm a smoke show, so I'm basically twenty-eight."

Robbie settles back into his chair, because it's not the right time. Not yet.

The words *I'm dying* are very straightforward. Over the last couple of weeks, though, he's been surprised at the difficulty of actually saying them. Five times since his trip to see Dr. Osborne, he's stood at mirrors and practiced.

I'm dying. I'm . . . dying. I . . . am . . . dying. I am dying.

The first one—contraction, no pause—is the most manageable. It's matter-of-fact, but serious, which is the most effective way to deliver challenging news.

"By the way," says Wade. "Robbie, did you rescue a cow in Iowa?"

"Did he what?" asks Blair.

"My parents google you a lot. My mom thinks you and Natalie Portman would make a good couple, too, in case you're wondering."

"Isn't she's married to a French guy?" says Cat.

"I read you bought an entire section out at the Super Bowl last year so homeless kids could go," says Martin.

"Oh my God," says Cat. "Seriously?" She takes out her phone and starts typing.

"Yeah, it was on CNN, I think," says Martin.

Robbie looks at the pinks and oranges over the horizon again.

"Did you know there's a site about you called The Legend of Robbie Malcolm?" asks Cat. "That Super Bowl thing is right here. No cow stuff, though."

"You can't believe everything you read on the Internet," he says.

And then Kenny asks Wade if he has "Shake It Off."

"Shake it what now?"

"Off," says Kenny.

"Yeah!" says Michelle. " 'Shake it Off'!"

"Wade, please say no," says Martin.

Wade looks at his phone. "Who sings this song of which you speak?"

"Um, Taylor Swift," says Michelle.

"Isn't that from, like, a bunch of albums ago?" asks Cat.

"That's the thing about kids," says Blair. "It's all new to them."

"Well, I typically only listen to music that's awesome," says Wade.

"Taylor Swift *is* awesome!" says Kenny.

"Swift burn," says Cat.

Wade sets his phone down. "You guys aren't gonna believe this. I *do,* in fact, have 'Shake It Off.' But listen, if I play it, I'm gonna need to see some dancing. *Legit* dancing."

The twins stand: zero hesitation. Cat stands, too. She has pizza crust sticking out of her mouth like a cigar. "Challenge accepted," she says.

Robbie considers stopping them. But how? And, frankly, why? What if this isn't so bad? His friends, they aren't quiet and somber. This is who they are.

Wade hits Play, and what follows looks less like dancing and more like an endurance challenge. Michelle is lanky and fluid, like her mom. But Kenny and Cat are disasters. They pump their arms and jump from side to side. Cat twirls. Kenny, whose bare chest is blotted with pizza sauce, transitions to something between flossing and the running man, and he nearly falls. Martin and Wade root them on, and Blair laughs so hard she barely makes a sound. "I won't be able to unsee this!" shouts Wade. "It's burned into my retinas!"

Three minutes later, as the song winds down, Robbie catches Dash's eye. Dash nods, and Robbie feels sad again, suddenly so, like he did in Dr. Osborne's office. Instead of being sad for himself, though, he's sad for his friends. They have no idea what's coming.

THEY COLLAPSE BACK INTO THEIR chairs to thundering applause.

"All right, fine," says Wade. "It ain't Lennon and McCartney, but Taylor can bring it."

"That song slaps, you snob!" says Cat.

"Play it again!" shouts Kenny.

"How about a videogame instead?" says Robbie.

It's clear that the twins want to say yes, but they look at their parents.

"Do they play videogames?" Robbie asks Blair and Martin. "I thought maybe they could play a little before dessert. And we could talk. Us. The adults."

"Is that what we are?" asks Cat. "I just lost a dance-off to two five-year-olds. One of them wasn't wearing a shirt."

"They play a little," says Martin. "Some *Mario Kart*. Kenny and I play *Madden*."

Dash is at the other side of the house holding two VR sets. The giant 4K TV behind him comes to life. A home screen appears— *Star Wars: Jedi Challenges*.

"This is a little more intense than Mario Kart," Robbie says.

"Kids, have you ever tried virtual reality?" They have no idea what he's talking about, but Kenny makes a longing sound as the Millennium Falcon soars across the screen.

"Wow," says Wade. "That actually looks cool. Maybe I can play?"

"Not now, Wade," says Robbie. This must've sounded harsher than he meant, because everyone's looking at him now, even the kids.

"Um, okay," says Wade. "Maybe later."

"Martin, Blair?" says Robbie. "Do you mind?"

When they give the go-ahead, Michelle and Kenny run to Dash, and there's no more slouching at the table now, no more fiddling with phones. Robbie clears his throat and is surprised to find that his hands are shaking beneath the table.

"Dude," Cat says. "What's up? Are we getting fired?"

Robbie stands. He fills his glass with red wine and passes the bottle to Blair. "This weekend," he says. "I know it may've come off as random or . . . sudden. I appreciate you making the time, though." Alarm has started to appear on their faces. He takes a sip. "The truth is, I need to talk to you, like I said in my invitation. And it has to be now."

Blair, Cat, Martin, and Wade look at one another.

"What's going on, Robbie?" asks Wade.

He's given speeches before, more than he can count. He's been on panels and been interviewed on television. His words, though, are usually prepared for him—pre-thought-through by a communications team. There are no talking points now, no slowly scrolling prompters. It's just Robbie, standing at a kitchen table, and it's a lonely feeling. "I'm sick," he says.

A TIE fighter explodes on the screen across the room. "I got him!" shouts Kenny.

"No you didn't!" says Michelle. "I got him!"

"We both got him! See? He blew up!"

Dash shrugs an apology. The headphones and goggles have made Michelle and Kenny deaf and blind to all of this.

"You're . . . sick?" asks Blair.

"Yes. And I wanted you to hear it from me. Because once it gets out—and it *will* get out, probably soon—it'll be everywhere. When that happens, everything will be different."

Wade is still holding his phone. Taylor Swift smiles from his iTunes screen. "What does *sick* mean?"

"I have pancreatic cancer," he says.

"You have *what*?" asks Wade.

"I'm dying."

"Robbie," says Blair, but she doesn't move. Neither do the rest of them. It was like this after his first diagnosis, in New York. Time simply froze. Martin rests his palms on the table. Wade's mouth falls open. He sets his iPhone down, and his wineglass nearly tips, but somehow, it doesn't. And then Cat runs to the sink and throws up.

Chapter 15

Cat liked them the moment she met them—Blair, Robbie, and Wade—instantly, the way little kids spot each other across playgrounds and become inseparable.

It was the first week of their freshman year, and they were running around the track behind Baltimore Prep. They'd each been encouraged by their parents to join the cross-country team as a way to get involved and make some friends.

Workouts were divided by gender—boys with boys, girls with girls—but the one-mile warm-up runs were coed. Cat hadn't figured out how good of a runner she was yet, so she was loafing toward the back of the pack. Wade was a few strides ahead in a Ringo Starr T-shirt, running alongside Robbie.

"Some people say he was just this random drummer who was in the right place at the right time," he was saying. "But that's bullshit. They totally gelled when Ringo joined. They *became* the Beatles."

"Um, okay," said Robbie. "Who are you again?"

Robbie was wearing the world's ugliest red Asics sneakers. Later, he'd tell them that he'd gone to a specialty running shop and had his stride videotaped, which was totally Robbie. Wade kept going on about the Beatles, but Cat was far more focused on Blair, who was running near the two boys. More specifically, she was focused on the way Blair's calf muscles flexed with every stride.

The backs of her knees, too, and the way her hair swayed as she ran.

At fifteen, Cat didn't officially know she was gay. She had, however, become increasingly aware of the female bodies around her and the persistent ache those bodies sometimes caused in her lower stomach.

Apparently she and Wade were on the same page, because Wade turned from Robbie to blurt, "Hey, why do you have all that paint on your shoes?"

That swaying ponytail again. A brief flash of her lower back. "What?" Blair asked.

"Your shoes. They're all splattered."

Blair looked down. "I wear them when I paint. I'm an artist."

Cat watched poor Wade struggle to think of something interesting to say next. Eventually, he went with "Sweet. Well, hi, I'm Wade."

"Blair," said Blair.

And then Wade looked back to Robbie. "You're the guy they made the special math program for. Robbie, right?"

Robbie admitted that he was. He'd tested so high on his high school entrance exam that he went to advanced-level math classes at Loyola University three days a week. Wade nearly tripped over a crack and asked Robbie how he liked them apples.

"What?"

"You know, *Good Will Hunting*. Matt Damon? Math?"

"Oh," said Robbie. "Yeah."

Introducing herself to three running strangers would normally have been terrifying, but seeing Wade try so hard to make friends was inspiring, so she sped up and pulled even with them. "Hey, guys," she said. "I'm Cat."

Robbie was breathing hard. "Kat with a *K,* or Cat with a *C*?" he asked.

"Cat like a cat," she said.

"Hey, Cat," said Blair, and Cat blushed at the sound of her name coming from Blair's mouth.

As far as beginnings go, it sounds simple enough. It wasn't, though, and Cat has thought about the confluence of factors that led to the four of them becoming so close. They each had some defining feature that would've made them otherwise groupless in the social hierarchy of high school. For Robbie, it was his brain. He was simply too smart for mainstream teenage society. Wade's nerdiness was too specific to fit into any particular subset of nerd culture. Cat didn't even know who she was yet. She was short and brash and smart and inexplicably angry at the pretty girls and mean girls alike. And then there was Blair, who was beautiful, but beautiful in a way that no one could quite figure out. She was smart, but she was artistic, too, which allowed boys like Robbie and Wade in while simultaneously keeping more conventional boys at a distance—popular jocks and class presidents.

They were groupless, so they made their own group. Cat liked them the moment she met them, and now she loves them.

THE WAVES OUTSIDE CAT'S BEDROOM window only make her headache worse, like the throbs and crashes have somehow been coordinated.

Dash carried her up here thirty minutes ago. She nearly fainted after she barfed, which was when she felt herself being lifted off her feet. On their way up, she saw that Blair was crying and Wade was at the kitchen table with his hands pressed to his forehead. The twins were yelling at the TV. Despite everything, Cat had to admit it felt nice to be held.

She shudders now—part sob, part dry heave—and thinks about the last time she saw Robbie before this weekend. He was in L.A. for a benefit, and they met for lunch. When the check came, he set a black Amex card on the table, and then he told Cat he thought their waitress was flirting with her earlier. They were near Hollywood, so the waitress in question was a stunning waitress-slash-model-slash-actress who glided across the restaurant like some celestial creature.

Cat laughed. "Well, duh. I've got an ass that won't quit."

"Don't joke," he said. "You should talk to her. Maybe go say hi."

Cat finished her mimosa and waved the suggestion away. That was more than a year ago. She hadn't started at *The Morning Gab* yet; she hadn't met Gabrielle. She was alone and lonely in a big, sprawling West Coast city where she'd never really felt like she belonged. "Come on, Cat," Robbie said. "What girl wouldn't want to be with you?"

THERE'S A KNOCK. WHEN SHE rolls over, the room spins, and Robbie is standing in the doorway. "I brought you some LaCroix," he says.

She takes the can as he sits at the side of her bed. "I made this about me, didn't I?" she asks. He smiles in the low light, and Cat searches him for signs of . . . *something*. Illness, she supposes, proof that he's dying. It's just Robbie, though, tired-looking, a little skinny. "You're not really sick, though," she says. "You were just joking."

"Some joke, huh?"

"Sounds like something Wade would do," she says.

"Hey, I resent that."

Wade and Blair are at the door now. They sit, too: Wade at the foot of the bed, Blair on the other side, opposite Robbie. Blair sets a cool hand on Cat's forehead, like a mom checking on a fever. "How're you feeling?"

"Been better," she says. "You?"

Blair's eyes are puffy, her face streaked. "Oh, you know."

"I'm sorry I threw up, Robbie," says Cat.

Downstairs, Kenny shouts about Ewoks.

"God, I'm sorry," says Blair. "I'll close the door."

"No," says Robbie. "Sit. Stop apologizing, all of you. We're at the beach. We're supposed to be having fun. Although, maybe a little less fun for you, Cat. I think we're only equipped for one death right now."

Blair tries to hold back a sob. "Sorry," she whispers.

"This part was always going to be hard," Robbie says. "But we have the whole weekend. We have this house. The convertible. And I've planned activities."

"Dude," says Cat. "Like what, minigolf?"

"Actually, yes," says Robbie. "Did you not read Dash's itinerary? Minigolf is tomorrow. Maybe Dairy Queen, too. And we're having a party on Sunday. An official one."

"A party?" asks Blair.

"Yes," he says. "Technically, we're all still Catholics. When someone dies, Catholics have wakes, right? Which are really just parties."

"Is that why we're here?" asks Wade. "Is that what this is? A wake?"

Cat's breath catches.

"Cat, stop," says Blair. "If you start, I'll . . ."

"It's better than a wake," says Robbie. "Because I get to be here to enjoy it." He waves his hand at the window, at the roaring ocean behind it. "Welcome to my living wake."

Blair's shoulders shake. Wade reaches for her but pulls his hand back.

"I've thought about it," says Robbie. "If I'd done this the old-fashioned way, I have a pretty good idea what would've happened."

Blair scoots into bed beside Cat now.

"The three of you would've come to my wake. I wouldn't be there, obviously. There'd be depressing music. Wintertime in Baltimore, probably, so cold and gray. There'd be a ton of people there you didn't know. You'd give my mom your condolences. My dad, too. They'd be on opposite sides of the place, so you'd have to find him. Then, afterward, you'd all go out for a drink. Maybe the Mt. Washington Tavern. You'd catch up. You'd have some laughs. It'd be nice. Then you'd hug at the door. You'd tell each other that you'll keep in touch. After my funeral the next day, you'd head home, back to your lives."

Cat can picture everything he's saying. She imagines being stuck in the middle seat on some Southwest flight, because she never remembers to check in early.

"And here's the part that makes me really sad," says Robbie. "There's a chance that'd be it. The three of you might literally never see each other again."

Cat looks at Blair and then Wade and wonders if Robbie is right.

"I didn't want to let that happen," he says. "*That's* why you're here. Plus, I wanted to get to say a proper goodbye."

"Shit, Robbie," says Wade. He holds his head in his hands, and Blair sinks into Cat.

"I have more planned than putt-putt and ice cream," says Robbie. "You'll see. All I ask is that you have an open mind. Whatever happens, just go with it. Okay?"

"Robbie?" says Blair. "You're sure, right? That you're sick?"

He sighs. "I started losing weight, and my abs kept hurting, like I'd had a hard workout, but it didn't go away. So, I went to my doctor. It's everywhere now. There's no stopping it."

"But you're so rich." Wade whispers this.

"God, Wade," says Cat.

"I know that sounds shitty," he says. "But isn't there something you can do? Steve Jobs, right? He was rich. I heard he went to see the Dalai Lama and had all these crazy experimental treatments."

Cat holds the cold can to her head, and Robbie says exactly what she's thinking. What they're probably all thinking. "You're right, Wade. Steve Jobs was very rich. But then he died anyway."

Chapter 16

The idea that Wade might be able to sleep was almost crimi-
nally naïve. He's in a strange bed in a *Citizen Kane*–size room,
the ocean outside won't shut up, he's lied to everyone, and his best
friend is dying. Also, Blair.

He's devastated about what Robbie told them, but still, here he
is, thinking about her.

He checks his phone for a message from Brandon, even though
it's the middle of the night, and then he opens Instagram again.
This time, he scrolls by Blair's pool picture and makes his way back
through time. When he stops, it's on an image from six years ago.
All four of them. Cat is doing a *Charlie's Angels* gun pose and Blair
is laughing. Wade has his arm around Robbie. They're in front of
the McNally Jackson bookshop in New York.

"In NYC for my friend's book launch. Go buy FEEDBACK by
Wade Stephens!!!"

Seeing Blair start to cry earlier in Cat's room had a complicated
effect on Wade. He wanted to hug her—to engulf her, actually—
as if to shield her from danger. He didn't, though, because he was
too upended by the memory of the night this picture was taken.
It was the last time he had seen Blair until today, and she'd cried
that night, too.

Robbie wasn't a billionaire then, but he was rich enough to pay for everyone to travel to New York for Wade's book launch, which included a reading at McNally Jackson and a party at a place called KGB Bar. Wade's publisher had hyped the book, and he'd gotten some nice prepub press, so all of the folding chairs at the store were full.

When he finished signing books, Cat, Blair, and Robbie were standing at the front of the store waiting for him beside a blown-up photograph of his book's cover.

"Dude," said Cat. "You're legit. You sold forty-four books. I counted. That one chick with the dreads bought two."

Robbie shook Wade's hand. "You were great, Wade."

"Funny, too," said Blair. "Everyone loved you."

"When you get famous, will you stop talking to us?" asked Cat.

Wade said he would, but gradually, so they'd barely notice, and he understood that he was happier than he'd ever been.

It was a nice night, so they decided to walk to KGB Bar. Blair and Wade lagged behind Cat and Robbie, who were a block ahead, sidestepping pedestrians and delivery guys on bikes. "The odds of them making it without Cat getting run over are pretty slim, huh?" Wade asked. He and Blair were at a crosswalk on Eighth Street.

"Robbie will take care of her," Blair said. And then she looked up at Wade. Her expression was one he'd never seen from her before. Later, he'd recognize it as something like admiration, maybe even attraction, but, in the moment, he was confused.

"What? Tell me I didn't just do that entire reading with something in my teeth?"

"Your teeth are fine," she said. "It's just . . . well, how was it?"

"How was what?"

She shoved him. "You just looked out on a store full of people and read from your published novel, Wade. What was that like?"

He'd been nervous, of course. But a few paragraphs in, all the faces aside from Blair's had dissolved. When he'd look up from time to time between sentences, there she'd be, head tilted, eyes focused only on him. "It was nice," he said. "I could get used to it."

The walk signal blinked. People bustled around them. The city was lit from above—from skyscrapers and glowing advertisements and satellites in space. Blair slid her arm into his. "Success looks good on you, Wade Stephens."

WADE GETS OUT OF BED now, abandoning sleep.

Outside, the pool lights are all still on. A Peppa Pig floatie drifts in the deep end. The hallway is quiet. He heads to Cat's room, where he finds Blair and Cat, asleep in Cat's bed. Cat is on her side, mouth open, butt pressed against Blair's hip. Blair is sleeping on her back, head angled toward him. Neither Blair nor Cat changed into pajamas, so Cat's still in her swimsuit and cover-up. Blair is in linen shorts and a simple V-neck T-shirt.

Wade could wake Blair and make sure she's okay. He could see if she wants some water and then usher her to her bedroom. But it's not his place to do these things. It never has been, and it never will be.

"WHAT IF I STAY AT your place tonight?"

KGB Bar was cool and offbeat, decorated with a Cold War–era motif, and the music was loud. Wade's brain went straight to logistics. "That's silly. Robbie got you guys rooms at the Plaza. It's, like, an historic landmark."

Blair's expression asked, *How stupid are you, Wade Stephens?*

"Wait, what?" he asked.

She smiled, said nothing.

The postreading party had been nice. There was a *Feedback* cake, and his agent, Brandon, gave a boozy toast about how this was the beginning of something amazing. But then it turned into what most parties turn into: a bunch of people drinking. A few times over the course of the evening, Wade saw Blair looking at him. He'd attributed it to wishful thinking. But then she came up to him and said . . . that.

What if I stay at your place tonight?

She pulled her hair off her neck and touched her glass to the skin there, cooling herself. She'd been dancing with Cat, and he could practically see heat radiating off her.

"You want . . . to stay with me?"

Blair laughed, flush and drunk and gorgeous. "I do."

"Cat made you drink too much, didn't she?"

"Yeah. That's what Cat does. It's not why I want to stay with you, though."

Wade looked around the bar. It was midnight. Robbie and Cat were chatting with people he didn't know. "What will we tell them?"

"They'll figure it out."

WADE ISN'T GREAT AT WRITING SEX scenes. He's too self-conscious to go into detail, because he doesn't want to sound like a pervert. But if he'd written this one, it would've been tasteful and understated and classy.

A tentative first kiss, as the female character steps out of heels. Clothing removed in an organized fashion. Small sounds of quiet pleasure when ears are bitten and collarbones nuzzled. Then the male character says "Holy shit" the moment he's finally inside of her.

After, lying in bed, Wade couldn't stop smiling. He tried. *Stop smiling, you moron,* he told himself, but he was no longer in control of his facial expressions. Earlier, at his reading, he'd been the happiest he'd ever been. It was trumped, though, by this, as Wade realized that everything in his life was now good. What a staggering realization happiness can be, like what lottery winners must feel as they read and reread their numbers. His book had just come out. Blair McKenzie was naked beside him. Even his apartment was good. It had been transformed from a shitty studio the size of a Yemeni prison cell to something stylish and Bohemian.

"I really like that picture," Blair said.

It was as if she'd read his mind and agreed with him. She was looking at a Beatles print. He'd just bought it a few days before from a street vendor. It was a black-and-white photograph from 1968 of John, Paul, George, and Ringo mingling with fans outside a churchyard. *Rolling Stone* had just called Wade's novel "a fun little blast of rock & roll," and he was flush with enough cash to buy things on the street.

"Thanks," he said. "It's cool, right?"

And then, with the love of his life beside him, he went ahead and laid out the next fifty years of their lives in his mind. Their wedding. Anniversary parties. A Margaret Atwoodian haul of published books. Baby showers and graduations and aging gracefully together. These images of the two of them came together so effortlessly that he wasn't even surprised when Blair said, "I think I'm pregnant."

After a moment: "What'd you say?"

"I think I'm pregnant."

"But it's been, like, five minutes."

She laughed. "No. I mean *before* that."

Wade sat up and said, "What?" again. He probably could've said it a few dozen more times. "But how? Who?"

Blair held the sheets in a twist over her breasts. She rolled onto her side and faced him. "Someone from work. We're . . . we're seeing each other."

"Seeing each other?"

"Kind of. His name is Martin."

A few minutes ago, she'd moaned into his ear and he'd wondered where in Baltimore they'd get married. Now it felt wrong to touch her.

"Are you going to say something?" she asked. Apparently, he hadn't for a while.

"Do you like him?" Wade meant *love,* but he couldn't bring himself to say it.

"I do," she said. "I think. It's only been a few months. He's one of the bosses. An account guy. I know, I'm dating an account guy. But he's sweet. He calls me Beautiful Blair."

In nearly any other city, Wade's bedroom would've been dark. But it was New York, so his bedroom was *never* dark, and he could see tears gathering at the side of her face, staining the pillow. "You're crying," he said.

"I know," she said. "I don't really know why. I'm just scared, I guess."

"Why are you scared?" he asked. "You said you like him."

"Because when I tell him, he's going to want to marry me. And then that'll be it. That'll be the rest of my life. Am I ready for that?"

Wade didn't answer. Instead, he spent some time torturing himself with revisionist fiction. What if this Martin guy *hadn't* gotten Blair pregnant and, instead, Wade had, just now? He imagined a phone call a month later. *Wade, it's Blair. You're not going to believe this.*

As his heart broke, Wade understood that everything that had seemed so good just minutes before really wasn't good at all. His apartment was, in fact, a dump. *Feedback* would be gone and forgotten in weeks. His next book would take years to write and no one would want it.

"You don't have a spare pregnancy test, do you?" Blair tried to laugh.

"Fresh out," Wade said. "You'd be surprised how often this happens."

He got dressed in his terrible little bathroom so Blair could have privacy. Then, at 2:15 A.M., they went to the Duane Reade at the end of his block. A benefit of New York City living: you can get a pregnancy test twenty-four hours a day. They bought some sodas, too, and a box of powdered donuts and a tacky cat figurine wearing an "NYC is Puurrfect" T-shirt for Cat.

By then, the test itself was an afterthought. They both knew what it was going to say.

THERE'S ENOUGH PIZZA AND PASTA downstairs to fuel a revolution. Wade's plan is to heat up a few slices of pepperoni and sit next to the pool. Maybe he'll find a bottle of something exotic-looking in the bar.

When he steps onto the main floor, though, he hears something he hadn't expected: light sabers. Then he sees Blair's husband virtually battling Darth Vader on the flat-screen.

"Oh, shit." He considers bolting to the kitchen, but he finds himself making eye contact with a teenage boy. The kid's face is on a laptop, which is open and aimed toward Martin, who's just now struck Vader's left shoulder with his light saber. Martin pulls all the VR crap off his head. "You see? How awesome is *that*?"

A confusing ten seconds follows. Martin is looking at the boy on the computer, but the boy on the computer is looking at Wade. Martin turns and sees Wade standing in a pair of old athletic shorts and his Beatles T-shirt. "Um, hey," says Wade.

Martin pauses the game. "Oh, Wade. Hi."

"Did you just kill Darth Vader?"

Martin looks embarrassed, like he's been caught watching porn. "I think I just wounded him," he says. "This is my son, Brian. Brian, this is Wade. He's one of Blair's old friends."

The boy on the computer waves. "Hey," he says, his face briefly pixilating.

"So, that's it, Bri," says Martin, "virtual reality *Star Wars*. What do you think?"

"Those graphics are hype," says Brian. "VR's where it's at. The processing speed on that screen is dope, too. Gotta be 4K."

Martin looks at Wade. "Any idea what any of that means?"

"Bits and pieces," says Wade.

Martin crouches at his laptop. "I'll call you on Monday, okay?" he says. "Five o'clock, your time? Good?"

"Yeah, cool." Brian's voice is unsteady, the way a boy's voice sounds right before it starts to change. "Later, Dad."

"All right," says Martin. "Love you." The laptop makes a *bloop* sound, and the boy is gone. Martin's hair is messed up from the VR equipment. "Brian's my *other* son," he says. "From my first marriage. He's in San Francisco with his mom. I don't get to see him very often, so we Skype. I thought he'd get a kick out of all this."

"That processing speed *is* pretty dope," says Wade, and they smile at the floor.

"Did you happen to see Blair up there?" asks Martin. "Is she still . . . ?"

"I stopped by Cat's room. Doesn't look like they're going any-where anytime soon."

"I wasn't sure if I should wake her," Martin says. There's a small plastic bucket of Amstel Lights on the coffee table. Martin offers Wade one. "I brought them from home. Seems silly now, right? This place has everything."

Wade takes a beer.

Martin tries to wrangle some of his hair down, but it pops right back up. "I'm sorry about your friend, Wade," he says.

Wade thanks him and resists the urge to drink his beer as fast as he can.

"And it sounds like congrats are in order," says Martin. "Blair told me you sold your second novel."

"Thanks," says Wade. "It's . . . exciting."

"She'll have to hang on to that signed copy of your first one. Sounds like it'll be worth something."

Six years ago, Wade hadn't gotten the chance to sign Blair's book at the reading or the after-party. Instead, he ended up sign-ing it in his apartment, while she was in his bathroom taking the pregnancy test from Duane Reade. "Maybe someday," he says.

"The kids and I are leaving tomorrow," Martin says. "Blair will be staying. We thought maybe us staying, under the circumstances, would be a distraction. And the kids might be confused. Probably best to give Blair—and all of you—time to be together."

Instagram really is a strange thing. You can look at a guy for years, keep vague tabs on him, envy him, be infuriated by how good-looking he is. And then you meet him one day and he's just some guy. He's a little shorter than you imagined he'd be, and, just like you, he has no idea what he's doing.

"I'd appreciate it if you'd look after her for me," Martin says.

"Look after her?"

The monitor on the wall flips to screen saver mode, the Millennium Falcon again. "This is going to be hard for her. You're all very special to her. *You* in particular. I can tell. You two have a . . . a special bond."

The silence that follows is the kind that could quickly become destructive, killing them both and sucking Delaware into a black hole. But then Martin asks, "Do you wanna play a little?"

"You mean *Star Wars*?"

"Yeah. It makes you dizzy at first, but you get used to it."

Wade puts the other headset on and pulls the goggles over his eyes. The game surrounds him, teasing out toward the limits of his peripheral vision. "Whoa," he says.

A selection board appears. Martin toggles to Lightsaber Battle. "Do you want to be Luke or Vader?" he asks.

"I should probably be Luke," Wade says. "You *are* pretty old."

The controller vibrates in Wade's hand, activating his pretend weapon, and Darth Vader stands before him. Except it isn't Darth Vader, it's just Martin. And, for the next two hours, they drink beers and battle in the TV room with the pitch-black ocean behind them.

Saturday

Chapter 17

Robbie sees the beach ball before he's even sure it's a beach ball. It's just a dot at first, bouncing along the shore. But, like the banner planes hauling their messages across the sky, it gets clearer as it gets closer.

The ball drifts off into the surf and bobs. A lady wading just past her knees plucks it from the water and tosses it over her shoulder. It catches some wind and blows back toward the sand where it ping-pongs off a fisherman's Yeti cooler and a lifeguard stand, and then comes to a rest on the beach behind the house.

The color is unusual for a beach ball. Instead of the standard rainbow swirl, it's just a yellow smiley face. It's partially deflated, which makes it more of a blob than a ball, and it's dirty, too, like it's traveled a great distance. A breeze blows a chill into the air, tipping it over, and the smile turns almost completely upside down.

A little on the nose, isn't it? he thinks.

"How're you doing, boss?" Dash asks.

Robbie closes his eyes then opens them slowly. "Good. Really good. Wow."

They're on the balcony outside Robbie's room, and a clear mix of liquid morphine eases into Robbie's right arm. It burns for a second, then throbs, then becomes a feeling like not caring. "I see why people get addicted to this."

"You should be careful. This stuff can kill you."

It's charming that this is still where Dash's head goes: protecting him. "All things considered," Robbie says, "it probably wouldn't be a bad way to go. You'd just drift away, right? You wouldn't feel a thing."

"Forgive me, boss," says Dash, "but you're stoned."

Robbie puts his syringe away and looks at his hand. Each finger has its own heartbeat.

"Everything's going pretty well so far, I'd say," says Dash.

"Well, I think Cat may be an alcoholic," says Robbie. "Wade is a huge liar, and Blair and Martin's marriage is falling apart."

"Right," says Dash. "But aside from that, Mrs. Lincoln, how was the play?"

Robbie smiles. He's sitting in a cushy chair with his feet up. It's just past eight A.M. and the sky is clear blue. Off the balcony, he can see his new convertible parked next to Martin and Blair's minivan. Martin is in the driveway loading things into the Odyssey.

"The LeBaron really is pretty cool, huh?" Robbie says.

Dash seems to doubt this. "I would've gone with a Lamborghini, but what do I know?"

"The hula girl on the dashboard is what got me," Robbie says.

"The look on the guy's face when you offered him seventy-five thousand dollars for his thirty-year-old Chrysler made the whole thing worth it, if you ask me." The medicine keeps dulling things. Dash sips from a bottle of water. "So, I need to mention something, boss. Yesterday evening, on the beach, when I was doing my rounds, I saw a woman. She was taking pictures of the house. She was out there again this morning."

"Was it our persistent friend from New York?"

"Can't say for sure," says Dash. "But she had red hair, so it seems likely."

CNBC is on back in his room; Robbie can hear it through the screen door. He wonders how the story will be reported when it eventually breaks. Somber tones and wild speculation seem like a safe bet. "Can't hide forever," he says.

"I'll keep an eye on the situation," says Dash.

The beach ball is back in the water now, marooned between the waves and the shore, spinning on its head. "This next part," he says, "phase two. It'll be easier with Martin and the twins gone. Logistically speaking."

"I thought the same thing," says Dash. "I'll miss Michelle and Kenny, though. Especially Kenny. Yesterday, he told me his swim trunks have built-in underwear to hold his ding-dong."

"You think you'll ever have kids, D?"

"Sure. I'm only twenty-eight, but, you know . . . someday, right?" Discomfort flashes across Dash's face. *Someday* is a word he gets to be very casual about. "I mean, I'm . . ."

"It's fine, Dash. I get it."

Robbie would've had kids someday, too, he supposes, and he bets he'd have been a good dad, definitely better than his own. "We should go down to breakfast. They're waiting for us on the beach. Is everything ready for phase two?"

Dash pulls the three manila envelopes from his messenger bag again and sets them on a small table. His friends' names are written neatly in black marker: Blair, Cat, and Wade. "All ready on my end."

"Good. After golf, we'll hand them out."

Dash nods.

"They're gonna hate me, aren't they, D?"

"Nah," he says. "They're your best friends."

"They'll be mad, though."

"I think you should prepare for that," says Dash. "You have to look at it from their perspective, boss. The things in those envelopes are very sensitive. They'll understand, though. You're helping them, right?"

Robbie sticks a Band-Aid over a red dot of blood at the crook of his elbow. "What'd I say about telling me what I want to hear?"

Chapter 18

Wade is a way better miniature golfer than he has any right to be. As his pink ball bounces off the wood border, rolls between the horse statue's legs, and breaks gently along the raised mound of Astroturf, he dreads what's about to happen. Because shouldn't he be letting Robbie win? Shouldn't he, under the circumstances, at the very least be less awesome at this?

Cat rolls her eyes when his ball drops into the hole. "Oh God," she says.

"Is that three in a row?" asks Martin.

"Four, actually," says Wade.

"You keep getting it in with one hit!" shouts Kenny.

"That's legitimately impressive," says Martin.

"Don't encourage him," says Cat. She sets her ball on the putting mat and takes a sip from her flask. "Wade is inexplicably good at useless things."

"Ouch," Wade says. "But yeah."

"Ping-pong," says Robbie. "Darts. Cornhole. Quarters. Skee-Ball."

"Don't forget Beatles trivia," adds Cat. Her ball bounces off the horse's hoof and rolls backward. "Wade, what's the fifth song off their fourth album?"

And now Wade dreads this, too, because he's about to sound like a huge nerd. "In the UK or the U.S.?" he asks.

"My point exactly," she says.

Cat kicks her ball into the hole and checks her phone. She keeps doing that, Wade's noticed, checking her phone. They all do, because they're phone-obsessed zombies, but Cat's doing it more than the rest of them. Wade checks his now. Still nothing from Brandon.

"Is this really what you wanna do, Robbie?" Cat asks. "We could be doing *anything*."

Robbie is resting on a plaster chair shaped like a mushroom. "Where else would I wanna be?" he asks.

When it's Kenny's turn to putt, the boy swings wildly, knocking his ball across four holes. It comes to a stop by a ship full of Viking skeletons.

"Maybe not so hard, bud," says Martin.

"I hate this stupid game!" Kenny shouts.

"So, you guys know this place?" asks Martin. "Was it here back in the day?"

"Yeah," says Cat. "Viking Golf was our jam, especially before we got fake IDs. They've made some upgrades. It looks nice. Blair climbed on that Viking statue's shoulders once. A bike cop almost arrested her."

Martin points at an eight-foot-tall plaster statue. "*That* Viking?" he asks. "Really?"

Blair leans on her putter. "I guess there's a lot you don't know about me," she says, and everyone pretends not to notice her tone, which is just short of anger. Wade hasn't seen Blair so much as look at Martin all morning.

"Remember the guy who used to run this place?" asks Cat. "The smoking guy with the Lynyrd Skynyrd T-shirts. You think he's still around?"

"No," says Robbie. "He's dead. Lung cancer." That word—the C-word—strikes an ugly chord. "His daughter runs it now. Jane. She's here somewhere. I saw her when we walked in."

"How do you know all this?" asks Cat.

Robbie taps his ball, which stops a few inches from the hole. "Oh, right. I didn't tell you guys. I bought it a couple of weeks ago."

Cat looks up from her phone. "You bought what?"

"This. Viking Golf."

"You bought a putt-putt golf course?" asks Cat. "In Delaware?"

"We had fun here," Robbie says. "I thought it'd be a nice thing to have."

They all look at Robbie now; no one seems to know what to say. He's smiling. If Wade's not mistaken, he looks a little stoned.

Hole eleven features a treasure chest that you either have to go through or around. Wade goes around and sinks his ball, and Cat gives him a sneaky middle finger. And then Michelle points at her brother, who's holding his crotch. "Uh, Daddy," she says.

"Oh. Hey, buddy. You gotta hit the potty?"

Kenny seems to genuinely not know. "Maybe?"

"That's definitely a yes." Martin hustles Kenny away, off to the restroom shack, which is when a woman stops by. She's as tan as the lifeguards back at the beach. She's wearing a Viking Golf T-shirt and pink running sneakers.

"Hey, everyone," she says.

"Hi, Jane," says Robbie. "Speak of the devil. Everyone, this is Jane. She runs Viking Golf."

"Prestigious, I know," Jane says. "Welcome." Everyone introduces themselves. When Wade shakes Jane's hand, their eyes meet. He likes her sneakers, which he briefly considers telling her but then doesn't.

"Robbie said you all used to come here," Jane says.

"I like what you've done with it," says Cat.

"Thanks. We're getting there. We painted, added some new obstacles. Check out the octopus on the last hole. It's pretty cool. We installed a Sonos system, so we can play music."

Wade notices Phil Collins now. He's mostly drowned out by the go-carts next door.

"And there's ice cream!" says Michelle.

"Sweetie," says Blair. "*Shhh.*"

"You're right," says Jane. "Want some? I can hook you up. I know the owner."

Michelle's eyes light up, but Blair tells her to wait for Kenny. And then, to Wade's horror, Jane says, "You're the writer, right? Robbie told me about you."

It's a feeling like having your pants yanked down in a high school cafeteria. Wade's palms flood, and his face burns. The surest way to cripple writers is to acknowledge that they're a writer. "Oh," he says. "Yeah. I guess."

"What kind of stuff do you write?"

Another fact about writers: None of them know how to answer this question. "Comedies," he says. "But not ha-ha comedies. They're about serious things, too. Sort of domestic stories, but with a music angle. But not . . ."

"He's really good," says Blair. "He just sold a book, actually."

Blair thinks she's helping, Wade knows, but she's only made it worse.

"Oh, wow," says Jane. "That's great. What's it about?"

"I was wondering that, too," says Blair. "What *is* it about, Wade?"

He considers coming clean right here in the shadow of a giant purple dragon. But then, thank God, Martin and Kenny return. "Gimme my putter!" the boy shouts.

"Hi, I'm Martin." Martin shakes Jane's hand.

"This is Blair's husband," says Robbie.

"Oh, there are a lot of you," says Jane.

"Kenny, Mommy said we can have ice cream," says Michelle.

"Ice cream?" says Kenny. "Serious?"

Blair sighs an apology, and Jane laughs. "Well, I tell you what, Wade, I'll look you up at Bethany Beach Books." She turns to Blair and the twins. "Come on, y'all. Let's make it happen." Blair, the twins, and the minigolf woman walk off together.

"Robbie, you told her I'm a writer?" Wade asks.

"I didn't realize it was a secret," says Robbie. "Cat, I think you're up."

Apparently, though, Cat is done playing for the day, because she smashes her iPhone against the plaster dragon, screams, "I hate this fucking thing!" and then heaves it across the go-cart track.

Chapter 19

"Look at us," says Cat. "Coupla gals gabbing in the bathroom. Just like old times."

They're in the powder room back at the beach house, looking at themselves in the mirror, which is weirdly clean, like, stare-into-your-soul clean.

Clichés of womanhood be damned, Blair and Cat have stood side by side looking into bathroom mirrors more times than Blair could ever count, from the girls' restroom at Baltimore Prep on through sketchy ladies' rooms in bars and clubs when they were young and passing cigarettes back and forth.

Cat's reflection now has blotchy pink skin and wild eyes, and Blair feels bad for not keeping better tabs on her friend. "Wanna talk about it?"

"Oh, talk about what?" Cat asks, and they smile.

An off-white bidet sits between their reflections, which is difficult not to address. "Ever use one of those?" Cat asks.

"There was one at a hotel once," Blair says. "I was intimidated, though."

Cat splashes her face and rubs water from the half-moons under her eyes. "I hear they're very refreshing."

Blair holds Cat's eyes in the mirror, because she's not going to joke her way through this.

"In my defense, I needed a new phone anyway." Cat squints at herself. "And, I mean, who hasn't wanted to throw her iPhone across a go-cart track, right?"

Everything is quiet on the other side of the bathroom door. The others haven't returned yet. Immediately after her phone smashed on the pavement and disappeared beneath a pile of go-cart tires, Cat started marching home. Blair sent the kids back to Martin and chased after her friend.

"What's going on, Cat?"

"I'm in love with someone," she replies, "but I hate her. I only hate her because she doesn't love me back, though. Also, I quit my job. I *think* I did. If you can quit a job over text. I feel so Gen Z."

"Oh, Cat. Why did you—?"

"And Robbie's sick. And I've been drunk for two days. And I'm on so many hormones that my body feels like it's vibrating. I almost stole a baby from Trader Joe's last week. I had an escape route mapped out and everything. And I should really get this mole checked. Do you think it looks bad?"

Blair touches the mole on Cat's shoulder—a glorified freckle. "I have a hundred of those," she says. "Everyone does."

"It's like we're all time bombs," says Cat. "All these little blemishes and scars. Which ones are the bad ones?"

"You're trying to have a baby, aren't you?" Blair asks, and Cat nods. "Your ovulation comment yesterday. I got suspicious. Women don't just *know* that. Speaking from experience here."

"I'm gonna have a science baby," Cat says. "All the cool girls are getting them."

Blair is six inches taller than Cat, but her friend looks even tinier now in flip-flops, hair in a messy bun, shoulders slumped.

"I'm looking at a catalog of perspective sperm daddies next week. Hot, right? It's anonymous, but you can sort dudes by their voting habits, so that's nice. God bless California."

Blair squeezes Cat's hand. "And this woman you love and hate? Is she . . ."

"I thought she was," says Cat. "Guess I was wrong. I told her I started the process—like, the drugs and all that. Yesterday morning, before I flew here. She stayed over at my place. She never stays over, so I guess I got carried away. It just felt so domestic, though, you know. Wholesome. Just the two of us, cuddled up."

"What did she say?"

Cat opens her flask and takes a sip. "She said, 'What are you talking about?' She acted like we'd never even talked about it. You don't think Michelle and Kenny heard me say 'fuck,' do you?"

"I think most of Fenwick Island heard you say 'fuck.'"

"Shit," says Cat. "Sorry."

Blair pumps from a shell-shaped bottle of lotion next to the faucet. "Come here," she says and dabs two white dots on Cat's cheeks. "This'll make it a little better."

"I want what you have, Blair. I have for a long time."

It's like a quiet blow to the stomach, and Blair half sits on the bathroom counter, absorbing it. "Cat," she says.

"Your little family. I want one. I want people who love me, too. I want a house. I've only seen your house on Insta, but it looks nice. I even kind of want your minivan."

"No you don't," says Blair. "Not the minivan."

"I mean, yeah, it's horribly ugly," says Cat, "but when you drive a minivan, it means you have *people*. I have a stupid Honda. *I* can hardly fit in it. If a semi crashed into me on Pacific Coast Highway, the EMTs would scrape me up and be like, 'Well, at least she was utterly alone.'"

There are noises now: a door opening downstairs, footsteps, and voices.

"You're smart and hot and artistic and a good mom," says Cat. "Shit, Blair, you're my model of womanhood. Have I ever told you that? Is that creepy? You and maybe Angelina Jolie. And Ruth Bader Ginsburg, too, but for different reasons."

"Cat," says Blair. "No, it's not creepy. But you can do better than me."

She hears "Mommy?" It's Michelle's voice, muffled, not terribly urgent-sounding, but Blair knows it'll only get louder. "I think my marriage is over," she says.

"What?" asks Cat.

"This weekend," she says. "It was our last chance. It was *his* last chance."

"Does Martin know that?" asks Cat.

Blair picks up Cat's flask and takes a drink. She'd hoped for something stronger than mimosa, but it'll do for now. "No," she says. "I decided last week, on my own. I told myself that if we came here and kept just limping along, I was going to leave him. I can't even remember the last time we had sex, Cat. I can't even remember the last time he looked at me. Like, *looked* at me. And now he's leaving. Last night, after Robbie . . . told us. He took me out on the deck and said, 'What would you think about me and the kids going home?'"

"Shit," Cat whispers. She holds out her hand for the flask and takes a drink. "Are you sure? Are you okay?"

"Mommy?" Michelle again, shouting from downstairs. "Mommy!"

Blair rubs lotion on her own face now. "Do you remember that morning at the Plaza in New York, after Wade's reading?"

"Yeah," says Cat, "of course. You were still wearing your dress."

Six years ago, Blair and Cat were in yet another bathroom together looking at themselves. Blair had just told Cat about sleeping with Wade, about being pregnant, about everything. Cat was sitting hungover and wide-eyed next to the sink, sipping iced coffee from Dunkin' Donuts.

Blair squirts some more lotion into Cat's hand now. "That whole time we were talking, I was thinking about how jealous I was of you."

Their eyes meet in the mirror. "Jealous of me? Why?"

"Because you were free," says Blair. "I was standing there pregnant. And I knew that part of my life was over. That part where you're in charge of yourself—of everything. But *you,* you could do anything you wanted. Sometimes I'm *still* jealous of you. I love Michelle and Kenny; I do. But one of them will be freaking out in Target or something, having a full-on meltdown over Legos, and I'll think, *I wish I was Cat.*"

There's a knock at the bathroom door. They've found her. "Mommy?" It's Kenny now, but Michelle is there, too, Blair can tell.

"In here, guys."

"What are you doing?"

"I'm talking to Cat."

Cat makes her voice cheery. "Hi, twins."

"Cat, we looked for your phone but we couldn't find it," says Kenny. "Why did you throw it and say the f-word?"

"I was just working through some stuff," says Cat.

"Daddy says we're leaving in a few minutes," says Michelle. "Come say goodbye."

"Can we have string cheese?" asks Kenny.

"Can you just give me a second?" asks Blair.

There are breathing sounds, whispers and giggles. "Are you guys going potty together?"

"Kenny, I'm counting to three. One . . ."

The twins scurry from the bathroom door, and Blair and Cat look at themselves again. Cat still has a glob of lotion under her eye, so Blair rubs it in for her. "I haven't gone to the bathroom in peace in five years," she says. "All I'm saying, don't take freedom for granted."

"Here's the thing, though, Blair Bear," says Cat. "Freedom gets lonely after a while."

WHEN CAT IS GONE, BLAIR stands in the soft lighting, looking at herself—at Adult Blair. She's a mother in the suburbs. She's careful and always worried about something. She bugs her friends to wear sunscreen and drink water. She's tired and restless and feels weirdly alone, even though she's almost never, technically, alone.

Cat left her flask on the counter next to the lotion. It's about a quarter full, so Blair drains it easily in three gulps, like Young Blair would do.

She unzips her cover-up halfway, exposing the top of her new bikini. No one other than her has seen it yet, because it was too chilly on the beach at breakfast to take off her cover-up. She unzips a little farther now, and then all the way, and then she takes her phone out and opens her email. She goes to the message from Mr. McGee.

I think you should send me something beautiful to paint.

She takes her cover-up off, letting it slide from her shoulders onto the floor. Unsmiling, scowling almost, she snaps a picture of herself and examines it on her screen. She takes a few more and examines those, too. She's spent her career picking through photography selects, and she's quickly able to identify the best one.

There are voices outside the door—her friends and children and husband—but she blocks them all out. Imaginary Taylor Swift is in the mirror now, where Cat's reflection had just been. *You've gone this far, right?*

Blair taps the paper clip icon and attaches the photo of herself. Beneath it, she types, How's this? And then she hits Send.

Chapter 20

"Look, we made you something," says Michelle. Michelle and Kenny hand Robbie wrinkly pieces of paper with squirrels drawn on them. Michelle's squirrel is colored in carefully, and she's written "Thanks Roby" across the top. Kenny's work is messier than his sister's, with purple crayon tornadoes and scribbled smiley faces. It's clear, though, how proud of it he is, and Robbie can't help but imagine an alternate universe. World's #1 Dad.

"Do you like it?" Kenny asks.

"Wow, you guys," he says. "They're fantastic."

Except for Blair, they're all out in the driveway next to the idling Odyssey.

Cat hugs Michelle and then Kenny. "I'm gonna miss you little jerks," she says. Wade shakes Martin's hand and high-fives the twins. Martin checks his watch. The neighbor's corgi stares down at them as they wait.

"Where's Mommy?" asks Kenny, and everyone looks up at the house.

Martin and the twins leaving wasn't part of the plan, and now that they are, Robbie is faced with having to say goodbye to them. The fact that it's a *goodbye* goodbye isn't lost on any of the adults, and as Robbie shakes Martin's hand, Cat looks to be on the verge of tears.

"Thanks for having us, Robbie," says Martin. "It was great to meet you."

"Can we come here again sometime?" Michelle asks.

"Of course you can," says Robbie.

"Will the game room be here?" asks Kenny. "The pinball and stuff?"

"That's the plan. It'll all be here, ready and waiting."

"Will you be here, too?" asks Kenny.

Cat turns away and takes a few steps toward the ocean.

"You're sick, right?" Kenny asks.

"A little bit, yeah," he says.

"But you'll get better," says Michelle. "People get better when they're sick."

According to Dr. Osborne, hope means different things to different people. To a couple of five-year-olds, maybe hope means they'll all see each other again soon and everything will be fine. "Absolutely," he says.

"There she is," says Michelle. "Hi, Mommy. Are you going swimming?"

They turn back to the house and, for a moment, no one says anything. Blair is standing on the front steps holding a can of hard seltzer. Her cover-up is open, swaying gently in the breeze. She's wearing a small red bikini.

Cat wipes her eyes and laughs. "My God, Blair."

As Blair walks barefoot down the steps, Robbie sees the muscles in Martin's face go tight from surprise, like it's the first time he's seen his wife. Beside him, Wade looks away, embarrassed.

"Okay, everyone," says Cat. "Maybe we give the Hardens a little privacy."

They walk back toward the house together, Cat, Robbie, and Wade. The fine white gravel crunches beneath their flip-flops. Wade shakes his head. "I can't believe he's just gonna leave."

"What a fucking idiot," says Cat.

Chapter 21

As Michelle and Kenny climb into their car seats, Blair wonders how one actually leaves one's husband in this dumb century, in the era of co-parenting and amicable uncoupling. A calendar invite, maybe, or possibly an email. `Martin, let's have a quick touch base. I'm leaving you.`

Martin will marry again, because men can marry at will. She pictures him shaking hands with Mr. McGee in the driveway. They won't be friends, exactly, but friendly, and of course, Martin will call him Nick and not Mr. McGee.

The kids might actually be better off. Instead of one good home, they'll have two. They'll have their real dad, all hyperinvolved and loving, and their artistic stepdad. A perfectly blended modern family, like a TV show. She stands at the Odyssey's open sliding door, imagining an entirely new life, and it's thrilling. She checks the kids' belts.

"Why aren't you coming with us?" Michelle asks.

"We're giving Mommy some adult time," says Martin, looking back from the driver's seat. Waze is open on his phone, his path forward laid out.

"Cat and Wade aren't like normal adults, though," says Michelle.

"They're more like us, but big," says Kenny.

Blair takes a sip of her Truly, kisses their warm foreheads, and tells them she loves them. As the sliding door closes slowly, Blair decides that she likes this version of herself: a mom in a bikini with a drink in her hand and no idea what comes next.

"I'm actually jealous," says Martin. Blair stands at the driver's side window now. "Dash is setting up one of those Cadillac Escalades to bring you home."

"Lucky me," she says.

He touches her shoulder. "I know it's sad," he says. "But this is good for you guys. You'll all get to be here with him."

She nearly tells him that it was supposed to be good for *them,* but it seems useless now. Maybe a light would flicker in his eyes— some hint that he recognizes the importance of this moment—but then it'd just go dim again, and he'd push Go on the nav. "Goodbye, Martin," she says, and she lets him kiss the side of her closed mouth.

WHEN HER FAMILY IS GONE, Blair walks back into the silent mansion. She passes the game room, then climbs the stairs to the empty kitchen. Her Truly is finished, so she grabs another one from the fridge. Cat, Robbie, and Wade are outside by the pool. She'll join them soon, but not yet. Instead, she goes up to her room.

Her travel bag sits on a stand next to her side of the bed. Martin has gone so far as to smooth out the comforter on his side. It looks as if her husband has been erased.

It's hot out on her balcony, which is directly in the sun. She takes her cover-up off again and enjoys the warmth on her skin. People on the ground look up at her. Let them look. She climbed a Viking statue once and was nearly arrested. She skinny-dipped with a lifeguard named Dustin and then made him cry a week later when she dumped him. She's the reason none of her friends graduated from Baltimore Prep. She had a brief affair with a professor in art school for no reason other than that she knew she could. She slept with one of her best friends while she was pregnant. It was a cruel thing to do, but she'd always wondered what it'd be like, and she knew it was her last chance to do it. Half an hour ago, she sent a bikini picture of herself to her kids' art teacher. Then, immediately after that, she sent him two more pictures without the bikini. And now she's standing on a deck chair, testing it for stability.

From there, Blair steps up onto the balcony railing. She puts one hand on the gutter that lines the roof and takes a moment to steady herself. The corgi next door watches from across the street with its foxy little head tilted. She puts a finger to her lips. "*Shhhhh.*"

She's surprised how easy it is to pull herself onto the roof. Yoga, apparently, works.

Little black tar balls from the shingles stick to her feet as she steps gently to the edge. Her friends below are oblivious. Robbie and Wade are sitting by the pool. Cat bobs in a donut-shaped floatie. A banner plane passes, and Blair imagines its sign fluttering in the wind: Nice to See You Again, Young Blair.

She walks back to the center of the roof, takes a deep breath, and starts running.

Chapter 22

In the late spring of their senior year, Cat told Blair, Robbie, and Wade that she was gay.

They were in Fenwick at Cat's grandma's place for the weekend. They were sitting on rickety deck chairs eating ham sandwiches. Cat exhaled after she said it, a burden released, and for several seconds, her friends were silent. Then Wade said, "Well, yeah." Blair and Robbie laughed.

"Yeah?" said Cat. "That's it? I come out, and you say *yeah,* you dick?"

"Cat," said Blair, "we know. We *have* known. We were just waiting for you to tell us."

She looked at Robbie, who smiled. Cat knew that Robbie had feelings for her. They weren't the big, tortured, swoony feelings that Wade had for Blair, but she could sense them when they were together, like a gentle buzzing sound in the room. He shrugged a little shrug.

Cat was so emboldened by her friends' immediate, blasé acceptance of her truth that she came out to her parents when she got back to Baltimore. They were at the kitchen table at dinnertime. Their neighbor, Mr. Henderson, was cutting his grass next door, and the hum of his mower came through the window. Cat's dad looked at his hands, and her mom immediately burst into tears.

"Um," said Cat. "You guys didn't know?"

Eighteen-year-olds are naïve. Cat had expected tenderness and love, but what she got was silence and then tears, which quickly turned to shouts and one slammed door. Her dad wouldn't look at her. Her mom just kept crying, like there'd been a death in the family. They've evolved since, both of them. Her parents came to terms with Cat being gay, and they eventually apologized for their initial reactions. Her dad texts her rainbow pictures every June, and her mom shyly asks her if there's "anyone special" in her life when they talk on the phone. But on *that* night, as Cat ran out of the house, the last thing her mom said to her, still through tears, was "Couldn't you have just *not* told us? Would that have been so hard?"

Cat headed for Blair's house. She felt like a teenage runaway with her Nike bag full of hastily packed Baltimore Prep uniforms and mismatched pajamas. Mr. Henderson waved and shouted hello over his orange lawnmower.

Cat had called ahead, so Blair was waiting for her on her front porch. She'd been drawing a perfect blue waterfall in her sketchbook. She stood and hugged Cat.

"They hate me," Cat said.

"No they don't."

"They do. I could tell."

"Well," said Blair, "I don't. Wade and Robbie don't. You've got us, right?"

It was Blair's idea, that following weekend, for the four of them to go to the Baltimore Pride parade. "You should go," said Blair. "*We* should go. All of us. It'll be fun."

Cat smiled. She was eating cereal. Blair's family had good cereal—the name-brand stuff with real raisins. "You think the guys would want to go, too?" she asked. "It wouldn't be, like, too much for them?"

"Nah," said Blair. "Robbie and Wade'll be fine. The people there, they're your people now, Cat. And you're *our* people."

While attending the parade had been Blair's idea, it was Cat who decided they should both wear their school uniforms. She's gone over that weekend and the days that followed many, many times in her head, and she's decided, ultimately, that was what did them in: the uniforms. But she was young, and she was pissed at her parents, and she was pissed at her school for being so . . . Catholic. A checkered skirt and a white polo would teach all of them a lesson.

When Wade picked them up, Robbie was in the passenger seat. They got out of Wade's car and looked up at Blair and Cat, waiting on the porch. Along with their uniforms, both girls wore temporary Pride tattoos on their faces, which they'd gotten from the hemp shop near Towson University, and rainbow socks pulled up to their knees. Robbie and Wade seemed to understand the danger of this more than the girls did.

Robbie sat on the hood of Wade's car and took a breath.

"Oh shit," said Wade.

Cat stood defiant, though, sipping one of Blair's mom's Diet Cokes. The Baltimore Catholic Preparatory High School logo practically glowed on her chest. She folded her arms and looked down on the boys—Robbie, the soon-to-be valedictorian, and Wade, the winner of the school's St. Francis de Sales Prize for English & Literature. "Oh shit, what?" Cat asked.

"You think this is a good idea?" said Wade.

"We do," said Cat.

"Probably the best idea we've ever had," said Blair. And then she held up a handful of Pride tattoos. "Now, where do you guys want these?"

THEY FOUND PARKING BY PENN Station and walked together. On Charles Street, just past the University of Baltimore, they could see the crowd gathered near the statue of George Washington.

Cat had never really thought twice about the word *Pride;* it was more like a brand name than an actual emotion. But as the music played, and as the rainbow flags waved from cars and awnings and brick rowhouses, that was exactly what she felt: pride.

People laughed and smiled when they saw Blair's and Cat's outfits. They gave them high fives and thumbs-ups. Blair took Cat's hand and they swung their arms as they walked. Two steps behind them, Robbie and Wade were getting into the festivities, too. Maybe they were self-conscious at first, but when a beautiful man in booty shorts tossed them rainbow beads from a red wagon and told them to look alive, they happily obliged and dance-walked toward a giant speaker blaring "It's Raining Men."

The pride Cat felt only grew over the next two hours, swelling with each hug and burst of laughter and hilarious handcrafted sign. Somebody handed them beers in pink Solo cups. A *Hairspray* float ambled by carrying a papier-mâché statue of the director John Waters and dozens of plastic pink flamingos. Two Baltimore city cops accepted rainbow boas; one put his on his police horse. A lesbian Roller Derby team called Madam Sprinkles skated by to cheers. A group of men in matching gray suits launched glitter bombs into the crowd.

Blair, Cat, Robbie, and Wade moved slowly along the parade route, up Charles Street, checking out the scene. Each block had its own signs, music, and décor. The sounds that echoed up and down the streets were so universally happy—so totally positive—that when a smattering of hisses and boos cropped up near the Walters Art Museum, everyone turned to look. A group of grim-faced men and women stood in a tight pack, holding signs on long wooden sticks. These particular signs weren't like the others. They weren't colorful or festive, which only made them stick out more, their starkness against all that joy.

NOTHING TO BE PROUD OF

HOMOSEXUALITY = DAMNATION

STOP CONFUSING OUR CHILDREN

ADAM + EVE NOT ADAM + STEVE

<u>YOU</u> ARE A SIN

A few of them didn't hold signs at all, just crosses. People gave the group a wide berth, like fish swimming around predatory animals.

"More like sin-*sational!*" someone shouted. "You bitches weren't invited," said someone else. Another person yelled, simply, "Fuck off!"

Blair, Cat, Robbie, and Wade stopped. Cat could feel her friends' eyes on her. They were seeing how she'd react to this, what she'd do. Cat didn't really do anything, though. Instead, she stood calmly on the curb and looked at the protesters from across the street. Their expressions were so serious—so unsmiling and sure of themselves. Cat could see the disdain in their eyes. Blair had been right before. The people celebrating in Mount Vernon on that Saturday were Cat's people now. They would be for the rest of her life. But the people holding those crosses and ugly signs were a community, too. And they'd never go away.

"Assholes," said Wade.

Robbie put his hand on her shoulder. "Don't worry about them. Just look at the numbers. Statistically, they're minuscule." His Pride tattoo was starting to fade. The rainbow beads hung down to his belt.

"Come on," Blair said, guiding Cat across the street. "I have an idea."

The two girls stopped, and then stood face-to-face just a few feet from the people and their signs and crosses. Cat could smell Blair's breath: a little like beer, but still sweet. To those around them, it must've looked like something was about to happen, because people stopped walking; they hushed and gathered.

"You should kiss me," Blair said.

"I should what?"

"Come on, you prude," said Blair. "Kiss me, because screw these awful people."

It was Blair's idea for them to kiss on Charles Street at the Pride Parade their senior year of high school in front of joy-killing, Bible-thumping homophobes. But it was Cat who leaned in and closed her eyes. It was her first kiss, and, against a soundtrack of cheers, it felt perfect. It was warm and soft, and Cat still thinks about it sometimes.

None of them heard the rapid-fire shutter snaps of the photographer's camera. None of them had any idea that a photo of Blair and Cat kissing would appear on the front page of *The Baltimore Sun* the next morning, above the headline "Celebration and Protest Converge in Largest Pride Parade in Baltimore History."

Later that week, the photo that earned them their nickname and cemented their friendships forever was reprinted for a story about Blair and Cat being expelled from Baltimore Prep. It was printed yet again—a third time—two weeks later in a *Sun* editorial about church and state and the limits and consequences of free speech, and then again just before Christmas in the *Sun*'s special year-in-review issue. But before any of that, on the night of her expulsion, in her parents' garage, in a little art studio built by her dad, Blair McKenzie re-created the photo in beautiful watercolor.

She eliminated the protesters, though, replacing them and the entire background with a sun-kissed Baltimore cityscape and clouds in rainbow hues, because, again, screw those awful people. This became Blair's aesthetic as a painter—her artistic hook. She'd take real-life photos and stylize the worlds behind their subjects.

While that original painting now hangs in Cat's apartment in L.A., an eight-by-twelve re-creation of it ran, against very strict orders from the school, as the cover art for the spring issue of Baltimore Prep's literary magazine. This earned the magazine's editor, senior Wade Stephens, immediate expulsion. That same day, Robbie Malcolm, the smartest student in the history of the school, with a copy of Wade's issue in hand, quit Baltimore Prep and never went back.

Chapter 23

Wade assumes it's a bird, which triggers some seagull flashbacks from his youth—stolen turkey sandwiches and ransacked potato chip bags. The scream, though, pulls him back. It's Blair, and she's falling from the sky. And, despite the fact that she's about to crash face-first into a swimming pool from God knows how high, her scream is a scream of joy.

The splash is shocking, hitting Wade and Robbie in their faces and sending Cat whipping side to side on her floatie. "Holy shit!" she says. "Was that Blair?"

Dash runs to the side of the pool. "Did she just . . ." He leaves the question hanging, because clearly she did.

Wade squints at the blurry figure at the bottom of the deep end. She doesn't seem to be moving. Cat leaves her floatie to rescue her friend just as Wade dives in. He fears an unconscious, broken version of Blair, lifeless. Instead, she's smiling, her eyes vivid in the shimmering water. She plants her feet on the bottom of the pool and pushes up. She, Cat, and Wade surface together, splashing one another in the process.

"You psycho!" says Cat, laughing.

Blair flings her wet hair off her face. "I think I destroyed my boobs."

"You deserve it!" says Cat. "You could've died."

"Nope," says Blair. Her smile is radiant and wild. "Fully alive."

Cat dunks her, then they tread water, half hugging. "Are you okay?" Cat asks.

Blair nods. "Yeah. I am."

Wade suspects this exchange has nothing to do with Blair jumping off the roof.

"Get in, Robbie!" calls Cat.

"Yeah, come on, Robbie," says Blair. "I haven't seen you swim at all."

Robbie is sitting at the table now. He puts his Harvard cap on, and it strikes Wade that he isn't smiling. His expression is distant, serious. Dash sets three envelopes on the table in front of him and then walks back into the house.

"Actually," says Robbie, "would you mind getting out for a minute? We all need to talk."

"So, um, what are those?" asks Cat.

The four of them are sitting at the table now. Blair and Cat have dried off and put on cover-ups. Wade is in a damp T-shirt. Their names are written on the envelopes, one for each of them.

"We'll get to those in a minute," says Robbie.

Wade sees Dash through one of the upstairs windows, looking down on them. Blair's and Cat's chairs are side by side. They're giggly still, leaning into each other, but Wade is pretty sure whatever's about to happen won't be good.

Robbie opens a laptop. "Blair," he says. "The studio upstairs, you like it, right?"

"Well, yeah."

"Good." He opens a file on his computer and moves it so Blair can see. "These are blueprints of your house in D.C. I've taken the liberty of having plans drawn up for building a similar studio there. Bigger, actually. I imagine it going upstairs, next to the master bedroom. Again, the lighting."

She laughs, uneasy. "What? Where did you get blueprints of my house?"

"You don't have a space to work, Blair," he says. "Not a real one. You've relegated your art to an afterthought. I think you miss it more than you'd like to admit."

She starts to say something, but Robbie stops her. "How about, for the purposes of time, we save discussion until the end? I have a lot to get through."

"Is this a meeting?" Cat asks. "Are we in a meeting right now?"

"I'll email this to you, Blair," Robbie says. "Now, Wade." He taps his computer again. Blair's blueprints go away, and an image of a woman appears—light-brown hair, glasses. It's a page from Match.com. "This is Christina Allen. She's an English lit teacher at the University of Baltimore. She's thirty-two, and she has a cat. That's not ideal, I know. But she lives in Baltimore—in Federal Hill. She's new in town, from upstate New York. She loves to read, obviously. And she's looking for someone who loves to read, too."

"Okay," says Wade. "Why are we looking at her?"

"Next week, you're meeting her for coffee. A date. It's been arranged."

"What're you talking about?" asks Wade. "I don't even know this person."

"She read *Feedback,* actually," Robbie says. "That's a nice bonus."

"How do you know that?"

"I had her Amazon and Goodreads profiles reviewed." He scrolls down. A Goodreads page appears. "Three years ago, see? Four stars. Not bad." *This one surprised me!* is typed above the little yellow stars. "The two of you are an ideal romantic match."

"Based on what?"

"Math," says Robbie. "Science, too, but mostly math. Everything's math. Rounding some, you have a ninety-seven percent chance of liking each other. Those numbers are legitimate, too. I spoke with Mandy Ginsberg last week. I asked her to have her team run some numbers for me. They went beyond what Match does for its normal subscribers. You and Christina connect on virtually every recordable metric. You even have the same birth signs."

"Who in the hell is Mandy Ginsberg?" Wade asks.

"Oh, sorry," says Robbie. "She's the CEO of Match.com."

Cat laughs. "Is this a joke?"

"Robbie," says Wade, "I'm not meeting some rando because you did long division."

"You're alone, Wade," says Robbie. "You've exiled yourself. You'll never be happy if you keep living the way you're living."

Cat slides Robbie's computer closer. "She's kinda cute, actually," she says. "Bookish. But she lives in Baltimore. Wade's in New York."

Wade is starting to sweat, because Robbie is looking at him the way he did yesterday in the kitchen when he was lying about his book deal.

Robbie closes his laptop and slides the envelopes in front of them. "I want to warn you. The things I'm about to say are going to be difficult to hear."

"What's going on, Robbie?" asks Blair.

"I have people working for me who aren't on the Malcolm Capital payroll," he says. "Contractors. Their job is to tap into sensitive information about . . . well, a lot of things. People, mostly. Competitors and adversaries. In my world, there are always adversaries. It's like war. And information is the most effective weapon."

The sliding door opens from the kitchen. Dash steps out onto the deck holding a sheet of paper. He nods at Blair, Cat, and Wade and then whispers into Robbie's ear.

"Um, hey, Dash," Cat says. "What're you doing?"

Dash doesn't respond. Instead, he picks up the envelope in front of Blair and slides the paper inside, and then he goes back into the house.

"What did he just put in my envelope?" asks Blair.

The ominousness blooms like smoke. "Robbie," says Wade, "is Dash one of those *professionals*?"

"No. Not technically. He works with them, though. A liaison. I haven't been entirely forthcoming about Dash's job. Not all of his responsibilities are security related."

"What's in these envelopes?" asks Cat.

"Your lives," says Robbie.

"Our lives?" says Blair.

"Yes," he says. "And I'll be honest: they aren't good right now."

"Dude," says Cat.

"We're not in touch with each other the way we used to be," says Robbie. "That happens, we're not high school kids anymore. So, over the years, I've made it a point to keep up with the three of you. With your careers and your relationships. Last month, when I found out for sure that I'm . . ."

They wait for him to keep talking. Dash is downstairs now, watching through the kitchen window.

"Anyway," says Robbie, "when certain things became clear to me, I decided to dig in a little deeper on each of you. It was worse than I thought."

"What was worse than you thought?" says Cat.

Robbie nods at the envelopes. "We call ourselves best friends," he says. "But we aren't. Not anymore. Cat, when you came out, we were the first people you told. Blair, when you got pregnant and you were scared, you turned to Cat. Wade, when your dad almost died, we were all there. We all slept in that hospital waiting room that first night. Remember? We got through it together."

"Yeah," says Blair. "And now we're all here."

"Yeah," says Cat. "We're together."

"No," says Robbie. "This isn't about me. You've all been lying to each other. Keeping secrets. These envelopes prove it. Basically, your lives are a mess."

"Robbie," says Blair.

"I don't have time to be polite. No more secrets. No more bullshitting each other."

"Whatever," says Cat. "We're maybe not fucking billionaires, but come on, we're doing okay." She looks around. "Wade sold his book, right?"

"No, he didn't, Cat," Robbie says. "That was a lie."

"What?" says Cat. "Wade?"

Wade feels sick. Blair is looking at him, so is Cat. He doesn't say anything. He can't.

"*Feedback* was a failure," says Robbie. "It's barely sold ten thousand copies in six years. And I bought more than half of those. His publisher dropped him two years ago after he missed his fifth deadline." He points to Wade's folder. "His new book has been rejected by twenty-seven editors. He was evicted from his apartment. He doesn't have a job; he quit both of them. Wade is effectively a homeless person. I assume you're moving back to Baltimore, right? Frankly, I don't see where else you'd go."

Wade wonders if it's hurt that he feels. Sadness? Embarrassment? Whatever it is, it's like anger, like a fist, and heat builds in his chest.

"Wade?" says Cat. "How long has this been going on?"

"It's still with one editor," Wade manages.

"And now Cat," says Robbie.

She grabs the table, bracing.

"You're having an affair with your boss." Robbie's demeanor is beyond serious now. It's cold and corporate. Mean. "You have been for a year. Her name is Gabrielle Torres. And she's married to a man named Daniel. They've been married for sixteen years."

"Cat?" says Blair.

Cat has gone pale, her face a sickly shade.

"Why didn't you . . ." says Blair.

"And, as of yesterday, you're unemployed, too," says Robbie. "And you're in debt. Even more than Wade. You owe a hundred thousand dollars to the Fertility Center of California in Los Angeles. Cat, there's no way you can pay that back."

Cat's eyes spill over at their corners. "How do you . . . ?"

"You *spied* on us?" says Wade.

"Yes," says Robbie. "And, as a side note, none of you made it very difficult. Wade, your password is Paul McCartney's birthday. Your *only* password. You use it for everything. You need to change that. We accessed everything about you in minutes. You have six hundred and twenty dollars to your name. Cat, your former employer—the production company—their lawyers have advised Gabrielle never to speak to you again. Absolutely zero contact."

"What?" she says. "We broke up . . . yesterday."

"I know," says Robbie. "The text messages are in your envelope. She's been preparing for this, Cat. The show's lawyers have been aware of you for a while. As of yesterday, you've been cut off entirely. That's standard in cases like this."

"Cases?" says Cat.

"You're an issue for the legal and HR departments now," says Robbie. "Your work email, access codes, key fob, parking space. They're all frozen. They're preparing their defense, in case you sue them or her. They have a plan set up in case you go to the media, too."

"Defense?" she says. "Against . . . *me*?"

"A depressed, borderline-delusional former employee turned stalker," says Robbie. "That's also standard. If I were you, I'd stop texting her. Destroying your phone is the only smart thing you've done since you got here."

Everyone's quiet. Waves and another goddamn banner plane. Wade looks at the center of the table. "You bought all my books?" he asks.

Robbie nods. "Not all of them, but yes, many. Technically, most. I had analysts do it in small increments. I didn't want you to know. I didn't want you to feel dejected."

"Dejected?" Wade tries to laugh. "Oh jeez, why would I? It's just . . . my fucking career."

"I know how sensitive you are about your work," he says.

"Did you read it at least?" Wade doesn't know why, exactly, this matters, but it does.

"Of course. I loved it. You know that."

"What about me?" asks Blair. Her arms are crossed, defiant.

Robbie takes a sip of water. "Your marriage is in shambles, Blair," he says. "You've been researching divorce lawyers for months. And, as far as I can tell, you're having an affair with the art teacher at your kids' school. Nick McGee."

Wade looks at Blair. A blade of some new feeling slices through the other feelings tangled in his guts. This one is familiar, like some new version of rejection. "You're having an affair?" he asks.

"Blair?" says Cat.

She pushes her envelope away. "Anything else?"

"Yes," says Robbie. "About half an hour ago, you sent a series of pictures of yourself to him from what appears to be the powder room upstairs. They're . . . suggestive. Dash just informed me. That's what he put in your file."

Blair pulls the zipper of her cover-up to her throat. Wade meets Dash's eyes through the window now. Dash and Robbie didn't spy on them; they're *spying* on them.

"I don't get this," says Cat. "What's your p—?"

"There's more," says Robbie. "More for both of you, Blair and Cat."

Blair grips the armrest of her chair. "What?"

"I had him looked into, also," says Robbie. "The art teacher, Nick McGee."

Wade hates the sound of his name. He presses his temples until they hurt.

"There are others, Blair," says Robbie. "Other women. Moms, from the twins' school. You're not the only one he's . . . involved with. Three others. Their names are in there. This is his thing."

Blair stares at her envelope.

"What the fuck, Robbie?" Wade says. "Are you just rubbing our faces in this?"

"No. I'm protecting you. You need to hear this. You need to know the truth about what's going on in your own lives."

"What about me?" says Cat. "You said there's more shit about Blair *and* me."

Another sip of water. Robbie looks through the window at Dash, and the silence that builds at the table is jagged. Blair puts her hand on Cat's hand.

"What, Robbie?" says Cat. "Just say it."

"Cat, Gabrielle is pregnant."

"What?"

"About seven weeks. No one knows at the station; she hasn't told any of the executives, as far as we could tell."

"But she doesn't even want . . ."

"They've actually been trying," says Robbie. "Her and her husband. I think you need to come to terms with the fact that many of the things Gabrielle has told you simply aren't true. She's been living a normal life, in a seemingly loving marriage. *You* are her secret."

Wade stands, and when he does, his chair nearly slides into the pool. "Fuck this. And fuck you, you rich dickhead." He storms across the deck and whips open the sliding door. Dash is there in the kitchen. "And fuck you, too, Dash."

Dash holds his hands up, like surrender. "Wade, maybe you should just wait."

"What're you gonna do, Dash? Beat me up? Go fuck yourself."

The keys to the LeBaron hang from a hook in the kitchen. Wade grabs them, and he's down the stairs and out the front door in seconds.

"Wade! Wait." It's Blair, coming after him. "What are you doing?" she asks.

"I'm leaving."

"Where are you going?"

He looks around. "I don't even know. Somewhere that isn't here."

"Can I come with you?"

Chapter 24

The hula girl swaying on the dashboard is strangely hypnotic. As the wind whips through Blair's hair, she feels like she could curl up in the passenger seat and sleep.

"Ob-La-Di, Ob-La-Da" by the Beatles is playing. Wade found the White Album in the box of old tapes on the car floor. It's way too upbeat for the moment, but the rewind and fast forward buttons are broken, so they're stuck with it.

They haven't spoken since Wade hit the gas pedal. He's staring straight ahead. His face is mannequinlike, expressionless. Her heart hurts for him, but it mostly hurts for herself. For months, she's clung to a fantasy. A stupid fantasy, clearly—one of those early-middle-age do-over fantasies. The thing about fantasies, though, stupid or not: sometimes they're the only thing getting you through the day. And now her fantasy is over.

There's no starting over for people like her—no do-overs. Her rewind button is broken, too. She holds her hand out the LeBaron's window. The "Blair" and "Wade" envelopes are along for the ride, tossed onto the back seat. She grabbed them on the way out the door.

Beyond Fenwick Island, the speed limit goes up to fifty-five miles per hour, and Wade steps on the gas. An old wooden sign invites them back soon.

Blair wishes Wade hadn't lied to her. But, of course, she lied to him—a lie of omission. Cat, too. They're all liars. Blair takes her phone out and checks her email. Mr. McGee has written back. She feels stupid for thinking she was ever something special to him.

My God, look at you. You are so beautiful.

Her body in the images is angled just so, head tilted, stomach sucked in. This is what she's good at: being beautiful. Now, though, she sees how hard the woman on the little screen is trying. How long has Blair looked like someone who's trying so hard?

They pass a rusty pickup full of surfboards. Assawoman Bay is on their left, the ocean on their right. It's hot out, and the wind is loud and wild. "Where are we going, Wade?" she shouts.

Just the Beatles for a moment. Whoever's singing—Blair doesn't know enough about the Beatles to know if it's Paul McCartney or John Lennon—sings that "life goes on," and Blair would laugh at that if she could.

"Almost there," Wade says.

She doesn't ask where *there* is. She doesn't really care.

A few minutes later, another wooden sign welcomes them to Bethany Beach. At the center of town, Wade hits the blinker and turns right.

"Is this your escape plan?" she asks. "A ten-minute drive to Bethany?"

Wade drives up and down the boardwalk a few times looking for a parking spot. When white backup lights appear, he jumps two lanes, cuts off a line of cars, and slams on the brakes. "It's our lucky day," he says while someone honks.

He cuts the engine, and they sit watching the stream of people on the Bethany Beach boardwalk. Shorts and T-shirts and funnel cakes and sunburned kids with seashells. She thinks of the twins, because she's always thinking of the twins—because mothers are really just emotional hostages. They must be nearly home by now.

Nearby, a line of people wait to feed the group parking meter. Blair slides her hand into the pocket of her cover-up and feels her emergency twenty. "Got any quarters?"

"Eh," he says. "Let 'em tow it."

"Well, a drink, then?" she asks.

Wade taps the hula girl's head. She sways and sways. "Maybe in a minute. You wanna hit that bookstore first?"

Bethany Beach Books is tucked between a T-shirt stand and a frozen yogurt shop. Stacks of "Hot Summer Reads" sit in the window, their covers bleaching in the sun. "Really?" she says. "Now?"

He shrugs and grabs the door handle.

"Wait," she says. "I just realized, I'm not wearing shoes."

They look at Blair's bare feet, the tops of which, she now sees, are a little red. "It wouldn't have felt like I was storming off if I'd stopped for flip-flops."

Wade opens the door anyway. "Fuck it," he says. "It's the beach, right?"

Chapter 25

Wade was told in no uncertain terms that he could not use Blair's painting as the cover to the school's literary magazine.

"There's no wiggle room on this, Wade. I'm serious."

Father Garringer didn't seem happy to be saying this, but he was saying it nonetheless. He was the youngest priest at Baltimore Prep. He barely seemed older than the seniors; like a kid who'd bought a white collar at Party City. He taught English and oversaw the magazine. He wore thrift store blazers over his black shirts. The kids all thought he was cool for a priest.

"But, Father, it's good," said Wade. "It's *really* good, right? Look at it."

The *St. Paul Street Journal* was published twice a year, before Christmas break and at the end of the school year. It was made up of student short stories, essays, and poems. The final issue was all laid out and ready to go to the printer. The cover Wade had initially chosen was a photograph of bright green leaves taken by a fellow student. He was proposing switching it out with Blair's painting of her and Cat kissing.

"Yes, it's good." They were in the dusty English Department office. "But in this case, that doesn't matter, Wade."

"Isn't that *all* that matters? It's art." It was a painfully naïve sentiment, particularly in that drafty old building. It wasn't just a good painting; it was a protest.

"This magazine isn't going to break from the school, Wade," said Father Garringer. "Even for the sake of *art*."

When he walked out of school that day, Wade had already made his decision. He'd switch the cover himself and take the file to the printer. Then he'd leave piles of them in the student center, outside the gym lobby, at the doors to the cafeteria. He'd slide copies into every faculty mailbox. His magazine, and Blair's painting, would be everywhere.

On the day he distributed the magazine, when Wade was told to report immediately to Father Milton's office, Wade was nervous, but he was proud, too. He had his line all ready to go. "I don't support the church. I support my friends."

Now, ALL THESE YEARS LATER, whenever he's feeling particularly shitty he heads to the closest bookstore. Sometimes he buys a book, but usually, like now, he just wanders.

He starts at the beach reads—*literally* beach reads. Their covers have pictures of loungers and seagulls and women shown from behind looking at oceans. He touches spines, opens books and smells them. He moves along the fiction wall. He always goes to fiction, because who wouldn't want to escape all this?

He starts at *A* and goes from there. Megan Abbott to Michael Chabon, and on and on.

These bookstore therapy sessions are meant to be solo operations. Being trailed now by a beautiful barefoot woman in a short beach cover-up is throwing everything off entirely. Particularly because she keeps asking if he's okay.

"Are you gonna talk to me or what?" Blair asks.

People keep looking at her. She seems not to notice. Her feet make little slapping sounds on the floor. She pokes an Emily Dickinson doll. Wade is embarrassed for himself. He's sad for Cat, because it sounds like someone has hurt her. But frankly, he's pissed at Blair. "I'm not *not* talking to you."

"That's a double negative."

"Well, I'm not a very good writer."

"Your folder?" she says. "The stuff Robbie said? It's true?"

He nods. "Yours?"

She leans on the Local Interest shelf. "Mostly. I'm not having an affair, though. Not technically."

Wade has no idea what that could mean. He thinks of Martin. His feelings for the man are a study in rapid emotional evolution. In twenty-four hours, Wade's gone from envying him to kind of hating him to begrudgingly liking him to now feeling sorry for him.

"What are you gonna do?" she asks.

"About what?" he says. "About the dumpster fire of my career or about the fact that I'm a thirty-five-year-old, grad-school-educated vagrant?"

"Start with the second one."

"Like Robbie said. Baltimore. My parents' basement."

"Oh, Wade," she says.

When they make it to the letter *S,* Wade stops. For the last six years, in whatever bookstore he's been in, he's stopped at *S* and looked for *Feedback.* At best, this is an exercise in masochism, and now he feels the familiar sting of not seeing it.

"I always look for you, too," she says.

And, suddenly, Wade finds he's having trouble staying pissed at her.

A woman from the bookstore walks by, an older lady with glasses on a rainbow chain. "You two looking for anything in particular?"

He can't help himself. "Do you have *Feedback* by Wade Stephens?"

Her friendly expression turns blank. "I'm not sure. Let me check the computer."

When she's gone, Blair frowns a frown that asks, *Was that really necessary?*

They continue inching along. Toward the end of the alphabet, they stop again, standing now at Violet and Vonnegut. The bookstore lady is behind the register, typing. "Says we're out," she calls. "Lemme check in back, though. You never know."

"Wade?" Blair says. She's shivering in the blasting AC, because she's basically in a swimsuit, and he wishes he had a jacket or hoodie for her. "Did you lie about selling your book because of me?"

"Yeah."

"Oh, Wade."

He wishes she'd stop saying that. *Oh, Wade.* "I was trying to impress you. I have been since I was fifteen."

"I wish you didn't feel like you had to."

"I show up at the house yesterday," he says. "It's this *mansion* owned by a billionaire. And there you are, the most beautiful woman I know. Your kids are beautiful. Your husband . . . shit, even *he's* beautiful. I wanted you to think I was somebody who actually belonged there."

She's about to say "Oh, Wade" again, he can tell. Before she can, though, Wade's phone rings. He pulls it from his swimsuit pocket. "Oh shit," he says.

"Who is it?" she asks.

"It's my agent."

Chapter 26

G abrielle is *not* in love with her husband.

Cat knows this, because Gabrielle has told her over and over again.

He was a mistake. I was young. I know who I am now.

The moment she met Gabrielle, Cat knew Gabrielle was gay. At least, she knew Gabrielle was . . . *something*. Curious, maybe? Bi? It was confusing, because the moment she met Gabrielle, Cat also knew that Gabrielle was married to a man.

Cat has been a video production producer for twelve years. She's bounced around, working for different studios and stations and production houses. A year ago, she was recruited through LinkedIn to work on *The Morning Gab,* L.A.'s second-most-popular morning talk show. Cat did her research, which included googling the show's star, Gabrielle Torres.

She was on TV, so she was pretty. There was a picture on some site of her and her husband, her high school sweetheart, an affable-enough-looking guy. But then, on Cat's first day at the show, the HR generalist, a girl named Annie with a nose ring, took her on a tour of the studio. After a trip through the cubes to meet the staff, they got to Gabrielle's office. Annie knocked. "Gab, you available? I've got someone for you."

"Yeah, come on in."

Annie opened the door, and there she was, and there was . . . the look.

It lingered longer than a normal look, as "the look" always does, full of interest and heat, like a sudden hyperfocus. In a world of straight people ogling each other, getting this unmistakable look from another woman never fails to briefly take Cat's breath away. That's what happened on that morning, the day she met Gabrielle: Cat's breath was taken away.

"Hey there," said Gabrielle. "And you are . . . ?"

In trouble, Cat thought.

AND NOW CAT IS RUNNING.

She hates the word *jogging.* Cat is *running,* dammit. And because she threw her iPhone across a go-cart track two hours ago, she's running without music, so the only thing competing with her stupid brain is the sound of her own slamming feet.

When Cat runs, she usually starts slowly, easing in for a half mile or so. Today, though, she just bolted, like a starter gun had gone off.

Blair, Robbie, and Wade quit cross-country for good after that freshman season. Cat, though, stuck with it and thrived, lettering the next three years. Nine races out of ten, she was the shortest chick out there, but she could fly.

She cruises along the beach now, gliding over packed sand. She hits Bunting Avenue, which runs parallel to the ocean, and passes more beach mansions. She veers over to the other side of Fenwick Island—the bay side—scaring up shorebirds and annoying vacationing dogs. She stops briefly at the plot of land where her grandma's house once stood. That house was small and pink, with a little garden that attracted sneaky rabbits. Now, though, because the land was more valuable than the house, a big gray mansion stands before her. A boat named *Daze at Sea* is parked out front.

Fucking rich people, she thinks, and then doubles back the way she came.

She passes Dairy Queen and runs in the direction of Ocean City, then back toward the beach again. It's hard to say how far she's gone for sure—no phone means no distance-tracking app— but she barely slows until she's on sand again, weaving around towels and umbrellas. Finally, at the edge of the water, she stops.

Sweat drips down her nose. She puts her hands on her knees. Her heart feels like it might burst.

"What if we could run away together?"

Gabrielle said that once to Cat, in bed, in the loungy, dreamy, post-orgasm-y stage of sex when up is down and down is up and nothing particularly matters. Cat rolled onto her stomach and kissed the crook of Gabrielle's elbow and listened as she lazed through more what-ifs. What if I'd met you when I was younger? What if nobody knew who I was, and I could just do whatever I wanted? What if I just left him? What if it was like this every day?

CAT TAKES HER SHOES AND socks off. She looks up and down the beach, getting her bearings. She spots the beach mansion maybe two hundred yards up the shore. Dash is standing on the back deck. Four sandpiper birds sprint by on blurry little legs looking for sea junk to eat.

Wading into the surf, she lets the chilly water sting up to her midcalves. About an hour has passed since she took off running. It'd be nice to be gone longer, but as she stands in her sweat-soaked running gear, she knows she has nowhere else to go.

"What am I gonna do?" she asks the ocean.

"Wow, you were really flying!"

Cat turns, and there's a woman sitting on a towel, ten or fifteen feet away. She's not in a swimsuit. Shorts and a T-shirt. Hiking shoes sit next to her towel. She has bright red hair, pulled into a ponytail. "I mean, that had to be exhausting, right?"

Cat tries to be polite. "It wasn't so bad."

"How far did you go?"

"Six miles, I think."

The woman whistles and stands up, gathering her towel and shoes. "I run a little, too, but nothing like that. And in this heat, no way. I'm more of a sweater-weather gal."

The first prickly edges of suspicion gather. Cat starts walking, but the woman walks with her, stumbly in the sand. "So, you from around here?" she asks.

"Just in for the weekend."

"Ah. Vacation town, right? Doesn't feel like anyone's really *from* here. That's what I've noticed."

A banner plane: two-dollar drinks at Big Chill Beach Club in Bethany Beach.

"You with friends, or . . . ?"

Freckles run up her arms. She's a girl who really shouldn't be out in this kind of sun. Cat says yes, but cautiously.

"Cool. Like, a reunion? Old friends?"

"I should really get—"

"I'm here alone," she says. "Getting the lay of the land. I'm from New York. This place kinda reminds me of the Hamptons. Not as awful, though. Fewer rich people ruining everything."

The house is just up ahead now, casting shadows over the dunes. Dash isn't on the deck anymore. Cat stops walking and curses herself, because she's basically just led this woman who may be crazy right here.

"This is you, huh?" She nods up at the house, another whistle.

Where in the hell is Dash?

The woman pulls at her hair tie, adjusting her red ponytail. "It's actually the most expensive house in Fenwick Island. Did you know that? There are some bonkers places down in Ocean City, and over in Rehoboth. That's where most of the megarich people go. But *this* thing: it's the crown jewel of Fenwick."

A second hit of suspicion, sharper. "I really need to get inside," says Cat.

She takes a notebook out of the back pocket of her shorts, flips some pages. "Four million," she says. "You believe that? Well, four-point-two-five, to be exact. Zillow.com. Cool site. You can look up any house you want. All you need is an address."

Cat looks up again, willing Dash to appear.

"All things considered, though, four-point-whatever is nothing for a guy like Robbie Malcolm, right?"

Cat takes a step back. She holds her Adidas sneakers like weapons.

The redhead laughs. "Relax, Cat. I don't bite. My name's Casey Green. I'm a journalist. Can I interest you in a Gatorade?"

Chapter 27

More now about writers and their neuroses. A writer can tell right away when his or her agent has bad news, often before that agent utters a single word.

Just before an agent ruins a writer's day, he or she will inevitably pause and take a quick, stabilizing breath. When you hear those two things—the pause, the sharp intake of oxygen—honestly, you might as well hang up and start drinking.

Wade answers his phone now, out in front of the bookstore, and he tries to sound casual. "Hey, Brandon, what's up?" But then there it is: the pause, the breath, and the muscles in his body go slack as he leans against a placard advertising Italian ice.

"So, I heard from the guy," says Brandon. "He exists, turns out. It's a pass. I'm sorry. He just . . . he said he didn't see the . . . he didn't see the sales potential."

"The sales potential?" says Wade.

"Yeah. I wanted to be like, 'Seriously, man? Your office is attached to a fucking Quiznos, but you're worried about *sales potential*?'"

Wade doesn't say anything.

"I know, Wade. This fucking business. I need to get out of it. I would, too, but my mom would murder me. Also, my husband is a stay-at-home dad now. Did I tell you that?"

Wade looks into the bookstore through the front window. He sees Blair waiting for him.

"Wade, you there?" says Brandon. "Listen. I know I'm shit with the bad news. But I'm not gonna be a dick about this. He said you're a good writer. And he meant it. I could tell. And he's right. You are, Wade. A *damn* good writer. This just—this just isn't the book. You're gonna sit down, and you're gonna get after it again. Fresh start. The Wade Stephens reboot. Wade Stephens 2.0. And when you do? *That* will be the book. You hear me?"

Brandon may be right. Maybe Wade really *is* a good writer. Maybe there's a book somewhere inside his brain that the world would actually want. He'll never know, though, because this is it. Wade is done.

"So, take the holiday weekend," says Brandon. "Get some rest. Recharge. Do some shots. That's what I'm gonna do. Then, next week, we can brainstorm. We'll look at trends. Vampires. Serial killers. Time travel. I'm just riffing here. We'll start over. Cool?"

Wade doesn't feel like saying "cool." Wade doesn't feel like saying anything, really, including goodbye, so he just hangs up.

Back inside Bethany Beach Books, Blair's shivering still. She gives him this expectant, hopeful look that only makes it worse. "So?" she says.

"I believe I'm ready for that drink now," he says.

"Oh, hey, there you are! Thought I lost ya."

It's the clerk again. Her voice is so cheery it's startling, like sudden Christmas. She's holding a copy of *Feedback*. "Look what I found! Most of them got sent back to the publisher forever ago. But I found one. See? Little dusty, but good as new."

Blair and Wade look at each other, and then Blair takes a twenty from the pocket of her cover-up. "We'll take it."

Chapter 28

Back in Fenwick, Robbie is taking a walk. He doesn't particularly know where he's going, but it's good to be out, just him. Dash offered to come, because that's Dash's job, but Robbie told him to stay put and wait for his friends to come back.

"You're just gonna . . . *walk*?" Dash asked. "What if there's—?"

Who knows what dangers Dash had scrolling through his head: ransom-seeking kidnappers, hit-and-run drivers, redheaded journalists with axes to grind? Robbie held up his hand, and that was that. He stepped out onto the grand front steps and chose a direction.

Being alone is something Robbie's gotten used to. It's perfectly normal for thirty-five-year-old men to be single. When you're a billionaire, though, it's a matter of public speculation. He's had three romantic relationships that could be considered "serious." All three started after he was rich, which made things complicated, because he knew that not one of those three women would've been interested in him in real life. A socialite, a former sitcom actress, and the daughter of a cartoonishly outspoken British politician.

If you saw Robbie, unless you specifically knew who he was, you wouldn't look again. He knows this about himself, his forgettableness. Not short, but not tall either. Brownish hair, a slight build. Introverted. Humor can be a saving grace for average-looking men—a loophole in evolutionary science—but Robbie is too reasonable to be funny.

The last of those serious girlfriends, Hannah Ashbury, in an accent so posh it sounded like something from an *SNL* skit, told him once before a charity gala in Trafalgar Square that they absolutely *must* get married. "Don't be daft, Robbie. I make you appear better-looking than you are, and you make me appear smarter than I am. It's called teamwork."

So, he walks alone.

He started keeping tabs on his friends about the time Wade's book came out. As he slowly bought up copies of *Feedback,* he found himself thinking about Blair and Cat, too. How were they doing—*really* doing? He mostly followed them through their social media accounts at first. Then he had members of his communication's team aggregate their activity into monthly reports.

As things slowly spiraled for Blair, Cat, and Wade, he planned to do something about it. He didn't know exactly what, though, so he kept tabling it. Then he got cancer. Now, as he walks, he's afraid they won't come back. What if he's overplayed his hand? What if he's proven that he's more hassle now than he's worth? He'll be gone soon anyway.

THE INSIDE OF DAIRY QUEEN smells like sugar and French fries. The line is maybe fifteen people deep.

The place hasn't changed. The same ads are on the walls, the same drippy AC vent by the restrooms. They used to come here at least once per Fenwick Island trip. It's impossible to think about them here and not think about them laughing. Cat and Blair especially, who caused scenes in their bikinis. Blair jumped behind the counter once and started helping the stunned manager dip vanilla ice cream cones into chocolate sauce. It makes him sad to think about how happy his three friends were then.

The line moves fast, and when it's Robbie's turn, he can't remember what his go-to order used to be. He remembers theirs. Blair and Cat would get one small Oreo Blizzard and split it. Wade was a Mister Misty guy.

The girl behind the counter waits, bored. She has a purple streak in her dirty-blond hair. "Oh yeah," Robbie says. "Butterfinger Blizzard. Small."

"Anything else?"

He takes out his wallet. Everyone around him is sand-covered and sun-dazed and happy-looking. A little girl in her young mother's arms is trying to pronounce "Peanut Buster Parfait." Two old people wearing matching sun hats hold hands. He hands the girl his American Express card. "Yeah. Whatever all these people want."

The girl doesn't know what to do.

"Actually," he says, "keep it. Pay for everyone until close, then cut it up before you go home."

Back outside, Robbie finds that he's looking directly at a church. It isn't big and grand-looking like a lot of churches. It's just a white building with a slanted roof. He tries to remember if it's always been there. That's the thing about churches: your eyes breeze right over them, like they're not even there.

The sign out front says ALL ARE WELCOME. He figures that includes him, too.

Chapter 29

"So, what're you feeling?"

That's a hell of a question. Cat is feeling shell-shocked, depressed, hungover still, sticky with sweat, and physically depleted from running. She feels abandoned and betrayed by Gabrielle. She feels violated by Robbie, and she's more confident than ever that she'll die alone while eating a microwavable meal. She keeps all this to herself, though, because Casey Green is just asking about Gatorade.

"There's orange," Casey says. "My personal fave. Red, three different blues, one of which is—" She squints at the label, standing on her toes. She's short, too, like Cat. "Arctic Blast? Whatever that is. Finally, yellow."

They're at Royal Farms standing before an enormous glass drink cooler.

Royal Farms isn't like a normal quick shop—it's more of a mini supermarket that also sells pastries and fried chicken. Cat grabs a handful of napkins next to a case of donuts and mops at the sweat on her forehead. "I'll take orange," she says.

"Damn right." Casey grabs a Diet Coke, too, and holds up a credit card. "Anything else? I've got the official *HypeReport* corporate card. Sky's the limit."

"No thanks," Cat says. She's starving—stomach-eating-itself

starving—but murdering some fried chicken right now probably wouldn't be a good look. And, yes, despite everything, Cat finds that she's concerned about her appearance. As she stands dripping next to a rack of beef jerky, she's beginning to realize that Casey might actually be pretty.

At the register, an old lady in a "Kickin' Chicken" T-shirt rings them up.

"So, *HypeReport,* huh?" says Cat.

"The one and only," says Casey.

They've wandered away from Royal Farms to a green space across the street next to a playground. "Is that one of your techniques over there?" asks Cat. "Ambushing vulnerable people?"

"Well, you hardly look vulnerable. But, yeah, kinda. How'd I do?"

"A little skeevy," says Cat, "if I'm being honest."

They sip their drinks.

"I see your point," says Casey. "Apologies. But I really wanted to talk to you."

"And why's that?"

"I assume you know *HypeReport*'s work?"

"I do," she says. *HypeReport* is a digital news and entertainment site that mixes hard news and celebrity gossip with plain old clickbait. "I love your quizzes. Saw one the other day: 'Eight Simple Questions to Find Out What Kind of Zoo Animal You'd Be.' Groundbreaking."

This is Cat's go-to move when presented with a reasonably attractive woman: be awkward and a little mean. Casey is undeterred, though. "I know it's not as hard-hitting as your work at *The Morning Gab.* Associate producer, right? Coffee runs and scheduling the catering, that kinda thing?"

Cat startles at the sort-of reference to Gabrielle. She startles again at the *not*-sort-of reference to herself. The logical question is

"How do you know where I work?" but the last few hours have altered her sense of what people should and shouldn't know about her.

"The quizzes, though," says Casey, "and all the celebrity rumor stuff. Not my side of the house. I'm in the news division. Financial reporter. How was the Malcolm Capital jet, by the way? Gulfstream G650, right? Those things are plush."

A woman with a little girl appears; they're both eating ice creams from the Dairy Queen up the street. "Pean prf-yay," the girl shouts. "Prrffffyay!" The mother gives them a tired nod and places the girl on a starfish rocking swing. Cat thinks of Gabrielle with a baby on her shoulder, her nose nuzzled against its tiny head, and she can barely breathe.

"You with me, Cat?"

"What?"

"Kinda went spacey on me there. The jet. I got ahold of the flight manifest out of L.A. That's where I got your name. I like Cat more than Catherine, by the way. You're definitely a Cat."

"Thanks?" Cat says.

Casey finishes her soda, and Cat's pretty sure what's coming next. "Robbie's here, isn't he?"

Saying no seems silly, so Cat says nothing.

"My question is, why? I mean, a billie goes dark for a month, just vanishes off the face of the earth . . . then he turns up *here*."

"What's a billie?" Cat asks.

"Oh yeah. Forgot. You're a civilian. Billies are billionaires. It's what we call them."

Cat wishes she had more napkins. The little girl on the playground toddles toward the jungle gym; her mom gives chase.

"And this particular billie is in Delaware of all places," Casey says. "On a beach in a recently purchased multimillion-dollar dwelling. And, he's with *you*. From my standpoint, that makes you a pretty interesting lady, Cat Miller."

"We're old friends," she says. "Just . . . getting together."

Casey chews her lower lip. "Sounds nice." She reminds Cat of the nerdy girls in the library back in college. They were always thoughtlessly dressed, bundled up in thrown-on hoodies or baggy sweaters, hair falling across their faces.

"I should really be getting back." Even as she says this, Cat knows she doesn't want to. Not yet. Maybe not ever. How far could she make it, she wonders, in sneakers and running clothes, if she just started walking westward?

"He's not who you think he is, Cat."

"What?"

"Robbie. He's not who *anyone* thinks he is. In my experience, billies never are."

Chapter 30

You shouldn't eat ice cream in church. This seems like a good general rule. But when Robbie opens the heavy door, there's no one there, so he decides it's probably okay.

He hasn't been in a church in years. There are the standard pews and hymnals and stained glass. When he looks up at the altar and pulpit, though, something's off. No crucifix. No fit Jesus. Instead, there's just a bare cross.

He slides into the back row and thinks about his last day of high school. By sheer coincidence, when Wade was making his death march through the halls of Baltimore Prep to be expelled, Robbie saw him. The seniors didn't have much to do those last few weeks of school. Robbie was alone in one of the math rooms going over extra problem sets when Wade's head bobbed by. Robbie knew what was happening. He'd heard the announcement over the loud-speaker: "Wade Stephens, report immediately to Father Milton's office."

Later that morning, as he and his classmates watched a film version of *Macbeth* in Father Garringer's AP English class, Robbie stood and asked if he could be excused.

He hadn't had a cellphone back then, so Robbie went directly to Father Milton's office and asked his secretary, Mrs. Doogan, if he could use the phone. When his mom picked up, she sounded harried. Robbie could hear office noises in the background. "Hi, Mom. Nothing's wrong. You may need to come down to school, though."

"Why?" she asked. "What's happened?"

"I'm about to quit school. They may want you here, in case there are things to sign."

Mrs. Doogan looked up from a stack of paperwork, eyebrows raised.

"Robbie, what?" his mom asked. "Robbie?"

"I'll explain later. And I'm sorry. But I'm also not sorry." He set the phone in its cradle and addressed Mrs. Doogan. "Is Father Milton available?"

If Father Garringer was the most approachable priest at Baltimore Prep, Father Milton was the scariest. Not only was he the dean of discipline, he was the head wrestling coach, so, presumably, he knew how to hurt people.

"Robert," Father Milton said after Robbie told him he was quitting. The wrinkles that bracketed the priest's mouth were deep enough to slide dimes into. His hair was Brillo-pad thick and silver. "You're the valedictorian. Need I remind you of this fact?"

"No, Father, you don't."

"And how do you think the folks up in Cambridge will react to this? Not a lot of high school dropouts running around Harvard, I'd assume."

Robbie had been accepted early, offered a full scholarship. The school had even sent him a welcome package, which included a teddy bear wearing a little "H" sweater. In the coming weeks, Robbie and his mother would explain the situation to Harvard's admissions department. They'd receive a phone call during which the dean of admissions told Robbie how excited they *still* were to have him enrolled there for that upcoming fall. Blair, Cat, and Wade would have similar conversations with the schools to which they'd been accepted. The four friends would take their GED exam together on a rainy Saturday morning at the Towson Library. They would go out for pizza afterward. Robbie didn't know this yet, though, so he felt genuine fear. He held his hands firmly in his lap so Father Milton wouldn't see them shaking.

"Are you going to give that up for . . . for *this*? For *them*?"

"They're my best friends," Robbie said.

The old man grumbled. "You know how many of my friends from high school I keep in touch with today?"

Robbie wasn't meant to respond.

"Exactly zero. That's how it works. You leave this place; you find new people. You move up and on. Particularly someone like you, Robert. That kid I kicked out earlier today, your buddy Wade? You think you're going to be friends with *him* in ten years? Twenty? And those two girls? The ones who made fools of themselves in front of the entire city? What, you're all going to be old pals, you think?"

Robbie wasn't meant to respond to this either. But if he had, he might have said something like "I really, really hope so."

Father Milton reached for a mug of coffee, sniffed it, then set it back down. "Face it, son. Some things are more important than friends." From that particular angle, the portrait of Jesus on the wall behind Father Milton appeared to be looking at Robbie. "And these friends of yours? They've got a hell of a lot less to lose than you do. So I'll ask one last time. Are you sure about this?"

Chapter 31

A realization has set in, and under the circumstances, it's annoying. Casey Green is definitely pretty. Cat thinks of the library girls again, how she'd sneak glances at them over the tops of her textbooks. Occasionally, from a distance, she'd choose one and fall a little bit in love, even though Cat never actually spoke to any of them.

They're at a beach shop on Coastal Highway called Sea Shell City. Casey holds out her arm. "Do I look sunburned to you?" she asks.

It seems like permission to look at Casey. At her hitched stance and curly red hair. At her sensible footwear and bulky iWatch. Her freckles exist in bunches, like concentrated efforts of nature. "A little pinkish, maybe," she says.

Casey hasn't mentioned Robbie once since they got here. A few minutes ago, she said that ominous shit about him on the playground and then pointed at Sea Shell City down the road and suggested they take a walk.

"So, like, what's the deal?" Cat asks.

Casey frowns at a pencil case made of crab shells. "I wonder if my niece would like this."

"I can't tell if you didn't hear me," says Cat, "or if you're doing more journalist tricks."

"I'm working on an article," she says.

"About Robbie?"

"Yeah."

"Lots of people write articles about Robbie, right?"

"Sure. I have a fresh angle, though. One I don't think he's gonna be thrilled about."

Cat wonders if she should say something like "I have no comment at this time," like people do in movies. Instead she says, "Why are you talking to me, though? I'm nobody."

"You're not *nobody*," Casey says. "You knew Robbie *before*, pre-billie, when he was just a high school nerd. In a piece like the one I'm writing, you could provide insight. A counterpoint."

"He wasn't really *that* nerdy." Cat is unsure why she feels the need to say this. "You'd assume he would be, I guess. The genius thing. But our friend Wade was *way* nerdier."

Casey looks like she's taking mental notes. "We've seen it before, right?" she says. "Some powerful guy does something shady, and every news organization on the planet goes live with 'Breaking news: rich fucker behaves like rich fucker.' Click, click. Shock, shock. But Robbie Malcolm is different. He's one of the *good* ones, right?" She makes air quotes around *good*.

"But he *is,* isn't he?" asks Cat. "The charity stuff, the . . ." She nearly brings up the escaped cow but doesn't, because there's no way it's true.

Casey rolls her eyes. "PR. These guys? Their public-facing images are completely orchestrated. In real life, they're capable of shit you wouldn't believe. All of them."

Cat feels herself get defensive for her friend. Her friend whom she loves. Her friend who is sick. Her friend who . . . used shadowy operatives to pick through her life.

"*That's* why I'm talking to you, Cat," say Casey. "You can help me tell a full story. You can make this piece legit, not just another takedown from some left-leaning news site."

"Wait," says Cat. "How do you know I've known him for a long time?"

"You said you were old friends, remember? Plus, I'm a professional. I googled you. You're really funny on Twitter, by the way."

This is both creepy and flattering, because Cat tries very hard to be funny on Twitter.

"High school classmates, right?" Casey says. "Baltimore. In the piece, you'd be Catherine Miller, longtime friend. I'll mention that you go by Cat, though. You know, for color."

They leave Sea Shell City and walk back out onto Coastal Highway, which is loud and busy.

"So, what did Robbie actually do?" Cat asks.

They head in the general direction of the beach mansion.

"For starters," says Casey, "being a billionaire in and of itself makes him an immoral, resource-hoarding monster, right?"

"Jeez," says Cat. "Left-leaning, huh?"

"So were Woodward and Bernstein." A roaring pack of motorcyclists passes. "Did you ever wonder how Robbie made all his start-up money, Cat?"

"Well, he's a genius," she says. "Right?"

Another eye roll. "So was my high school chem teacher. He lived in a fourth-floor walk-up in Queens. Robbie's, what, thirty-five?"

"Yeah."

"Two things are needed to generate the kind of wealth Robbie has: time and money. Since he's young, he hasn't had much time. So let's focus on money. In that business, it takes an insane amount of capital to make billions. Wealth begets wealth."

"Capital?" Cat says.

"Fancy word for money."

"Oh."

"You've heard the expression 'The rich get richer,' right? Being rich is actually a moneymaking operation. When you have a lot of money, that money grows. If you have a little bit of money, that money grows, too, but just a little. It's about percentages."

Cat thinks of word problems swirling in her mind in high school.

"Robbie didn't have a cushion," says Casey Green. "No trust fund springboard. His parents: solid middle-class America. They have the kind of money that just grows a little. Billionaire money, though? That had to come from somewhere."

"Okay," says Cat. She draws the word out. "Where, then?"

Chapter 32

"You know what? I actually feel good."

Blair wonders if this could possibly be true.

"Here's a secret," Wade says. "Writing sucks."

Her new copy of *Feedback* sits on the bar top with their envelopes. They're a few blocks from the bookstore at Big Chill Beach Club, an open-air bar overlooking the bay.

"Imagine having homework every day," he says. "Then, when you're done, you sit in your apartment and wait for people you don't know to tell you why they don't like it. *That's* writing. I hate it. I don't have to do it anymore. Shit, I feel better than good. I feel . . . relieved."

A DJ is setting up at the other end of the bar, and Blair tries to block out everything Wade has just said, because if she doesn't it might tear down the façade she's been building around herself her entire adult life. But then again, maybe that's what today is: an epic teardown. "Same," she says.

"Same what?" he asks.

"Same. Painting. I hate it, too." And wow, Wade was right, because what Blair feels right now is pure, uncut relief.

"But you're fantastic," he says.

"I'm not, though."

"Of course, you—"

She stops him. "Wade, I'm not. I've sold a handful of canvases at art fairs. I painted one really good thing in my life, and I was eighteen when I did it."

Blair's own mediocrity and the fact that she may very well hate making art are not new revelations. She's managed to bury them, though, because aren't thoughts like those just part of being an artist? But yesterday, as she stood in her beautiful new studio, the facts were undeniable. Imaginary Taylor Swift was there whispering in her ear: *You know you don't deserve any of this, Blair. Right?*

The bartender stops by and asks if they want another round. Wade hands over his credit card and opens a tab. "I'm moving to Baltimore," he says. "Maybe Visa won't find me."

"When the twins were born," Blair says, "and I went on my *artistic hiatus*, I acted like I was making a sacrifice. But, like you said, I was relieved. It meant I didn't have to sit at half-finished canvases anymore trying to convince myself that I'm actually still good."

The DJ taps a mic. He's wearing a Hawaiian shirt. Blair wonders what happened to them, all of them. Things were supposed to be better than this.

"Well, shit," Wade says. "I'm glad I'm retiring, because if *you're* not good enough, I'm *definitely* not good enough."

Blair picks up *Feedback,* wipes away some condensation from the bar top. "It doesn't matter how many copies Robbie bought. It's a wonderful little book, Wade."

He tips his glass. On the cover, Wade's name runs sideways in a punk rock font along the neck of an illustrated guitar. She was so happy for him when it came out, and then sad for him when it went nowhere. That's the problem with having friends like these: you absorb their goods *and* their bads, which is why she sits now in a damp cover-up, feeling the Rejects' collective pain.

Their new drinks arrive, but they're not finished with their first ones.

"The good news is," Wade says, "now I can focus on my *true* calling."

"Which is?"

"Getting rejected by women."

Blair laughs, which feels good.

"It's tough out there, Blair. Chicks nowadays want guys with jobs and places to live."

"What about the Match girl?" she asks. "She looked nice. Maybe Robbie's right. Maybe you'll like her."

Wade starts in on his second drink. "Maybe. But, Blair, what's in it for her? I'm an unemployed former novelist. I'm about to move into my parents' basement."

A hostess passes and waves at the bartender. She's wearing neon-colored sneakers, bright, like Jane wore earlier at Viking Golf. Blair thinks about her now, the way her face changed when she met Wade—how her eyes briefly lit up.

"I feel like I asked you this," she says, "but I don't think you ever answered. What's your new book about?"

He looks at his drink. "You're just gonna make fun of me."

"No, I won't," says Blair.

"It's about the Beatles."

"The Beatles? *The* Beatles? I actually might make fun of you."

"It's hard to explain."

"Try me," she says.

"I borrowed things from their songs," he says. "A few titles. Some snippets of lyrics. A couple of their characters, like Lucy and Eleanor."

"Who?"

"Lucy in the Sky. Eleanor Rigby."

"Oh. Can you even do that?"

Wade shrugs. "I wrote stories based on those things. There's one called 'Tangerine Trees,' another called 'Speaking Words of Wisdom.' 'All the Lonely People.' At first it just reads like a normal story collection. One-off pieces. Gradually, though, they start weaving together. By the end, you get it. They're all connected."

She looks at his author photo: an airbrushed and serious-looking Wade from six years ago. "That sounds good. What's the title?"

"*All Together Now,*" he says.

"*All Together Now*? Is that a song?"

"Not a particularly famous one," he says, "but yeah. It's on the *Yellow Submarine* soundtrack from 1969. By then, there was all this tension in the band. Lots of arguing, creative differences. Yoko, et cetera. They'd be broken up within a year. Done forever. But they had this song, 'All Together Now.' It's this great, catchy little thing. John and Paul have a call and response. George and Ringo goof off in the background, playing cymbals and clapping. They sound so happy—you can hear it—like four old friends having fun. You could listen to it a thousand times, and you'd never know the whole thing was about to fall apart."

Blair's eyes fill—sudden, like an allergic reaction. "I want to read it," she says.

He tells her maybe someday, and they watch the water. A boat jostles kayakers and paddleboarders. People laugh and lounge and hold hands.

"But enough about me." Wade nudges her envelope. "What are you gonna do about all this, Blair McKenzie?"

Her maiden name sounds so natural coming out of his mouth she hardly notices. She dips a finger into her new drink, tastes the sweetness. It's a good question.

Chapter 33

"Oh, hi there. I didn't know anyone was here."

A woman in worn jeans and a purple T-shirt stands before him, and Robbie feels like he's been caught breaking and entering. "I'm sorry. I should've . . . knocked."

She laughs. "Knocked? You don't have to knock at church. That's why we leave the doors open." She notices his Blizzard. "What flavor'd you get?"

Busted, Robbie tells her Butterfinger and offers to throw it away.

She looks around at all the empty pews. "Eh, we'll let it slide. DQ does a mean business on Sundays thanks to our eleven A.M. service. I'm a Heath Bar fan myself."

She sets a hand on his pew. Her long hair runs in a braid down her back. Her T-shirt has a picture of a cartoon dog on a surfboard. LIFE IS GOOD. "Anything I can help you with? I'm Mary Louise, by the way."

"Robbie," he says. "I was just on a walk."

"Well, when one finds oneself here," she says, "it's usually not an accident."

"Do you work here?" he asks.

She laughs again. "I'm the minster. This is my church."

"I'm sorry. It's hard to tell without—"

"You're Catholic, right?" she asks.

"Former," he says.

She sits, and Robbie slides over. Mary Louise is maybe sixty—no frills, undyed hair, a plain, wrinkled face. A beam of sun has just shone through the stained glass, projecting colors onto the altar. "Lotta folks like you find themselves here. Half our congregation is former Catholics, I'll bet."

"Well, Catholicism has had some branding issues these last few decades."

She smiles. "I can always tell a Catholic. They get a little taken aback by me—a woman, in an outfit like this—getting to be in charge. We Presbyterians are more relaxed about all that. Plus, those collars look itchy."

Robbie doesn't know much about Presbyterians. Not knowing much about something is unfamiliar territory. He likes that word, though, *relaxed*—a word he doesn't remember Father Milton ever using. "Presbyterians," he says. "What's your thing, if you don't mind me asking?"

"Our thing?"

"I don't mean to generalize. But Jews have neurosis. Catholics have guilt and itchy collars. What do you have?"

Mary Louis thinks. "A personal relationship with God. I guess that's *our* thing, if you had to pin me down. Fewer sacraments, too. You guys love those things."

A silence settles. She's right; Robbie didn't accidentally end up here. Mary Louise waits, like she could sit here all day ribbing Catholics. "About the sacraments, though," he says.

"Mm-hmm."

"Confession is an interesting one," he says.

"I agree. Bless me, Father, for I have sinned, right?"

"Right. It's very transactional." Robbie sets his DQ cup next to a book of hymns. "Black-and-white. Value exchanged. If you've done something wrong, you tell a man about it and it all just goes away. You're forgiven."

Mary Louise angles herself to face him, her expression less casual now. "Well, Robbie, you're in luck. You don't need a priest for that. You don't need me, either. That's how *we* do confession. If you think you've sinned, and if you're sorry, just tell God. If you're serious about it, he'll forgive you."

"Just like that?"

"Just like that."

Robbie doesn't quite believe Mary Louise, to be honest, although he wants to. It was easier when he was a kid. He sat in church and he believed, because that was just what you did. A bunch of motorcycles pass outside, shaking the place.

"That sounds nice," Robbie says. "But what if I'm sorry about something I haven't actually done yet? Can I be forgiven for that, too?"

Chapter 34

"Do you know what a viatical settlement is, Cat?"

The two women stare at each other. Cat is fairly certain Casey meant this to be dramatic, like a journalistic mic drop, but no, she has no idea what a viatical settlement is. "Um," she says.

"Right. A viatical settlement is a financial practice that allows people with terminal illnesses to sell their life insurance policies before they die, for cash payouts."

"Terminal illnesses?" Cat says.

"Dying is expensive in America," Casey says. "A lot of people can't afford it. Medical bills. Credit card debt. Underwater mortgages. You have to go into debt to die. So what do you do? You find out you're dying, right? Soon, you'll be gone. But you need money *now*. Well, if you're desperate enough, you sell your life insurance policy, usually at a big loss, for quick cash so you can stay afloat till you're dead. Remember the financial crisis—'08, '09?"

"Sure."

"Millions of people who had some pretty decent money suddenly found themselves broke as fuck. Some of those people were sick. Some *got* sick. That's what humans do: they get sick. But, suddenly, their liquidity: gonzo. Zip. But what they *did* have was life insurance. Big stacks of money, just waiting to be cashed in."

Cat is still mostly lost. "What?"

Casey stops walking. They're standing on the sidewalk now. "Back when the economy went to shit, Robbie Malcolm went after dying people. He went after people who found themselves sick and in trouble and in debt up to their asses in a world that had just been flipped upside down."

"Went . . . after them?" says Cat. "How?"

"He set up a shell company that sought those people out and offered to buy their life insurance policies—sometimes for pennies on the dollar. And he made millions."

"He stole money from dying people?"

"He didn't *steal* it, no," says Casey. "They gave it to him. And then he used it to take little, floundering Malcolm Capital to a whole other level. He turned their blood money into billions for himself. He generated capital. And then he *grew* that capital."

"Is that illegal?"

"No, ma'am," Casey says. "It's gross. It's predatory. It's gonna put one hell of a stain on Robbie Malcolm's bullshit sterling-good-guy, man-of-the-people image. But it's perfectly legal. God bless America."

Cat walks to a tree, leans against it.

"Helluva story, huh?"

"Why haven't you run it yet?" Cat asks.

"I was about to," says Casey. "Last month. We fucking had him. It was good, too. Quick. Concise. Our legal team was reviewing. The fact-checkers were running through it. Then something strange happened."

"What?" asks Cat.

"Robbie vanished." She makes a *poof* sound, and Cat tries to act however a person acts who doesn't know anything about anything.

"I figured somebody must've tipped him off, right? It happens. These rich guys have their ways. They have lackeys and spies, like third-world dictators. They hack into email and dig through shit. I assumed he was just gonna go away for a bit, wait out the news cycle. Give a bunch of money to AIDS research or whatever. But then I found him."

"Here?"

"No, before here. Before I found you in L.A., too, actually."

"Where?" asks Cat. "How?"

"Same way I found you." She taps Cat's arm. "His plane. Tough to hide those things. They aren't stealth bombers."

"Okay."

"You ever been to Rochester, Minnesota, Cat?"

"No, why?"

"Kind of a random place for a billionaire to hang out for a few days, right? Unless, of course, that billionaire is visiting one of the most esteemed medical institutions on planet earth. The Mayo Clinic."

In retrospect, Cat should've ended this when she had the chance. She should've chugged her Gatorade, thrown her empty bottle in Casey Green's face, and declared "No comment."

"My boss and I," Casey says. "We decided to hold the story, because, well . . . seems like maybe there's more story to tell."

Chapter 35

Last Friday night, Blair and Martin went to a fundraiser at the twins' school.

The gym, which had been decorated for Casino Night, was loud and packed with tired parents, and everyone was hopped up on free chardonnay and domestic beer. A banner on the wall read, WIN OR LOSE, WE ALL WIN.

Blair and Martin did a few laps upon arrival. They played four hands of blackjack and chatted with other couples about school things—proposed parking lot expansions, a head lice outbreak in the fifth grade. Then, all around them, spouses drifted apart. This happens at events like these; men find other men they know, and women find other women with whom they're comfortable enough to talk trash about their own kids.

Blair checked her phone. A new email had arrived from Mr. McGee five minutes before.

I know we've agreed not to speak tonight, but, holy shit, you look amazing.

Her eyes found him right away, drawn by some animal chemistry. Mr. McGee stood about seventy-five feet away by the makeshift bar under the basketball hoop. He was chatting with the other art teacher, a mousy-looking woman named Mrs. Grayson. Blair smiled, Mr. McGee smiled back, and Blair wondered if it was obvious they were smiling at each other.

She put her phone away and ate a little square of crabmeat from a silver tray. She needed to hide her phone because if she didn't, she knew she'd keep checking it. Over the last few months, their emails had been near constant, ranging from friendly recaps of the day's events to back-and-forths that left her breathless, and sometimes she had to put her phone in a drawer and commit to not looking at it again for thirty minutes.

Blair bumped into two mothers she knew, and the three of them lost twenty dollars each at the roulette table. They told Blair she looked beautiful, and she told them they were very sweet.

She took a flute of white wine from a passing waiter and was confronted by her own reflection in a trophy case. She knew she looked good. Men had been glancing at her all night, some subtly, some not. It was fine, though. The night was about being seen. And not just by Mr. McGee, but by Martin, too. By the world at large.

Before getting in the car and coming there, though, Blair had practically had to force Martin to get ready. He was sitting on the couch watching a Nationals game with Kenny. Her husband looked up at her, arm around their son. His eyes briefly went to her black dress, which fit her as perfectly as any dress ever had. "Is this one of those things we *have* to go to," he asked, "or one of those things we *should* go to?"

Later, as she mingled and chatted, Blair saw Martin from a distance. He was talking in a circle of dads, smiling and laughing politely, his tie loose. He noticed her looking at him, and their eyes met. This was animal chemistry, too, Blair supposed, a practical, less frantic version of it. Mates finding each other in the jungle. He made a face—a goofy eye roll and a half smile—the look he gave her when he wanted to leave soon. The silent language of marriage.

Blair won five dollars at the slot machines, which were actually a set of mounted iPads open to a slot machine app. Mr. McGee glanced at her again, a few times, in fact. Other men continued to as well, and she cataloged all of them, because glances like those have always had an inherent value to Blair, like currency.

"That dress is great, by the way," Martin told her as they walked through the dim parking lot. He stifled a yawn. "I meant to say that earlier. You look really pretty."

He put his hand on Blair's lower back. Blair reminded herself: *His hands; I like his hands.* She thought of the first time those hands had been on her body. They'd slept together for the first time after their third date. Afterward, still breathing hard, Martin laughed in bed beside her. When she asked him why, he ran a hand from her bare clavicle down to her hip and kissed her shoulder. "Jesus, Beautiful Blair, can I take a picture of you and send it to every guy I went to high school with?"

The man who'd said that wonderful thing was walking beside her. That feeling—the simple joy of being with her—was still in there somewhere, right? It had to be.

They'd been late to arrive at Casino Night, so the Odyssey was in one of the farthest corners of the school's big parking lot. They never drove it when the kids weren't with them, but when Martin got home from work that night his Infiniti was on fumes. Blair noticed the streetlight directly above the Odyssey happened to be out. The handful of spaces on either side were empty, the cars from before gone now. Their minivan was as hidden as it reasonably could be in a parking lot just outside Washington, D.C.

Blair took Martin's hand, squeezed. The dress she was wearing, the watery glasses of wine, the looks she'd gotten, the hundreds of emails from Mr. McGee stored in a special folder in her inbox, the memory of sex with Martin—they'd combined to make the evening feel like it had been set on a low simmer. The Odyssey's windows were tinted black. The bench seat in the back folded down flat.

"We should have sex in the Odyssey," Blair whispered.

Martin laughed. "What?"

She was turned on, but vulnerable; emboldened, but embarrassed, too. "Why not?" she said.

He looked around. "Should I list the reasons? This is our kids' school. We could get caught. Arrested."

The parking lot was empty. No one would ever know. She persisted. "I want to, Martin. Come on."

He reached into his pocket for the minivan's key fob and laughed again. The minivan's lights flashed as the vehicle unlocked. "Stop it," he said. "We'll do it at home." But, of course, they wouldn't, and she knew it. The second they walked through the door, the twins would bound down the stairs, wide-awake and yelling. He opened the door for her. "Hop in," he said. "You can pick the music."

"WAIT, YOU'RE TELLING ME HE turned down minivan sex?"

Blair nods and sips her drink.

"Wow," says Wade. "And the dress? It was . . ."

"Hot, yeah."

"I'd have risked it," he says. "Helluva way to get arrested, too, right? YOLO. The kids say that, I think."

The DJ has just put on a big pair of those firing-range-looking headphones that DJs wear. He's bobbing his head.

"This guy's gonna play Jimmy Buffett, isn't he?" Wade points with a stirring straw. "Probably 'Cheeseburger in Paradise,' too. And I'm gonna spend the rest of my life in a Delawarean prison for stabbing a beach DJ."

"You really are a snob," she says.

"Ten minutes, y'all," the DJ announces. "Ten minutes and we get this thing bumpin'."

Wade grimaces, then swivels to face Blair. "So, Mr. McWhat's-his-face? You haven't . . . you haven't actually . . ."

"No," she says. "I would have, though. I was going to."

Wade taps his glass against hers. "You know I'm not an optimistic person, right?"

"Of course."

"And silver linings are complete bullshit."

"Right."

"But this whole thing," he says, "maybe it's good. Robbie's meddling was weird and fucked-up. But what if it was a blessing? You found out *now*. It's not too late. You haven't crossed the point of no return. You sexted, right? Big whoop."

"It was more than that, though." Wade is right, but he's also not right. You can have sex without intimacy. But then you can read a sentence in an email so intimate it makes you consider the logistics of uprooting your life and running away with an elementary school art teacher. She looks at her envelope. "I sent him things. Pictures. I just don't understand how he could lead me on like that."

"I have another secret for you, Blair. Men are awful. Total fucking creeps, across the board. The lot of us."

"Well, not *all* men," she says.

"No," says Wade. "All of us. I don't think women fully grasp that. Someone should do a podcast as a general service to female society. The level of depravity that surrounds you every day is terrifying."

Wade may be nearly drunk, but he's smart. Blair looks around. There are men everywhere, of course. They look at her like at Casino Night, like at . . . always. When she was a teenager, Blair noticed that men divided her into pieces when they looked: legs, ass, boobs, face. They did this when she was fifteen, and they're doing it now. A familiar moment passes in which she briefly feels naked.

"Think of it as a spectrum, if you will. A creep spectrum. We're not all Harvey Weinstein and R. Kelly, but we're all on it. The art teacher certainly is. I am. Not as high up on the spectrum as him, though. Somewhere between the art teacher and Mister Rogers."

A low, clubby baseline starts; a guy in a Phillies cap walks by and leers at Blair's bare feet.

"My point is," says Wade, "and I can't believe I'm saying this, because I've fantasized about him dying tragically for the last five years, but Martin's a good guy, Blair. I like him. He's super low on the creep spectrum. Barely registers. Last night, we hung out. He's a terrible videogame player. Really awful. But he's nice. And he loves you. Yeah, he's not doing a good job of showing it lately. I get that. Rejecting minivan sex and then leaving you here today . . . probably not hall-of-fame moves. And I know that you feel ignored. But he can work on that. Talk to him. Along with being awful, men are really stupid. Sometimes they need to be told exactly what you're thinking. If you want, *I'll* tell him. Here, give me your phone. I'll tell him that every guy in this cheese-dick bar is in love with you, so he needs to get his shit together."

"You're not calling him, you idiot." She pokes the ice in her grapefruit crush and smiles. "I like drunk Wade, by the way. I've missed him. He's surprisingly upbeat."

"I know," he says. "I'm off-brand here. But, just saying, it could be worse, right? Two adorable kids, a minivan with sick rims, a husband with an annoyingly good body for a guy his age. Seriously, did he get pec implants or something?"

"He does Pilates," Blair says.

"He does what?"

"Every morning before work. We have a machine in the basement."

Wade holds his glass to his forehead. "I take back everything I just said. Fuck that guy."

Blair laughs, and Wade finally picks up his envelope and starts tearing into it.

"You're gonna do that now?" she asks. "Here?"

"Yes," he says. "Then you're opening yours, and we're gonna be done with them."

"Can I ask you a favor first?" she says.

"What, dammit?" he says.

Blair knows that he's saying it like this because whatever she asks he'll do. That's the way it's always been. "Jane," she says. "From Viking Golf today. I want you to go out with her."

Wade stops tearing. "You want me to what?"

"She liked you. I could tell."

A flash of teenage Wade—embarrassed, trying to hide a smile. "I talked to her for five seconds."

"Women get this look, Wade," she says. "I saw it."

"You're crazy. Besides, she lives here."

"So what?" she says. "It's a few hours."

Blair can see that he's thinking of a million reasons to say no. "But you told her I have a book coming out. I don't."

"She seems like the kind of person who will understand." Blair holds his eyes now, like she did in the mirror with Cat earlier in the powder room. "I think you're unhappy because you've made a decision to be alone, because it's easier to sit in your apartment and write about the Beatles and think about me than it is to take a chance on something."

Wade goes still, like he's been put on pause. "Fucking A, McKenzie. I liked you better when you were jumping off houses in bikinis."

"Shut up," she says. "You're gonna do it, okay? For me."

Wade groans, defeated, and she watches him open his envelope. The contents are mostly rejection emails, forwarded from someone named Brandon Ross. Some bank and credit card statements. One of the balances is startling. A notice of eviction.

"Sorry, Wade," she says.

"All stuff I know." He nods at her envelope. "Your turn."

Blair knew that there were a lot of emails, but seeing them together in a stack makes her light-headed. They're in chronological order, so, collectively, they read like a story. She looks at that first email, with the thumbnail pictures of her best portfolio work. She flips ahead. She catches stray words—some of them quite dirty.

"Is it bad?" asks Wade.

There are three other sections separated by red tabs, each marked with a different woman's name. They're names she recognizes—other moms from school, like Robbie said. "Jesus," she whispers.

She shouldn't look. There's no point; the names themselves are proof enough. Blair can't help herself, though. She skims the emails. The dates generally correspond with the dates on her emails, and the stories correspond, too: simple, innocent messages at first, then . . . less innocent. Blair sees a selfie of a woman she knows named Stephenie Downs. She's in her bra and underwear. A few selfies later, she's wearing less than that. She has a son named Trevor who's in third grade. Then there's Grace Arrington. She has a daughter in the twins' class. Blair doesn't let her eyes settle on the images. The next woman, Agatha Haven. Blair and Agatha volunteered together last year at the school's library. Shit.

"You okay?" asks Wade. "Do we want shots? We need Cat. I don't know how to order shots. Do you just say, 'Give me shots'?"

"No," she says. It's unclear, even to her, which of Wade's questions she's answered. "You're right. Men *are* awful."

"The other women?" he says. "Did they . . . did they send pictures, too?"

Blair nods.

"I bet yours are way better," he says. "Wait, was that nice or creepy?"

"A little of both."

"I'm glad we're friends again," he says. "I've missed you."

"Are you really not in love with me anymore?" she asks. Another blushing flash of fifteen-year-old Wade. Blair doesn't ask the rest of what she wants to ask. She doesn't ask if they can go back to the way it was, when he was in love with her and expected nothing in return.

She doesn't have to, though, because Wade picks up his drink and says, "Blair McKenzie-Harden, I promise, no matter what, for the rest of my life, I will always be in love with you."

And then "Margaritaville" by Jimmy Buffett blasts through the speakers. It's not "Cheeseburger in Paradise," but pretty damn close, and Wade says, "Let's get the fuck out of here."

It's a short walk back to the LeBaron, which sits waiting, un-towed, ticketless. The hula girl moves in the evening breeze. They ditched their envelopes in the trash on the way out, so all they have is Blair's copy of *Feedback*.

"Are you good to drive?" asks Blair.

Wade kicks the front tire and laughs. "Not even close."

"Same," she says. "Shit. Cat's right. We *are* bitches."

"Do they have Uber at the beach?" Wade takes his phone out and discovers that they do. "Seven minutes," he says. "Good luck, hula girl."

They people watch on the boardwalk. Funnel cakes and hot dogs and people taking a break from whatever it is they do.

"Wade," Blair says, "what about Robbie?"

"What about him?"

"Are we just gonna go back? Act like nothing happened, like we're okay with it?"

Wade nods. "We don't have to act like nothing happened. But, yeah, we're going back. He's a rich dickhead. But he's *our* rich dickhead. And right now, he needs us."

Blair knows he's right. "Okay, then give me your phone."

"What?" he asks. "Why?"

She holds out her hand. When he hands it over, she holds down the Home button. "Search the number for Viking Golf, Fenwick Island, Delaware."

He looks confused.

"I'm asking Jane out for you," she says.

"Oh yeah," he says. "Shit." Then he points to the gift shop next to the bookstore and laughs. "Holy crap. We totally have to get that T-shirt for Cat."

Chapter 36

"I'm glad you're back, Cat."

Robbie is at the edge of the pool in a hoodie; his feet are in the water. Dash nods hello from the corner of the deck and goes back to scanning the beach.

Ten minutes ago, Cat said goodbye to Casey Green. "Listen, I get that you don't want to betray him," said Casey. "Powerful dudes, they've always got this wall of people around them who keep their mouths shut. But if you want to talk again, here." Casey slid a glossy business card into Cat's hand.

"I'm sorry you had to find out like that," says Robbie.

He's talking about Gabrielle, which is funny, because for the first time all weekend, Cat isn't thinking about Gabrielle at all.

"Robbie," she says. "We have a problem."

Robbie and Dash exchange a look. Later, Cat will think about this—about how Robbie seemed to know exactly what was happening, because, of course, Robbie Malcolm knows everything.

"All right," he says. "Let's wait for Blair and Wade, though, okay?"

CAT TAKES A QUICK SHOWER and finds a second bathing suit in her duffel bag, clean and dry. She shivers in the air conditioning and grabs a beer from the fridge before rejoining Robbie and Dash on the deck.

The late-day sun is still warm on her shoulders, and she notices her "Cat" envelope on the table where she left it. For the sake of her career, she should look at it. She should also look at it so she can fully process what her life has come to. And she will, but later.

Cat fills her lungs with a big gasp of air and dives into the deep end.

Forty-five seconds or so. That's how long she's underwater. It feels like longer, though. She kicks and paddles the length of the pool, reaching out, feeling along blindly for the wall. The world is dark and silent and weightless, like space.

She wonders what's going to happen. To her. To Blair and Wade. To Robbie. She wonders what's going to happen to them after all of this. After Robbie dies. Will this be the thing that finally pushes them all the way apart?

Her lungs burn, but she stays under, still reaching. Finally, her fingertips find the smooth wall and she pulls herself up. When she opens her eyes, she sees two pairs of feet—one bare and pretty, the other pale and in worn-out flip-flops.

Blair and Wade are back.

Wade is smiling, and he's clearly been drinking. He holds out a T-shirt. "We got you a present."

He unfurls it like a flag so she can read what's screen-printed across the chest. FBI: FEMALE BODY INSPECTOR. "Get it?" he asks.

It's subtle, but yes, she does.

"Hey, Robbie," he says. "I shouldn't have called you a rich dickhead. You're rich. And you're definitely a dickhead. But it was a mean thing to say."

"Um, yeah," says Cat. "I think we might wanna hold off on apologizing to Robbie for a sec."

Chapter 37

C at does her best to explain. She doesn't totally understand
what she's saying, but Robbie lets her talk. Blair and Wade
listen, confused but clearly disgusted. She uses layperson terms.
There are some small inaccuracies, some missed details. But she's
mostly right. She's right enough.

Corporate security flagged Casey Green last year. She was dig-
ging around Malcolm Capital's history and filings, contacting former employees, challenging nondisclosure agreements, making
impassioned pleas about freedom of information. She's a good
journalist, smart and crafty. Honestly, though, Robbie didn't expect her to show up on Fenwick Island. Another miscalculation on
his part.

She's out to hurt him, without question, and by all reasonable
accounts, she hates him. Still, though, he's impressed, particularly
that she went to Cat first. Cat is the most emotional of the three,
the most vulnerable, and she's also Robbie's favorite.

"It sounds like a medical procedure," Cat says. "Like *vasectomy*."

Robbie runs his fingers over the surface of the pool. "Viatical
settlement."

"Right! Viatical settlement. Apparently it's shady."

"They're fairly common in the financial world, though," he
says.

"So were credit default swaps, Robbie," says Wade. "How'd those play out?"

They all look at Wade, surprised. "What? I read the news."

Robbie is at the edge of the pool. Blair, Cat, and Wade are in the water, floating on noodles, so the three of them form a bobbing triangle with Robbie at the apex.

"So, you screwed over sick and old people?" says Blair.

"It's more complicated than that," he replies.

"Is it, though?" asks Cat. "Because, kinda sounds like you were screwing over sick and old people. Like, if I take a hundred bucks from some lady on the street, but then I give her fifty bucks back so she can buy groceries, I've still taken fifty bucks, right?"

Robbie can think of at least four counters to this comparison, but, again, she's right enough.

"Fucking capitalism," says Cat. She looks up at the house. "Shit. Maybe I'm just as bad. I flew here on a fucking private jet. A guy drove me here in an Escalade."

"And sick people, too?" asks Wade.

"*Very* sick people," Robbie says. "Terminal. That was where the *real* money was. People who needed funds immediately. People who didn't have time to shop around for the best rates. Desperate people."

"Fuck," says Wade, like an exhale. "Goddamn, man. *Dying* people?"

"Yes. Me, leveraging the terminally ill to make money. And now . . . the irony isn't lost."

Robbie looks at the water. He's ashamed, but this is what he wanted: everything finally out in the open.

"This journalist," says Cat. "She said you did things to hide your identity so people wouldn't ever know. And it worked, for years. You hid behind, like, shell companies. She said that's how she knows you *knew* it was wrong. That's the whole crux of her article, apparently. Like, when billionaires do fucked-up shit, the argument is always 'That's just how it's done.' But if that's just how it's done, why would you hide?"

"She's right," says Robbie. "I knew it was wrong."

"But you're Robbie Malcolm," says Blair. "You're better than that."

"I'm not better than anyone," he says. "I saw a hole in the system. Free money. I knew my mother would be ashamed of me. I knew you guys would be ashamed of me. But I also knew I could make millions. And I knew that if I made millions, I could take it and . . ."

"Make billions," says Wade.

Robbie nods.

"Jesus," says Wade. "How much is enough? It's not like you needed to do it. You were going to be rich anyway. Shit, you were *already* rich, right? Malcolm Capital was up and running. You're a genius; you were gonna be fine."

Robbie watches the ripples in the water.

"You felt bad, though," says Blair. "Didn't you?"

Robbie slides his hood off. The sun is setting—all those colors again. It would be so gorgeous under different circumstances. If he weren't dying. If he hadn't cheated people, and if Wade were a bestselling novelist, and if Blair were happy, and if Cat had a baby on her hip and a woman who loved her, and if everything had gone in different directions entirely.

"You did," Blair says. "You felt bad. That's where all the other stuff comes from, isn't it? Your charity things. Your foundations. You've been trying to make up for it."

"Penance," says Wade. "You Catholic motherfucker."

"When I was funneling the money from the settlements into Malcolm Capital," says Robbie, "I came up with an expression. I made it a rally cry for the philanthropy department. 'If we do *well,* we can do *good.*'"

"That's actually catchy," says Wade.

"It didn't work, though," says Robbie.

"What do you mean?" asks Cat.

"I gave away millions," he says. "I did a lot of good. But I still felt like shit. I was going to tell you all this, by the way."

"When?" asks Cat.

"After I showed you your envelopes. But then you all left."

The beach below is mostly empty. The incessant banner planes are gone. With no beachgoers to pester, even the birds have piped down. The result is genuine quiet.

"It's kinda funny, actually," Wade says. "All this time. All . . . *this*." He nods at the house, at the pool. "You're just as messed up as us."

"I can fix it, though," says Robbie.

"Fix what?" asks Blair.

"And how?" asks Wade. "A hundred Our Fathers?"

"No," he says. "I have plans for making the money thing right. But I wanted to start with fixing the three of you. Your lives. That's what I'm trying to do. That's what the envelopes were about."

"You're just gonna fix our lives?" asks Cat.

"If you let me," he says.

They're suspicious, because they have no idea how the world really works.

"For starters," he says, "Wade, I'm going to do two things for you. And I've already done one of them. You're lonely and you're depressed, and you know it. Your career has stalled. But the woman I found for you on Match is perfect. Statistically, you are as ideal a couple as there can be. All you need to do is meet her and be yourself. And I'm going to make sure your novel is published. Everywhere. Sold in every bookstore in the world, reviewed wherever you want."

"You can just do that?" Wade says.

"Yes. And Cat. You're breaking yourself financially with this fertility regimen. And the odds aren't even that good; I don't like the math. I'm taking it over for you. A more aggressive plan. And I'm going to get you another job. Again, like with Wade's book, I just have to make a few calls. I have contacts at every television, film, news, and entertainment conglomerate in the world. You could have your dream job before you get out of this pool. I should've done this for you years ago. You've been floundering. You're more than an associate producer on some talk show."

Cat bobs silently.

"Gabrielle treated you badly, Cat. As far as I'm concerned, that's the same as treating *me* badly. If you'll let me, I can have her ruined. Her chances for national syndication, gone. I could have her essentially blackballed. If we want to go a step further, I could have her marriage ruined, too. Easily. As far as I can tell—according to the information we have—her husband has no knowledge of her relationship with you. I could send him everything."

"Shit, Robbie," says Cat.

"Blair," he says. Robbie is rolling now, energized. "Ditto for the art teacher. Dash has every email McGee has sent to you and the other women. If the twins' school saw that, he'd be fired immediately. And we could track his next move, too. When he applies for new jobs, the headmasters of those schools will get his entire file, hand delivered."

Blair hugs herself, like she's cold.

"And it's time for you to start working again," he says. "*Really* working. Cat was right. You're an artist. You're *our* artist. You saw the blueprints. Construction can begin immediately. Once you get new work together, whether I'm still here or not, I can ensure that it gets seen—seen by people who matter. I can get you space at galleries. Anywhere you want. D.C., New York, London. You can quit freelancing and focus on your work. You're lost right now, Blair. You're directionless. I can put you back in the driver's seat. All of you. You can have the lives you want to have—that you were *meant* to have."

Robbie takes a breath, calms himself. His friends are just looking at him, stunned.

"I've never heard you like this," says Wade.

"There's a version of me you don't know," he says. "This is him."

"I don't want to ruin Gabby's life, Robbie," Cat says. "I hate her, but . . . I love her. And I don't even know if I'd be a good mom. Look at me. Do you know how much I've drunk this weekend? I threw my phone across a go-cart track today."

"That's ridiculous," says Blair. "Cat, you'd be an incredible mom. But, Robbie, the rest of it—it wouldn't be real. Fancy jobs? Wade's book? Me in some gallery? It'd be fake."

"You can't just buy everything, dude," says Cat. "That's not how it works."

"It is, though," says Robbie. "Have you not been listening to me? Have you not paid attention to the world around you? That is *exactly* how it works. I know you don't want it to be like this, but it is. There are several hundred people like me in the world. We can do anything. We can get anything done. We control everything."

"I don't think I like this version of you," says Cat.

"And thanks and all, Robbie," says Wade, "but I am, at best, an okay writer. I get it now. I've accepted it. You being rich isn't gonna make me more talented."

"I don't even want to be an artist anymore," says Blair.

"And I'm not going out with that Match girl," says Wade. "That would be weird."

"He's going out with Jane tomorrow," says Blair. "To brunch."

"Jane?" says Cat.

"What are you talking about?" says Robbie. "Jane? From Viking Golf?"

"Oh, yeah, I liked her," says Cat.

"No!" says Robbie. "Goddammit. Why aren't you listening to me? That is not how I planned this. Listen, all of you. I don't have kids. Blair, you do, and maybe you'll have more. Wade, eventually you probably will. Cat, I can *guarantee* that you will. But I don't. And I won't, ever. I don't have a legacy. When I'm gone, my money will be distributed by lawyers. Casey Green will write a hit piece about how shitty I am. And then *that* will be it. *You guys* are my legacy. The three of you—the lives that I can help make for you. *That* is my legacy. For fuck's sake, can you please just let me have it?"

His hands again: shaking. Worse than that: tears. Jesus, he's crying.

"Oh, Robbie," says Blair.

"Can you just think about it?" His voice sounds weak, beaten. Blair, Cat, and Wade nod; they tell him that, yes, they'll think about it. They won't, though. Robbie knows them well enough to know that they're humoring him. Robbie doesn't want to die, but he's going to. And after more than a decade of getting whatever he's wanted, the one thing he wants now is slipping away. He pushes his hood back up, because he feels cold, as his friends drift slowly away from one another in the dead-still water.

A few minutes pass, the air cools even more. "Can I ask you guys something?" says Cat. Robbie wonders if she's changing her mind. "I know it's weird to think about food right now. But I'm starving."

"Yeah," says Wade. "Me too."

"I could eat," says Blair.

Cautiously, Blair, Cat, and Wade look at Robbie. They've cast his wishes aside, ignored his efforts to help them, but apparently he's still in charge of the schedule. "No," he says.

"No?" asks Cat.

"We're not eating?" asks Wade.

"Not yet," says Robbie. "We have something on the agenda first. It's something I've always wanted to do."

"What is it?" asks Blair.

They float, waiting.

"We're getting tattoos."

Chapter 38

The thing about old friends: they're really more like siblings.
You can be pissed at your siblings. They can betray you in untold ways, hurt, offend, and infuriate you. You can briefly hate them to their damaged cores. But they'll always be your brother or your sister, right? Whether you like it or not.

In fairness, as mad as she is at him—as hurt—Cat is incapable, even briefly, of hating Robbie or his damaged core. She's disappointed, though. She put Robbie on a pedestal; he's been on it since they were freshmen in high school. He's like the big brother she's always looked up to. The smartest person she knows. The long-distance, kind-of-famous person who checks in on her sometimes.

She's gotten used to seeing beloved public figures exposed. After all, it's nearly a weekly thing now—a trending hashtag. But this one hurts more than all the others, because Robbie is *her* beloved public figure. Blair and Wade are feeling this, too, Cat imagines. They're mad at him, hurt, blindsided. But Robbie is *their* brother, too, so a half hour later, all four of them are on bikes cruising side by side down Coastal Highway.

Obviously, it's the nicest bike Cat has ever ridden. Robbie bought the bikes last week and had them sized for each of them. You could argue that bikes are ill-advised, particularly for Blair and Wade, who were too drunk to drive themselves back from Bethany Beach, but they're pedaling in reasonably straight lines.

Just to be safe, Dash is following directly behind the four of them in the Range Rover with the hazards flashing.

"Doesn't this seem a little excessive?" asks Cat.

"Probably," says Wade. "Your bike looks like a kid's bike, by the way. Like it should have training wheels."

"Shut up."

They pass Dairy Queen. For some reason, a line is practically wrapped around the block. Blair is able to ride with no hands, which she's very proud of. "I haven't done this since I was a kid!"

"Please don't do that, Blair!" shouts Dash from the Range Rover. Blair, however—the roof-jumping mother of two—tells him to chill out. Someone whistles at her then—a guy passing in a Dodge Durango. "Need a ride, baby?" he says, and Wade stands on his pedals. "Dash! Go kick that guy's ass!"

Door to door, it takes fifteen minutes to get to Right Coast Tattoo. And, to Cat's surprise, the place is empty. The guy behind the counter—bearded, tatted to the gills, and wearing a Megadeth T-shirt—is reading *People* magazine. "Can I help you folks?" he asks, as if it's a bank and maybe they're there to discuss opening checking accounts.

"We're here for tattoos," says Robbie.

"You've come to the right place." He tells them his name is Francisco. Cat doesn't have any tattoos, none of them do, but she's always wanted one. Just as important, she's always wanted that tattoo to be administered by someone who looks like Francisco.

Wade, though, has become very nervous. "Um, like, where are we talking, here? On our bodies? And how big? Like, *big*? Like, biker big? Like, won't-ever-get-a-job-in-an-office-again big?"

"Wade, nobody's hiring you to work in an office," says Cat.

"But they could," he says. "I have word-processing skills."

For a few minutes, they toss out absurd tattoo suggestions.

"A rainbow," says Cat. "Or something Baltimore-y."

"Dolphin tramp stamps," says Blair, laughing.

"If I'm getting a tattoo, it should be Beatles-related," says Wade. "Like the *Abbey Road* album cover. Francisco, you know the Beatles, right?"

"Yeah," he says. "My grandpa was a huge fan."

"Boom," says Cat. "The Beatle burns keep coming."

"We're all getting the same tattoo," says Robbie. He asks Dash to get him his iPad. "I had a friend of a friend help with some design options."

"Of course you did," says Blair.

Everyone gathers around Robbie's screen. There are four versions of the same basic thing. Three letters, ornately drawn: BPR. It takes them a moment to get it, and then Blair says, "Baltimore Prep Rejects."

"Ah," says Cat. "Yeah."

Wade is tentative still, but coming around. "That's pretty cool."

Francisco agrees. "Designs're tight," he says. "What's it mean, the rejects thing?"

No one quite knows where to start, so Cat steps up. "I made out with *her* at a Pride parade. We were teenagers and a picture of it got in the paper, so we got kicked out of our Catholic school in Baltimore. You know, because Catholics. Then *he* turned her painting into the cover of our school's literary magazine, so he got booted, too. Then *he* quit . . . I guess just to help us stick it to the man."

Francisco nods. He's nearly as big as Dash. "Momma" and "Poppa" are tattooed on his wrists. "Damn," he says. "Shit's pretty hardcore. Lucky you didn't all end up in prison."

"Are you making fun of us, Francisco?" asks Cat.

"Little bit," he says. "But I'm here for it. I've inked people for a lot less than excommunication. And, if you want my two cents, that top right design's the one." He tugs his beard. "Nice'n clean. I can knock 'em out pretty fast."

Cat feels a rush. A couple of days ago, she'd have consulted Gabrielle, as if Cat's body was somehow co-opted. Fuck that. No one owns her. Not anymore. "I like it, too," she says.

Deciding on the physical location takes no time at all. Blair holds out her right arm and turns it over. She points to a spot between her wrist and the crook of her elbow. "How about here? Prominent, but subtle."

"I love it," says Robbie.

"And this is what you want?" Cat asks him. "Matching tats?"

Robbie nods. "Yes. I was never *really* a reject."

"What do you mean?" asks Wade.

"You three got kicked out," he says. "I just quit because I wanted to be included."

And for Cat, that's all it takes to forgive him completely. And when Blair says, "Oh, Robbie," and Wade says, "You're *totally* a reject," she knows that any doubts she had earlier that their friendships would survive this were unfounded.

"That looks like it'll really hurt, though," says Wade.

"I vote Wade goes first," says Cat.

Blair laughs. "Seconded."

"Thirded."

"Thirded isn't even a word, Robbie. Dash, help me out. That's definitely one of the most painful spots, right? All those nerve endings."

Dash stands between them and the entrance. He pulls the collar of his polo open, revealing a square foot of ink beginning at his jugular. "I can think of worse spots."

"Shit," says Wade.

Francisco claps once and tells Wade to sit. "It's settled, then. And don't worry, buddy. It only hurts for . . . well, for the entire goddamn time."

Chapter 39

Robbie and Cat are sitting on a padded table, their feet dangling a few inches off the ground. Wade is on a chair, with his freshly swabbed and shaven right arm resting on another padded table. Blair is next to him, holding his other hand, and like Cat and Robbie, she's clearly doing her best not to laugh at him.

"Scale of one to ten," says Wade, "how painful are we talking? Is it a bee sting? Or is it more like a burn? I read somewhere it feels cold."

"Would you let the man work, Wade?" says Cat.

"Has anyone ever passed out?" he asks. "Does that happen?"

"Why do you think the tables're padded?" says Francisco.

"Oh man."

"*Shhhh,*" Blair tells him, as if comforting a frightened terrier on the Fourth of July. "Don't listen. You'll be fine."

"But if you start to black out," says Francisco, "try'n keep your arm still."

"How can I keep my arm still if I'm unconscious?"

Francisco pushes a button, and his needle hums to life, like a small weapon. "Eh, I'm sure you'll be fine. If it gets too bad, we'll find a stick for you to bite on."

Robbie feels a nudge from Cat. She lowers her voice into his ear. "I like how he's totally fucking with Wade."

"Me too," he says.

"Your shirt's cool, by the way," Robbie tells her. "Very flattering."

Cat straightens, modeling her new "FBI" T-shirt. "I know, right? Look how hot I am. Wade's an idiot and apparently a tremendous pussy, but he knows how to pick out a gift."

Francisco lowers the needle. Wade looks away. Robbie scans the wall of tattoo art. There's a skeleton next to a panda. Dancing Grateful Dead bears next to a collage of illustrated naked women. Sports and car-brand logos and Harley-Davidson crests and American flags. A Rolling Stones tongue and a Union Jack. Robbie takes it all in—everything. The colors and shapes. The humming of the needle, the slight burning smell. The atmosphere. This particular moment in time, early summer, midway through his thirty-fifth year of life. He regrets not doing this more—observing the world around him—because there's so much to see.

He watches Blair and Wade. It's hard to know if Wade is really this scared or if he just likes being held by Blair. And then, almost matter-of-factly, as if mentally ticking through the rest of the weekend's agenda, Robbie thinks, *In two days, I'll be dead.*

Wade lets out a shrill cry. There's a small dot of ink on his skin.

"You got this, Wade," says Dash. "You're tougher than you think you are."

"Where did you find Dash, by the way?" Cat asks Robbie, leaning in still, just the two of them talking. "He doesn't seem like a typical bodyguard."

"That's because he isn't," says Robbie. "He was a football player at Harvard. He got drafted to play for the Bears. He didn't play very much. He was a third-team linebacker. Late in the season his rookie year, the Bears were getting killed on *Monday Night Football,* so they sent him in. Fourth play, Dash blew his knee out. He got carted off the field, went right to the hospital. He never played again."

"That's so sad," says Cat. "I had no idea."

"He was twenty-three and his career was over," says Robbie. "I thought maybe I could help him out. So I gave him a job. I'm glad I did."

Cat leans into Robbie again. She doesn't have anything to say this time; she just rests her weight on him, and he remembers how she'd sometimes do this when they were younger: just lean on him. Blair was right. Cat *will* be a great mom. He pictures it now: a baby, a girl with a shock of blond hair. A onesie with an irreverent statement on it.

"You can't control us, Robbie," she says. "I know you think you know what's best for us. Maybe you do. But that's not how it works."

How much easier would it be if they'd just listen to him?

"There's something I need to tell you," she says. "The journalist, Casey Green."

"Yeah?"

"She knows you're sick."

"Did you tell her?"

"No. But she's piecing it together. It's just a matter of time."

Another miscalculation—an underestimation, really. Of course it'll be Casey Green who breaks the news.

"She really doesn't like you," Cat says.

"I know," he says.

"Maybe I could talk to her for you. I could be your spokeswoman. I could tell her who you really are. Who we are. I could tell her our story."

"You'd do that?" Robbie asks.

"People should know that you're a good person."

Wade yelps again. "I think you hit a nerve. Maybe a vein. That really hurt."

Francisco stops. "Wait. Was it a nerve or a vein? Because if it was a nerve, I can't promise you won't lose this arm."

Blair laughs. Cat tells Wade to hang in there, and Robbie tells him that it's almost over, which probably isn't true, but lying isn't *always* a bad thing. For all his planning—for all the time and money spent putting all of this together—it turns out teasing Wade has been the most fun they've had all weekend.

Sunday

Chapter 40

"So, do you have a passion for miniature golf?"

Jane was about to take a sip of her coffee, but she stops, as if wondering if he's joking. In her defense, Wade isn't sure either. He just opened his mouth, and that was what came out. Talking really *is* hard.

"Passion may be an overstatement," she says.

One of the only things Wade actually likes about writing is that you can write and rewrite dialogue until it's perfect. In real life, we're all stuck with our own shitty first drafts.

They're at Catch 54, a cool seafood restaurant on the bay.

"Before this goes any further, you should know, I'm probably the best miniature golfer you've ever met."

"That's a bold statement," she says. "But we don't *just* have to talk about miniature golf. We can discuss other things, too."

"Really?" he asks. "Because I've got like thirty more minutes of minigolf material."

Jane smiles and sips her coffee. She's wearing a sundress and a pair of canvas sneakers. She's pretty and tan and tired-looking. He's guessing she's forty. "For example," she says, "let's discuss your hair."

He touches his head. "My hair?"

"Is it my imagination, or was it different yesterday?"

"Blair and Cat styled me this morning," he says. "They said I should try something more tousled. They also picked out this shirt. It belongs to Robbie." Which is definitely dialogue Wade would've edited out, because he's just confessed to being a man who can't groom or dress himself.

The waiter returns with a bottle of champagne that they didn't order. "Looks like you two have friends," he says. "Courtesy of Blair, Cat, and Robbie. It's sweet but not too sweet. Full-bodied. My personal favorite."

When the waiter is gone, Jane says, "I'd've been happy with a Miller Lite." She tears some crust off a piece of bread. "You don't do this very often, do you?"

"What's that?" he says. "Leave the house?"

She laughs. "Well, I was gonna say *go on dates,* but . . ."

Blair and Cat told him to be himself, which seemed like questionable advice. "How am I doing so far?" he asks.

"You're a natural," she says, then swishes champagne in her mouth. "What do you think *full-bodied* means, anyway?"

"No idea." Wade flags the waiter down and orders two Miller Lites. Through the window, they watch an old man on a little boat, headed out to fish.

"If it's any consolation," says Jane, "I don't do this a lot either. This is my first date in . . . wow, fifteen years."

"Really? Oh good, that's way more pathetic than me."

"Screw you," she says. "I was married. My former husband didn't have the same no-dating policy I did. So . . ."

Their Miller Lites arrive.

"Sorry," she says. "I do that. Sometimes I go dark."

The idea that she's struggling, too—that Jane might also be uneasy in her clothes and her own skin—makes him feel better.

When the waiter returns, he tells them that their bill will be taken care of by Robbie, so they order crab cakes and things with lobster in them. And then she asks him when his book is being published, because that was inevitable.

"It's not, actually," he says.

"But your friends said—"

"They were exaggerating. Actually, no. I lied to them. I told them I had a book deal. I didn't plan on it; it just sort of happened. I wrote a book. That part's true. But it got rejected by . . . well, by the entire publishing industry."

"Oh." She's quiet, which makes sense. Here she is, drinking champagne and beer across from another lying man. But then she says, "Is it weird that I'm kind of relieved?"

"What?" he asks.

"On the way here, I was like, *What am I gonna talk to some writer about?* I don't even read that much. I *try,* but suddenly it's eleven P.M. and I can't keep my eyes open. But a *failed* writer? No problem. I can talk to one of those all day."

The waiter brings an appetizer plate of cheese and fruit. Jane takes a little cube of something yellow. "So, did you *want* to go on a date with me, or was it your friend's idea?"

"The second one," he says. "But I'm glad I did."

"I suspected that might be the case," Jane says. "She told me you're the sweetest guy she knows."

Oh, Blair, Wade thinks. Pangs of guilt now. If he hadn't been so hung up on being in love with her, he could've been a much better friend.

Jane watches his face, like she's thinking things through. "Have you ever bought a house, Wade?" she asks.

"No," he says. "I've been living in New York. You can't buy in New York unless you've won a World Series or invented Twitter."

"Well, the ex and me, that's what we used to do: we'd buy, fix up, and sell houses. House flippers. He was the builder—the muscle. I was the realtor and the marketer."

Wade conjures an image of her ex. He's holding a hammer and wearing cargo shorts.

"Whenever we had a kick-ass house for sale," she says, "some gorgeous thing with a great view and all the amenities, I'd put tons of pictures up. As much info as I could list, like Viking ranges and hot tubs. I'd practically write poems about the places."

"Okay," he says.

"But when we were selling something that had . . . *issues*— maybe some red flags—I'd keep it short. Just the basics. If I were a house, that'd be me. The less you know, the better."

Wade gets it. He pictures himself as a human version of his studio apartment. Dust bunnies, weird water stains. Mysterious cracks and dodgy wiring.

Jane takes a sip of her beer. "Full-bodied," she says.

"Indeed," says Wade.

"You were just honest with me," she says. "Gave me a pretty full listing. Definitely some red flags there. I appreciate it, though. I feel like I should probably return the favor."

Her bottom teeth are a little crooked. Her fingernails are bitten and stubby, her sun-streaked hair has shades of gray at the roots. Wade leans in on his elbows. "Okay," he says. "I'm ready."

"I'm divorced," she says, "but we covered that."

Wade pretends to fall asleep. "Is that all you got?"

"Not just divorced," she says. "Like, walked-out-on-suddenly divorced. And not even for an upgrade. I got left for a middle-aged woman with a smoker's cough who rents out Jet Skis at a marina."

"Ouch," he says.

"I have two kids," she says. "And not cute, little ones, like your friend's twins. Tween boys. They're the two grossest human beings on the planet. I'm pretty much broke. And I'm a little bitter about it. I'm on antidepressants. My car makes this awful noise whenever I slow down. I think it's the brakes, but honestly, I don't even wanna know."

Wade finishes his beer, lets the moment breathe. "Well, it was nice meeting you."

Jane laughs so hard that a few people turn to look. "You bastard."

"I don't even *have* a car," he says.

Jane folds her arms and smiles. There's some butter on her lip. Over her shoulder, a fleet of waiters approaches. They're carrying more food than he and Jane could ever possibly finish.

Chapter 41

Two miles from Catch 54, Cat is walking along the shore. She sees something, though, that stops her: a little girl chasing after a beat-up smiley-face beach ball. The girl is down a ways, maybe a quarter of a mile, but Cat is certain it's the same girl she saw yesterday at the playground dripping a Peanut Buster Parfait all over herself.

"Hello again," Cat whispers to herself in the wind.

It's a beautiful, cloudless day, so the beach is already getting crowded. It'd be quicker to have gone a different way—up to the sidewalk and straight down Coastal Highway—but she's opted for walking along the beach instead. She's supposed to meet Casey Green in ten minutes, and she's a little nervous.

It's not a date, but it feels like one. While she and Blair fussed over Wade's hair and clothes earlier for his brunch with the minigolf lady, Cat kept glancing in the mirror. *If I were a gay girl from New York with questionable taste in footwear, would I like me?*

Blair and Cat figured out that Casey Green is gay in about thirty seconds, with the help of Google. Cat suspected as much, but it made her nervous to know for sure.

They found a list of Casey's bylines, many of which demonstrated her disdain for the wealthiest people in America. Then they stumbled onto a profile in *Out* magazine that had her on a list of young journalists to watch. Blair tapped Images along the search bar, and there she was, Cat's beach ambusher. It was a mix of professional headshots and more candid things from social events. *Shit,* Cat thought, because Casey Green cleans up nicely. She's never loved that expression—it seems casually antifeminist—but, dammit, it was true.

"Oh wow," said Blair. "Her hair is fabulous."

Cat looks at her new tattoo as she walks. It hurts, like a mild burn might, but it looks cool. She's a chick with a tattoo now, and it makes her feel different, like she has more of an edge than she did yesterday. Like maybe she doesn't have to be afraid of all the things that used to make her afraid. Like maybe she can, as Blair pointed out in the powder room, do whatever the hell she wants.

The little girl picks up the smiley-face beach ball and gives it a hug. Cat watches her for a few seconds. Cat has no interest in stealing her or biting her face off. The full-fledged assault that children have launched on her emotions for the last few months abates. Cat's just a harmless single woman watching a cute kid joy-scream into the wind. The optics are fine.

3BB Café is a crunchy little coffee shop between a kids' pottery-making store and a hot dog joint called Twilley's Willys. It smells like chai and granola, and an honest-to-God record player spins a wobbly Doors song. The shot of AC briefly freezes the surface of Cat's skin.

The place is so small that there are only three tables, and Casey is at one of them. She's facing the entrance, but she's looking down at her phone. In the single second it takes for her to lift her head and say hello, Cat holds her breath and waits. She's hoping to see the look—*that* look—the one she's seen from a handful of women in her life, most notably Gabrielle.

"Hello, Cat."

Did she see it? Maybe. Casey's red hair is pulled up neatly in a bun at the top of her head. Steam rises from her mug.

"Hey," Cat says.

A guy with a beard like a Russian poet appears. He's wearing a T-shirt that says "Death Before Decaf." Cat orders an iced latte and sits down.

"Well, don't you clean up nice," says Casey, and Cat laughs, because maybe it's not such a bad expression after all.

"I'm glad you texted," says Casey. "I give those business cards out a lot. It's exciting when someone actually uses one." A notebook and a pen sit on the table next to her iPhone. She taps the screen and opens a tape recorder app. "Mind if I record us?"

"Do what you gotta do."

A red circle throbs, digital sound waves flutter.

"Are you gonna, like, ask me questions?" Cat asks. "How does this work?"

"Probably," says Casey. "But in a situation like this, I think it's best to just let someone talk." She picks up her pen. "So, what'd you come here to tell me, Cat?"

Casey is wearing a bracelet. Just a simple beaded thing that she wasn't wearing yesterday. Cat imagines her at one of the beach hotels, looking at herself in the bathroom mirror before coming here and thinking, *Is the bracelet too much?*

"One thing," says Casey. "Does Robbie know that you're here? Did you get coached? I really *am* glad you texted, Cat, but I'm not interested in corporate spin. No Malcolm Capital press releases, okay?"

The turn is jarring, and Cat feels stupid. "What? No. Well, yeah, I mean, he knows I'm here. But coached? I don't even know what that means. I'm just a regular person."

"Right," says Casey, "a civilian. Sorry, I'm just used to dealing with—"

The poet-looking guy drops off Cat's latte. "Enjoy, you two," he says.

Cat takes a sip and looks at Casey's blank paper. She doesn't like

Cat, and it was silly to think that she might. Gabrielle was never going to leave her husband. None of those dreamy, studious girls from the library back in college ever thought once about her. Cat might as well have been invisible. She might as well be invisible now. She's here to deliver information—to help her friend.

"Robbie has stage four pancreatic cancer." Cat takes a breath, refusing to let tears fill her eyes. "He's dying."

It seems like Casey is about to write this fact down; she doesn't, though. "Oh Jesus," she whispers. "I thought maybe . . ." She puts her pen down. "I'm sorry, Cat."

"Thanks," she says. "And that thing you told me yesterday. About how Robbie made all that money. It's all true. Robbie knows it was shitty, and he feels bad. He's going to make up for it. I don't know how, exactly, but he will. And I know you think he's a bad person, like all the others."

Casey studies the little cactus on the table between them.

"But he isn't," says Cat. "He's my best friend."

"Okay, yeah," says Casey. "You definitely haven't been coached."

An odd compliment, but Cat will take it. She sets her right arm on the table. The light above catches the thin layer of healing ointment there, which makes the letters that Francisco burned into her skin shine. "The Baltimore Prep Rejects," she says. Because that's a good place to start.

Chapter 42

The afternoon plays out like a lazy vacation montage. Cat is quiet when she gets back from coffee with Casey Green. Blair looks at her expectantly, because she knows Cat was excited. Cat just shrugs, though, and says it went fine. When Wade returns shortly after, he keeps smiling, like he can't help himself. He thanks Blair and Cat for making him look like a presentable adult male. They press him for details, but all he says is "I guess I didn't make a *complete* ass of myself."

They go to the beach for a while. Blair and Cat get tan and freckled. Wade, though, remains as pale as ever, because Blair keeps making him reapply thick coats of the heaviest sunscreen she can find. They go to the pool after and take turns floating on rafts. Robbie joins them there. He's spent the morning resting in his room.

Blair checks her email as they eat sandwiches by the pool. She shows them Mr. McGee's latest message, because there are no more secrets between them.

Would it be greedy to request more pictures? Many, many more?

"Fuck that guy," says Cat.

"The creep spectrum," says Wade.

Blair thinks of Robbie's offer to ruin Mr. McGee's life. It's a sort of power she's not used to having, and she doesn't like it. She hits Reply and thinks of all the things she might say, but then she puts her phone away.

People have been setting up outside all day, arriving in coordinated waves.

Around ten A.M., some guys in a big white truck brought a few tables and chairs and set them out back between the lower deck and the beach. Next, two men strung strings of white lights pretty much everywhere. Some florists showed up after them, because what's a wake without flowers? The arrangements are lovely—big and colorful—and the entire back of the house smells like those first few days of spring. Technicians from a place called Beach Tech set up one big screen and two little screens, and then Delaware Vibes laid out a small stage, two microphones, speakers, and a dance floor.

The caterers came last. They're outside now, actually, from Mancini's, their favorite Italian place, again. The sliding door is open from the kitchen, and Blair smells bread and tomato sauce.

It's just after seven P.M., and Blair, Cat, and Wade are at the kitchen table eating grapes from an enormous fruit bowl. Blair and Cat are in summer dresses. Wade changed back into his outfit from brunch, because Robbie's clothes are nicer than everything he packed. Blair has brought some charcoal pencils down from the art studio, and she's doodling cartoon animal versions of her friends. The squirrels that Michelle and Kenny colored for Robbie are hanging up on the refrigerator.

"You made me into a donkey?" says Wade.

"Not just a donkey," Blair says. "Eeyore. Everyone loves Eeyore."

She makes Cat a cat, obviously. Robbie is a wise-looking owl in a Harvard cap. Dash, a panther. When she's done with Donkey Wade, she hangs her new sketches up next to the squirrels.

"God, Blair," says Cat. "You're really good at this."

They're silly, scratched out in minutes. Still, though, Blair feels a swell of pride.

"I like the squirrels best," says Wade.

"I feel like the guy squirrel is hot for the girl squirrel," says Cat.

"Nah," says Wade. "It'll never happen. She's all pretty and sexy in a dress and he's just wearing purple scribbles. She's an uptown squirrel. She's been living in her uptown . . ."

Blair and Cat look at him the way they've been looking at him for years. "Is this what we've been reduced to?" Cat asks. "Squirrel puns?"

And then, footfalls. Robbie comes down the stairs, trailed by Dash. Robbie is dressed up in a nice linen shirt and a summery sport coat. "It's about that time," he says.

Dash leads the Rejects out onto the deck. They've seen things come together piecemeal throughout the day. Now, though, fully set up, the grounds below are practically Gatsbyean. "It's beautiful," says Blair.

"Yeah but, dude, how many people are you expecting?" Cat asks.

"Just us at first," he says. "But it's a party. Parties draw crowds."

Blair feels Cat's hand squeeze her own. "This is gonna be tough, isn't it?" Cat whispers. Blair squeezes back but doesn't say anything, because the answer is obvious. They've known for two days now that Robbie is sick, but those two days have been full of things to distract them from that fact, like the beach and minigolf and Wade's delicate skin and all of their personal revelations and existential crises and blind dates and lurking reporters. Now, though, it's just them, surrounded by flowers and lights, and they're going to have to face what's actually happening.

"You all look very nice, by the way," Robbie says.

"You too," says Blair. "Very handsome."

"We're a sexy crew," says Wade.

"Yeah we are," says Cat.

Robbie smiles. "Everyone ready?"

They're not.

Chapter 43

Cat has decided to eat before drinking, which is the most adult decision she's made in years. *Look at me,* she thinks. *All grown up.*

It helps that she's starving. She eats pasta and pizza and a breadstick as big as her forearm. There's a glass of red beside her, but just for sipping.

They're at a table, just the four of them, and if it weren't for the beach and the four-million-dollar mansion, it could be lunch at Baltimore Prep. Four friends, eating, laughing. Nothing sad to see here.

But then Robbie clears his throat and stands up, and Cat immediately starts crying. "Shit," she says. "Sorry."

Blair takes her arm and pulls her chair closer. Their BPR tats align perfectly.

The big screen in front of their table turns on, and so do the smaller screens by the bar and over the buffet. A picture fades in: the four of them from high school. They're at Camden Yards, where the Orioles play, smiling from nosebleed seats in the sky. Robbie and Wade are skinny teenage boys, acne and Adam's apples. Blair is holding a hot dog suggestively, and Cat has her favorite O's cap pulled low over her forehead.

"A slideshow?" Cat says. "Really, you bastard?"

Robbie holds the back of his chair. "Can't have a wake without pictures."

Another picture: a cross-country team photo from freshman year. A bunch of kids stand in green hoodies with bright red leaves behind them. When the next picture fades in, they all yell-laugh. "Sweet Jesus!" says Wade. "Delete it!" It's a picture of Wade, the skinniest, palest fifteen-year-old boy ever, running as fast as he can in his cross-country uniform.

"You look like you're in agony," says Cat.

Wade squints at himself. "In retrospect, Blair, I get why you didn't want to be my girlfriend."

The horrible picture of Wade is replaced by a fantastic picture of Cat. She's in her cross-country uniform, too, standing on a podium in the winner's position, smiling.

Wade whistles. "Hide your daughters."

"Look at my cheekbones," says Cat. "I'm never eating carbs again."

Blair's next. A homecoming dress, lipstick that's a little too red.

"Where did you find these pictures?" Blair asks. "This was pre–social media."

"It was easier than you think," says Robbie.

A Halloween picture comes next: Cat and Robbie as Dr. Evil and Mini-Me. And on and on, in no particular chronological order. Their parents make cameos; other former Baltimore Prep students, too. In one picture, Father Milton looms over Robbie. In another, Wade holds up a copy of the lit magazine that got him expelled. There's a shot of Blair's painting from the *Sun*. Blair and Cat eating ice cream sandwiches. Wade and Cat playing ping-pong in Cat's grandma's garage. Blair's family's long-gone terrier, Dougie, makes an appearance.

"He humped my leg once," says Wade.

"Mine, too," says Cat. "He was a gentle lover." She isn't crying anymore. Each passing image makes her smile, and she considers how wonderful it'd be if this slideshow just kept going. She'd gladly sit here indefinitely, beneath a slowly setting sun, reliving their lives. Unfortunately, though, time is a stupid, finite thing. Wade's author photo fades in. Robbie in his hideous sneakers. The old Honda that Wade drove them all around in. Then, lastly, they see the picture of all four of them in New York at Wade's book launch. The screens hold on it for a few seconds, then the slide-show starts over.

"I have some things I want to say to each of you," says Robbie. "And I'm going to say them now, because . . . well, you never know when it might be too late."

"Oh shit," whispers Cat. This is already tougher than she'd feared.

"Wade," says Robbie.

Wade takes a breath and holds it.

"You never sold out. You knew that you wanted to be a writer, and you committed to it. All around you, people got real jobs, settled down. It would have been easy for you to give up. But you didn't. And I don't think you're going to. Because you're a writer, Wade. You've been a writer since we were kids, and that's what you're always going to be. You don't want my help. I understand that. Now that I've had a little time to think about it, I actually respect it. But regardless, you're *going* to succeed. I know you are."

Blair picks up her glass of wine. "The best writer we know," she says.

"And Blair." Robbie shifts, facing her. By chance, Blair's image passes on the slideshow loop: her black-and-white senior picture. "You're more than beautiful," he says. "You're smart and talented. You're a wonderful friend, and you're a good mom. You're loved. By us. By your kids. You're going to find yourself again."

Blair closes her eyes, and Cat kisses her cheek. She knows that she's next, but she doesn't want to be. "Dude," she says. "Maybe just . . . don't?"

"Well, you've come all this way," he says. "And don't worry. I don't have much for you. If you want, you're going to be a mom. And you're going to be fantastic at it. But you know that. So all I have to say to you is . . . everything's going to be okay."

It's silly. Cat knows that Robbie can't know this. It's just what people say: *Everything's going to be okay*. For some dumb reason, though, she believes him, because it's what she's needed to hear for a very long time.

Robbie smiles, swirls his wine. "If you look around, you'll notice that it's just us, right? That's not a mistake. Because you guys are my only real friends. Every person I've met since the three of you has come with conditions. Everyone has wanted something from me. Even if they didn't, I worried they did—*assumed* they did. Because of that, I've kept everyone at a distance. Everyone except for the three of you. That's fine with me. Because I don't need anyone else."

Robbie holds up his glass. Blair, Cat, and Wade do, too.

"To you guys," he says. "My best friends."

They touch glasses, and then Robbie sits back down. "That's it," he says. "The sad part's over." Cat doesn't believe him, though—not for a second. The sad part is just beginning, and she could lay her head on the tablecloth and not lift it for a week. She doesn't, though, because Wade says, "Um, Robbie, who are they?"

A man and a woman are standing with Dash at the base of the temporary stage, and they're both holding electric guitars. Dash touches his tablet, and the white lights strung all around them flicker to life.

Chapter 44

The two guitar players step to the center of the stage. The man is Black, heavyset, like an opera singer. He taps his microphone. "Mic check, mic check." The woman, who's white, does the same thing, and her voice is as sweet as a bird's. "Ooooo, sounds good on my end, baby," she says.

Blair, Cat, and Wade look at one another. *What?*

The man strums his guitar, and a burst of sound tears through speakers set up all over the deck and patio. It's loud, like rock and roll, and Wade stands up.

The two musicians look to be in their fifties, possibly sixties. Despite his sparkly sports jacket and her matching cocktail dress, they're perfectly normal-looking people. The man winks and holds his right arm up. "Straight outta Las Vegas, Nevada . . ." He hits his strings again, guitar-god style. "I'm the one and only Tyrone Cain."

"Damn right you are, sweetie," the woman says. "And I'm *Tilly* Cain."

Blair and Cat sit holding each other still. "Holy shit," says Cat.

"And together," says Tilly, "we're Tyrone and Tilly, the greatest two-top cover band ever assembled."

At first, it sounds like what two guitars falling down a flight of stairs might sound like. But Tyrone and Tilly fall quickly into rhythm, and the riffs form into a rapid-fire guitar medley. The beginning of "Beat It" becomes "Smells Like Teen Spirit." "Enter Sandman" eases seamlessly into "Seven Nation Army." They go back and forth, playing off each other. They fly through the intro to "Mr. Brightside," which leads into "Walk This Way" and "Sweet Child O' Mine." Then Tyrone and Tilly start their first full song, "Night Fever" by the Bee Gees. Cat shouts and pulls Blair to the dance floor. A disco ball sends glittery light into the sky.

"This is amazing!" says Wade. He and Robbie watch Blair and Cat dance. Dash is standing next to the bar like a bouncer. They demand he join them, and when he does, it's perfect, because he's a terrible, terrible dancer.

The screens are still running the slideshow. Their pictures fade in and out.

"Okay, lemme explain how this works," Tyrone says. "The missus and I have a whooooole set planned for y'all. Hit after hit after *goddamn* hit."

Cat screams and slaps Dash's ass, which makes a sound like a firecracker exploding.

"But this is *your* party," says Tyrone. "So, if you got requests, yell 'em up. Because ten bucks and a kiss on the cheek says you can't stump Tyrone and Tilly."

"Ice Ice Baby!" Blair shouts.

Tilly stops playing; her amp buzzes.

"Hmmm," says Tyrone. "What do you think, baby doll? We know that one?"

Tilly allows a moment of showbiz tension. "What is this, amateur hour?" she asks, and now she's playing chords stolen from Bowie and Queen. Cat tries to dip Blair. Dash saves them from crashing to the ground. Wade is so very lucky to have friends like these.

"You're gonna take care of them when I'm gone, right?" Robbie asks, and it's touching to think Robbie has that kind of faith in him.

"I'll do my best," he says.

It's like someone's hit Shuffle on an iPod loaded with every popular song of the last sixty years. Elvis to Justin Timberlake. Prince to Madonna. Tupac to Neil Diamond. Robbie and Wade have joined Blair and Cat on the floor. Robbie is tired, Wade can tell; a little weak, too; but the four of them dance, laughing and silly, to all of it.

"I'm in love with you!" Cat shouts at Tyrone during "The Chain" by Fleetwood Mac. Tyrone blows her a kiss and Tilly play-scowls. Forty-five minutes into the set, Blair says, "Look, it's the corgi!"

The little dog from next door stands by the bar, ears back, tentative.

"That little creep's been watching us all weekend!" Cat shouts.

"Must be theirs," says Wade.

An older couple—gray-haired, a little stooped—watch from the side of the house. Their expressions are as tentative as their dog's. Cat waves. "You folks want a drink?"

Their names are Donna and Dwayne, and their dog is Buster. Later, Blair teaches Donna and Dwayne the Macarena, and Cat holds Buster while spinning in circles. She introduces him as her platonic life partner.

As Robbie predicted, more people arrive. They come in curious waves from every direction—from nearby houses, from the other side of Fenwick Island, from bars and restaurants. Blair, Cat, Robbie, and Wade welcome them all.

"Play the Beatles!" Blair shouts.

She smiles back at Wade. Her shoes are off and her hair is wild. He's at the bar now, taking a short break from dancing. He orders a Miller Lite and considers texting Jane and asking her to come. He doesn't, though, because he's decided to try being cool for a change.

"The Beatles?" says Tyrone. He and Tilly are between songs, sipping drinks.

"The lame-ass Beatles!" shouts Cat.

"We might know a couple by them. Tilly baby, gimme a power chord."

Tilly counts up to four. "A Hard Day's Night" starts just as Robbie sidles up next to Wade at the bar. He orders a gin and tonic and tells Wade that he has a phone call.

"What?"

"Inside," he says. Robbie looks at his watch. "Might wanna hustle, though. It's time-sensitive."

Wade looks up at the glowing house. "Nobody even knows I'm here."

And then his friend takes him by the shoulders and gives him a good, hard shake. "Wade! Goddammit! Go upstairs! Dash is waiting for you!"

Chapter 45

"Where do you think *you're* going, doofus?" shouts Cat.
Wade dance-walks by, holding a beer.

"You can't leave, Stephens!" shouts Blair.

"Yeah, don't make us listen to this without you!" Cat says.

It's too loud for Cat to hear what Wade says back. As he heads inside, he makes a phone with his hand and holds it to his ear.

"Whatever," says Cat.

Wade may not be there to listen to the Beatles, but Donna and Dwayne are, and they're 100 percent into it. Buster is back at their feet, and the little family gently dances.

"Are you having fun?" Blair shouts into Cat's ear.

"I am!" says Cat, which is mostly true. Despite having spent much of today thinking about both death and Casey Green, she is managing to enjoy herself.

"Me too!" says Blair. "Can I have one of your drinks, though? I feel like you maybe don't need both of them."

Cat looks at her cocktails. Maybe that's how it goes with living wakes: one minute you're dancing with a corgi, the next you're double-fisting.

Blair takes the clearer of the two drinks, and they watch this ragtag group of strangers dance. Blair sucks from her straw and wrinkles her nose. "Oh good, tequila!" she says. "So, I'll either be flashing someone or falling down a flight of stairs later!"

"Do I get a vote?" asks Cat.

On the stage, Tyrone and Tilly are standing back-to-back, playing their guitars.

Blair leans close again. Her breath is sweet-smelling, like sugar. "So, I've been thinking!"

"Yeah?"

The song ends, and for the moment at least, Blair and Cat can speak without yelling. "I wasn't very nice yesterday," she says.

"When?"

"In the powder room," she says. "I was putting my stuff onto you. Kids are awesome. And if you want one, then I'm jealous of your little science baby." Blair touches Cat's stomach. "Because he or she gets to have *you* as a mom."

Cat feels this like a thump to the chest. "Stop it, you bitch. I can't cry anymore." Cat hugs her friend—a full-body hug. She tells her that she loves her.

"I love you, too. Also, you need to move back east. I've thought about that, too. Forget California. It's too sunny there. Move closer to me. I can be your science baby's cool aunt. I can help. You don't have to do it alone."

Cat imagines living on the East Coast again: cold and crowded, but comfortable and right. "I've heard worse ideas," she says.

"All right, all right," says Tilly from the stage. She stands crooked on sparkly wedge heels.

"Tell 'em what's up, baby," says Tyrone.

"We don't usually do two in a row by the same band. But, well, some bands deserve it. And this one's a stone-cold classic."

An electric piano has materialized. Tilly wheels it onto the stage. It's small, like a kids' toy, but it works. She plays a few bars while Tyrone stands back and watches. It takes a moment for Cat and the rest of the crowd to identify the beginning of "Hey Jude," and she instinctively looks for Wade, who played this damn song incessantly on his crappy car stereo in high school.

"Come on," says Blair. "Robbie looks lonely."

She's right: he does, their friend, swaying at the front of the stage. "You go. I'll join you in a sec." And now it's Cat's turn to take a break at the bar.

Donna takes Dwayne's hand. Two teenagers are making out beside the pool.

Earlier, at coffee, Cat told Casey Green everything. The details of Robbie's illness. The story of the Rejects. Years and years of friendship. Robbie's ham-fisted attempt to save the three of them. Casey took a few notes, but she mostly just listened. Her expression had lost the edge it had yesterday. She looked open and kind, and Cat was lulled into thinking maybe this wasn't just business after all. *Maybe,* Cat thought, *she does like me.*

When their meeting was over, Casey shook Cat's hand outside 3BB Café. A red strand of hair escaped her bun and fell across her face, and Cat heard her friend's voice in her head. *Come on, Cat. What girl wouldn't want to be with you?*

"Maybe we could get a real drink sometime," Cat said. "A *drink* drink. Not just Gatorade or coffee?"

Casey looked startled. "Oh," she said. "Cat, that's nice. But I'm a journalist. You're my source. I . . . we . . . we really can't."

Chapter 46

As advertised, Dash is waiting for Wade upstairs. He's looking at an iPad.

He looks different than he's looked over the last few days: more relaxed, less scary. "Hey, Wade," he says.

Wade holds out his fist for a bump. Wade is not really a fist-bumper, but it's been quite a day. The big TV on the wall is on, and the camera above it is active and alert. Wade sees himself on the smaller of two video boxes. The other, bigger box is blank. "Stand By" blinks lazily on the screen.

Wade focuses on his own image. It strikes him that *he* looks different, too. The clothes are part of it, sure. The shirt he's wearing— black, nicely fitted—is undoubtedly insanely expensive. His hair, too, still styled per Blair and Cat's specifications. It's more than that, though. For a long time, Wade has avoided looking at himself. The guy on the monitor, though, looks like someone who might just be okay with what he sees in the mirror.

Earlier, as their brunch wound down, Wade asked Jane if she ever came to Baltimore. "It's just a few hours away," he said, "depending on traffic."

The Miller Lite–champagne combo had made her practically giggly. "Baltimore?" she said. "That's in Maryland, right?"

"Yeah. Good seafood. Some casual gun violence."

Jane laughed. "You stupid bastard," she said.

"What?"

"Real Estate 101," she said. "Never invest in fixer-uppers. Nothing but money pits."

He can still hear the music outside. Tyrone and Tilly wrap up "A Hard Day's Night." The audience cheers. Then an edgy, electric version of "Hey Jude" starts.

"Shit," Wade says.

"What?" asks Dash.

"That's my song," he says.

"Ah," says Dash. "Well, maybe this'll make up for it."

"Who am I talking to here, D?" The screen still tells them to stand by.

Dash looks up from his iPad. "I don't want to spoil it. There's a friend of a friend Robbie thought you might like to say hello to."

Nothing happens for thirty seconds. Wade hums along to "Hey Jude." Then a woman's voice comes through the TV speakers. She has a British accent. "Mr. Walker, are you there?"

"Hi, yes," says Dash. "We're here. All ready from Fenwick Island, USA."

"Perfect. I'll connect you. He's in California at the moment."

Dash looks at Wade. "Great. Thanks for all your help with this."

"No thanks necessary," the woman says. "This is what we do, right?"

The "Stand By" message stops blinking, then disappears, replaced by a video image of a thin, older man in a T-shirt and a sport coat. His hair is grayish, floppy over his forehead. "Hello, hello," he says. He, too, has a British accent. A very, very famous British accent.

Wade is aware that Dash has stepped out of the room; the sliding door closes. "Hi," says Wade. Then he says, "Hello." Then "Hi" again. He forces himself to stop.

"Are you Wade?"

"Yes. That's me. I'm Wade."

"Lovely to meet you, Wade. I'm Paul McCartney."

Wade laughs and claps his palm over his mouth. It's the most unnecessary introduction in the history of videoconferencing. The man on the screen is Paul McCartney. Unmistakably so. Paul McCartney leans in toward the camera. "What's that you're listening to?" he asks.

"What?" says Wade.

"The tune. Is that . . . 'Hey Jude'?"

"Yeah, I guess it is. Have you heard it before?" Wade smiles at his own joke, marveling at the simple fact that he was able to make it.

Paul laughs, bobs his head along. "Once or twice. Not like this, though. It's very electric, by the sound of it. I dig it. Sounds like rock 'n' roll, doesn't it?"

"It does," says Wade.

Paul's face changes now; he looks concerned. "Oh, Wade. Mate. You don't have to cry. That's certainly not necessary."

Wade touches his face and discovers that's exactly what he's doing. He's crying. Crying in front of Paul McCartney. He's gone all weekend without crying. He's joked, and sulked, and drunk his way through all of it. He can't anymore, though, because, Jesus, he's going to miss his friend. The fact that there's a Beatle here, virtually in the room with him, only makes it worse. He's going to miss Robbie so much. "Shit. I'm sorry. I'm good. It's just, you're . . ."

"No need to apologize," says Paul. "People cry sometimes when they see me. Occupational hazard. Granted, they're usually women. But it's fine. I don't mind."

Wade laughs, because he's just been Beatle-burned by Paul McCartney. He takes perhaps the deepest breath he's ever taken, filling his lungs to their pink, delicate bottoms. "So, how are you?" he asks.

"I'm good, Wade. I'm playing a show in L.A. tonight. Hot here, but I love California. All the sunshine, you know. Quite a place."

"Right," says Wade. "Hey Jude" swells outside, and Tyrone and

Tilly sing the nah-na-nah-nah part, but Wade's able to let it fade into the background. "So, you know Robbie?"

"A bit, yes," says Paul. "Well, not really, to be honest. Similar circles, I suppose. He's been generous to some charities I care very much about."

"Oh," says Wade. "Makes sense."

"However, I was happy when he sent me—" Paul looks away, off camera. There's some noise, additional voices. He addresses someone. "Oh, there you are. Come, sit. You'll like this." Paul turns his attention back to Wade. "We have a bit of a surprise for the fans in L.A. tonight. Very hush-hush. An old friend is joining me for the encore."

A man with a beard and purple-tinted glasses sits next to Paul. He looks at the camera and smiles. "Hello there."

Wade's hands go to the top of his head. "Shit. You're Ringo Starr."

"I am!"

"I follow you on Instagram!" As this bursts idiotically from Wade's mouth, he's aware that he'll hate himself for it for decades, because *that* is what he's apparently chosen to say to the drummer of the Beatles.

"Well, thanks," says Ringo. "Are you the bloke who wrote the book about us?"

"I was just getting to that," says Paul. "It's not *about* us really. It's . . . what would you say, Wade? *Inspired* by us. Ring, he took what we did, and he made stories out of it. Fleshed our songs out, made them something else entirely."

"Right," says Wade. "That's *exactly* what I did. I'm so happy you got that, Mr. Mc—"

"Oh, stop. You've already bawled in front of me. Call me Paul."

"Okay . . . Paul."

"Call *him* Paul," says Ringo. "I'd prefer if you call me Sir Richard Starkey."

"I can do that," says Wade, laughing. "I would want to be called that, too."

"You think I'd like his book, Paul?" Ringo asks. "Wait, is that 'Hey Jude'? Have we heard this version? I don't know if I like it. No drums."

"I think it's someone outside," says Paul. "And, yes, you *would* like his book. *I* certainly did." Paul looks at the camera again—at Wade. "Some sweet little stories in there, Wade. Listen, Ring and I need to go. There are these buses, and traffic here is the most dreadful thing. But I wanted you to know that. *All Together Now.* Well done on that title, by the way. It fits, doesn't it? Anyway. You helped me remember a very lovely time in my life. I wanted to thank you for that."

Tears again. They won't stop. "You're welcome, Paul."

Ringo holds two fingers up. "All right, then. Peace and love."

"Bye now," says Paul.

"Wait," says Wade. "One . . . um, one thing."

They're looking at him. He has their attention. Wade has imagined talking to all sorts of celebrities—actors and actresses, writers, a few rock stars. Never Paul or Ringo, though. Never John or George either, even under the most hypothetical, imaginary contexts. He's never imagined talking to John, Paul, George, or Ringo in real life, because it's hard to imagine them even existing in real life, as if they're conceptual, too big, somehow, to actually exist. But, of course, they *do* exist. And they're waiting for him to speak. "My dad," he says.

"Your dad?" says Paul.

"Sorry. Yeah. My dad. He grew up loving you guys. The sixties, when he was young." Wade bites at his lip, holding himself together. "When I was little, I used to sit with him in this spot he set up in the den. He had a pretty sweet record player. We'd listen to your music. He had them all. The full albums, the little 45 singles, the . . . the fan club Christmas records. Everything."

The two men nod. Wade wonders how many times they've heard slightly different versions of this. He goes on, though, because he doubts he'll ever have their attention again.

"He was never much of a talker," says Wade. "Still isn't. But when we were listening to you guys—your music? We had a thing, him and me. He almost died when I was in high school. He had a heart attack. When he was recovering, I put all his Beatles records in a duffel bag, and I dragged his record player to his hospital room. Almost broke it, which would've been a disaster. But he refused to listen to you guys on my iPod."

The two men smile. "A purist, eh?" says Ringo. "He's right to be."

"We rocked out," says Wade. "In the hospital. Well, we softly rocked out. The nurses were pretty specific about the volume. But he says it helped him get better. *You four* helped him get better. And . . . you gave us something to talk about. My dad and me. So, I want to thank you. Thanks for doing that. And thanks for being . . . you."

"Well, that was lovely to hear," says Ringo. "I never get tired of that."

"You're very welcome, Wade," says Paul. "I'm glad we could do our part."

Chapter 47

Here's the thing about "Hey Jude": even if you don't like the Beatles—which Blair doesn't, not particularly—that nah-na-nah-nah part is killer.

It's just nonsense, like something the twins would've chanted when they were toddlers, banging pots in the kitchen. Depending on the moment, though, "Nah-na-nah-nah" repeated over and over has the power to make you either very happy or very sad, and in this particular context, Blair feels sad.

She wanders away from Tyrone and Tilly's crowd and finds one of the monitors near the food, which is still playing the slideshow. She eats a breadstick and sees herself. Homecoming. A pretty girl in a dress, all promise and lineless skin. She traces in her mind the path that led her from there to here.

Blair looks up at the house. She can see Wade through the big window, looking at the TV. Cat's at the bar. Robbie waves at her from a distance. As "Hey Jude" winds down, she tries to map out her future, which isn't easy. She's been told an Escalade will bring her home. Once she's there, though, what's she supposed to do? Will she just walk through the front door and set her bag down like nothing has happened?

"What's that, little man?"

It's Tyrone. His big baritone cuts through Blair's daydreaming.

Onstage, the two singers are crouched low. They're trying to hear a request from someone up front.

"Little louder, baby," says Tilly. "Can't hear you."

"Shake! It! Off!"

Blair hears this, loud and clear. Her children have screamed it.

Michelle and Kenny stand at the front of the stage in pajamas. Kenny's hair is sticking up, and Michelle has her Peppa Pig purse slung over her shoulder. Tyrone says, simply, "Coming right up," and the kids cheer. Blair is shaken by how happy she is to see them. Her babies. It's one of a million small miracles of parenthood: you have no idea how much you want to see your kids until you, in fact, see your kids.

Tyrone and Tilly start playing just as Blair spots Martin. Blair watches him as he finds her. In a different world, maybe they'd run to each other. Maybe they'd kiss. But not this world. They're married people, after all, and they both know that they're on shaky ground. He's here, though. He's come back. Martin smiles, tentative. Blair is happy to see him, too. She stands with her drink and her breadstick by a bowl of leftover Caesar salad and waits for her husband to come to her.

"There's zero traffic on Sunday nights," he says.

Blair laughs at this. Marital romance.

"Did Robbie invite you back?" she asks.

"No." He looks out at the crowd. "Wade did. He called me a few hours ago. Holy shit." Martin takes her arm by the wrist. "Is that *real*? Did you get a tattoo?"

"We all did. Wade called you?"

He winces at her puffy skin. "It looks like it hurt."

"What did he say?"

Martin still holds her wrist, rubbing his thumb gently at her pulse. "He said if I didn't come back I might lose you forever." Their twin children are currently screaming the word *shake* over and over at the foot of the stage. "So I came back."

Chapter 48

Wade needs a minute. After his call, he stands motionless, doubting his own five senses, because that couldn't have really happened.

He chatted with Paul McCartney and Ringo Starr. Paul had read his book and said nice things, although those nice things, specifically, have gone blurry, like when you wake up from a dream. He considers calling his dad but decides it's a story best told in person.

"Shake It Off" is blasting outside. He goes to the window and looks down on Robbie's living wake. He spots his people quickly. Dash first, because he's a giant. Then Robbie, who's talking to Cat. Wade smiles when he sees Kenny and Michelle beside them, dancing. Then, finally, there's Blair, the goddamn love of his life, talking to her husband. Martin is holding her by the wrist.

Wade hadn't planned on calling Martin. A few hours ago, he walked by the refrigerator. The squirrel pictures stopped him. He touched both of their rodent faces. This was more than angst or artistic malaise. Blair's family was at stake. So he found Dash, who had everyone's contact information at the ready. Wade didn't just call Martin, he facetimed him. He needed to look him in the eyes.

"Hello?"

"Hey, Martin," said Wade.

Martin looked alarmed. "Wade? Is everything okay?"

"Everything's fine." The screen glitched, but quickly resettled. "What are you and the twins doing tonight?"

"Making homemade pizzas and watching *Jumanji*. Why?"

Wade felt emboldened, suddenly—angry, even—at this guy's obliviousness. "Listen, Blair is the most beautiful woman I've ever met. She's a goddamn angel sent from heaven, and I've been madly in love with her since I was fifteen years old."

In person, Martin probably would've looked away, his gaze pushed downward by the overwhelming awkwardness of the moment. Staring into his phone, though, all he could do was look back at Wade. "Okay," he said. "That's definitely something."

"Six years ago, she picked you," said Wade. "She didn't just pick you over me. She picked you over every other man in the world. Do you even grasp the math of that? Do you deserve her? Probably not. No one does. If you have any idea what's good for you, though, you'll get your ass in that fucking minivan and get back here as fast as you can."

HE KEEPS WATCHING THROUGH THE window. Tyrone and Tilly finish "Shake It Off." Tilly adds a little shimmy at the end, her backside turned to the audience.

There's nothing left for Wade to do now but rejoin the party. He hesitates, because it's nice to have a minute.

He picks his Miller Lite back up off the coffee table and walks through the kitchen. As he rounds a corner, heading toward the stairs, Jane walks through the front door, and he stops dead at the banister, startled. She smiles up from the marble entryway. "There you are. I've been looking all over."

"What are you doing here?" he asks.

She climbs the short flight of stairs. "Robbie invited me. He said he was having a party."

Oh, Robbie, he thinks, sounding like Blair in his own head.

"My oldest is eleven," she says. "Almost twelve. I told them I'd be back in an hour. How much damage can two unattended tween boys do in an hour, right?"

Wade decides not to tell her what he's thinking, which is: *probably a lot.*

"Is that for me?" she asks. Jane doesn't wait for an answer; she takes the beer from his hand and sips. "Have you been crying?"

"What? Oh, yeah, maybe. I think. I just had a video call with Paul McCartney and Ringo Starr."

"Cool," she says. "My Uber driver was Mick Jagger. Nice guy in real life."

Jane is also wearing the same thing she wore this morning. Same pretty dress, same sneakers. He imagines her in her closet looking at all of her clothes and thinking the same thing that Wade thought a few hours ago. *I guess I'll just wear this. It's the nicest thing I've got.*

"So, why didn't you kiss me earlier?" she asks.

Wade laughs. "I was going to. I didn't want to be presumptuous."

"Well, you should've. I gave you the green light."

"You did?"

"Totally. You couldn't tell? Doe eyes? Head tilt?" Jane demonstrates both of these things. "Would it've helped if I'd pointed at my lips?"

"It may have, actually," he says. "I'm out of practice."

"No shit," she says.

Outside, there's another blast of sound from the speakers. To Wade's horror, Tyrone and Tilly have started playing "We Built This City" by Starship. "No way," he says. "This is literally the stupidest song in the history of music."

"Wade," says Jane. She's not doe-eyed this time, nor is her head tilted. But she *is* pointing at her lips. Literally. "Stop talking."

Wade kisses Jane. He kisses her to "We Built This City," which really *is* a stupid song. Beneath a thin layer of peppermint ChapStick, her lips are dry, but they're warm, too, and her hair brushes against his face and the palm of her hand finds the center of his chest.

"That was nice," she whispers. She's still holding his Miller Lite. "I should put this down."

"Probably on a coaster. This place is really nice."

They kiss again, longer this time. She pushes her body against his, and his hands move to her lower back, and it's funny, the twists that a night can take when you're a retired novelist and you're standing in a billionaire's mansion on the beach.

They ease apart again. Jane leans against the banister. "Shit," she says.

"That's a *good* 'shit,' right?" he asks.

Jane nods. "I haven't made out in a while. It's underrated." She runs her thumb across his lower lip. "I got ChapStick on you."

"I'll live," he says.

She's still up on her tiptoes, her sneakers creased. There's cheering and clapping.

"You wanna go outside?" he says. "There are more beers. Maybe they'll play a song that isn't a musical abomination."

"It's kinda nice in here. Don't you think?" She looks around the main floor—at the kitchen, at the fruit bowl, at the wine rack, at the insane TV. "So, do you have your own room, or . . ."

Wade laughs. "Really?"

"Wade, I haven't had sex in two years. It's a miracle I didn't throw you on the hood of a car in the restaurant parking lot this morning." She looks at her watch. "I have twenty-seven minutes. After that, I'm pretty sure my kids'll burn my house down."

Wade takes Jane's hand. "Well, you're in luck. I won't need nearly that long."

Chapter 49

Tyrone and Tilly are gone. They loaded their electric guitars and mini-piano and Tyrone's glittery sport coat into a rental car and drove off an hour ago. Offstage, they were soft-spoken and friendly. They drank cups of ginger tea and hugged everyone goodbye. Quiet followed, along with a steady ringing in everyone's ears.

The caterers and bartenders left shortly after Tyrone and Tilly. The white party lights burned for a while, but then Dash shut them off so everyone could get a better look at the stars, which are dazzling. The impromptu guests are gone, too. They left when the music stopped, oblivious to why they were there.

Now it's just the originals hanging together by the pool, drinks and leftover pizza crust scattered about.

"So, wait," says Blair. She's looking at Wade, leveling him with a squint. "You had *sex*." She whispers the word *sex*. The twins are crashed in a heap beside her on the big outdoor couch, their heads in her lap.

"Um," says Wade.

"Wade Stephens," says Cat. "Certified sex machine."

"Stop it," he says, clearly embarrassed.

Blair touches Michelle's head, thrilled, suddenly, at the prospect of Wade getting laid. She thinks of her night with him, in his little apartment six years ago. He was very sweet—gentle and attentive. He kept finding new places on her body and kissing her there, like she was the first naked woman he'd ever seen. "Well, she's a lucky lady," Blair says.

"*Get it,* girl," says Cat. "She shows up, hits it, then peaces out. She's my idol."

"You guys are drunk," says Wade.

"I wish Donna and Dwayne had left Buster," says Cat. She's alone on a deck chair, one bare foot hovering above the edge of the pool.

"Would you leave a dog with us?" asks Wade.

"Quiet, slut," says Cat.

Wade tears at a beer label. "Anyway, how is *me* having sex the thing we're talking about? I met Paul and Ringo tonight."

"I'd take sex over chatting with two old British guys any day," says Blair.

"Whatever," says Wade. "Robbie, that was amazing. Thank you." He looks at Blair and Cat, gives them a little nod. "And, speaking of thank you. We got you a gift."

"You didn't need to do that," says Robbie. "You're here, that's my gift."

"Oh, shut up," says Cat.

Wade hops up and runs back into the house. That afternoon, in the dead time after the beach and before the party, while Robbie took a nap, Blair, Cat, and Wade rode the bikes to CVS. You can print photos from your phone there in the back, next to the potato chips.

Wade comes back outside now. He's holding a sixteen-by-twenty framed photo, turned around so Robbie can't see. "It's a classic problem, right?" he says. "What do you get the guy who's got everything? Literally, like, everything. Like, planes—plural—and a beach house and a minigolf course? Well, the answer is pretty obvious."

Blair watches Robbie's face as Wade reveals the photo of the four of them from Friday afternoon. "You get that guy a picture of him and his friends standing in front of a Chrysler LeBaron," she says.

"Wow," says Robbie.

"You like it?" asks Cat.

"I love it," he says, and Blair can see that he really does.

They settle back into their chairs. The kids' feet are in Martin's lap, and he's snoring gently. Blair looks at her friends, one by one, spread out before her. Wade looks happy, buzzed still from Jane and his Beatles. Robbie and Cat, though, are both alone on their chairs, and she feels sad for them.

They listen to waves and faint sounds of fun coming from Ocean City, a half a mile away. Martin stirs in his sleep. Kenny is perfectly still. Blair curls a strand of his shaggy boy hair around her index finger. Then she imagines something that she's never imagined before: Robbie Malcolm kissing Cat Miller.

An idea comes together. Connections, like new synapses, form. It's ridiculous, but then again, what about this weekend hasn't been at least a little ridiculous? Blair thinks of Cat, emotionally shaky on Friday evening, announcing that she's probably ovulating. She thinks about a binder full of men in some clinic in L.A., their identities distilled to the most general physical characteristics and progressive voting habits. She thinks of captured sperm floating about, waiting. Blair looks at Robbie, practically lost in his big hoodie. Everything makes sense. It's perfect.

She sits up, careful not to wake her family. "You guys," she says. "Cat and Robbie should have sex."

Chapter 50

Blair said what she said thirty minutes ago out on the deck. *Cat and Robbie should have sex.* Several moments followed in which everyone looked at everyone else. And then Robbie said, "Wait, what?"

Wade and Dash laughed, because clearly Blair had been joking, like, *Yeah, right, maybe we should* all *have sex.* Blair was dead serious, though—Cat could tell.

"You're not kidding, are you?" said Wade.

Blair looked down at her zonked-out kids. "No, I'm not," she whispered. "It's perfect. We should've thought of this days ago. Cat wants a baby. This is how people *get* babies."

Wade leaned forward. "*This* is how people get babies?"

"I'm talking *biologically*," said Blair.

"You really *are* drunk," Wade said. "We all are. I think the twins are even a little drunk. Blair, I don't know if you remember this, but Cat is a lesbian."

Cat looked at Robbie. He held the photograph they'd just given him. She wondered, *Is this what he wants?*

"Cat, honey." Blair put her hands over her heart. "*You* know that *I* know who you are. But you said you're . . ." Blair trailed off.

Wade was a few steps behind. "She's what?" he asked.

"Ovulating," Blair said.

"Just for clarity's sake," he said, "that's when the egg starts to . . . ?"

"Wade, shut up," said Blair. She turned to Cat and Robbie. "Cat, if you *are* . . . and if you guys . . ." As difficult as full sentences had apparently become, Blair's point was clear. "This isn't about sexuality," she said. "This is about you two. It's about . . . friends."

Cat saw that Robbie looked frightened. *She* was frightened. Witches and psychics and space people in movies can sometimes speak with telepathy, and she was pretty sure Robbie was communicating with her through his mind. He was saying something like "Maybe this isn't as crazy as it sounds?"

"Cat could get a baby," Blair said. Her voice cracked next when she said, "Robbie could have . . . a legacy."

Now Cat is standing in her bathroom looking at herself in the mirror and wondering if she's even capable of doing this. Blair made some good points, and those points came directly from her heart. But this is more complicated than Blair realizes. Two days ago Cat thought she wanted a baby more than anything. Yesterday, she wasn't as sure. Now, shit, she doesn't know.

She squeezes toothpaste onto her electric toothbrush. She brushes until her gums ache, until her mouth is as clean and minty as it could possibly be. She's stalling.

Cat kissed a beautiful guy once in L.A. after college. It was at some huge house in the Valley—a friend of a new friend, that kind of thing—and it was New Year's Eve, and everyone was kissing everyone. His face was freshly shaven, and his cheekbones could've cut glass, and his lips tasted like alcohol. She thinks of it now, remembering the sexlessness of it. It was her one even remotely physical encounter with a guy, and she felt nothing, as if she'd made out with a cologne ad in *Vogue*.

This isn't some guy at a party, though. *This is Robbie,* she thinks.

And right now, Robbie is on the other side of the bathroom door, waiting for her. And maybe this shouldn't be about what she wants. Maybe it should be about what he wants.

Cat thinks of a baby. Not a conceptual baby, but a *real* one, a little girl. Her baby. *Their* baby. An infant, then a toddler, then a surly teen with braces. Cat would see herself in their daughter—little things, like her quirks and her hair. But she'd see Robbie, too. Every day she'd get to see her friend. It'd be like Robbie had lived on.

Cat takes a deep breath. "You can do this," she whispers to her reflection.

But . . . can she?

Maybe Blair is right. Maybe this isn't about sexuality. Maybe this is just two friends finding a solution. It is, however, undeniably about sex. And as she closes her eyes now and tries to imagine actually being with Robbie, she finds that she can't. As much as she loves him, her mind simply goes blank. The image of that beautiful little girl fades away, replaced by certainty. This isn't what she wants. She bets it isn't what he wants either.

Cat opens her eyes and sighs. No, on second thought, she can't do this.

And then she grabs the bathroom door and turns off the light.

Chapter 51

Robbie is in Cat's bed. He's wearing a T-shirt and boxer shorts, and he's positioned himself not at the center of the bed but on the right-hand side. Being at the center of the bed would seem too bold—too familiar and confident.

He pulls the comforter up to his waist and leans against the headboard. He thinks about how thorough and airtight his plans had seemed a few days ago. The house was closed on and furnished at lightning speed, along with the acquisition of Viking Golf. This second purchase he made on a whim, thinking it'd be fun to give the special little place to his friends. The dossiers on Blair, Cat, and Robbie were compiled quickly, too. Tyrone and Tilly were happy to come to Delaware. After all, it's 120 degrees in Vegas, and he offered them ten times their normal rate. Paul and Ringo were easy, too. The fact that the two Beatles happened to be together on this particular weekend was so perfect that it seemed predestined. Then Blair jumped off the roof. Everyone rejected his help. Wade hooked up with Jane. Now . . . *this*.

That's people, though. They aren't stocks. They aren't companies or commodities or complex financial principles. People are dumb and messy, and there's no good algorithm to predict what they'll do. Cat was right: Robbie can't control them.

Tonight will be Robbie's last night on earth. The logistics of that are all planned out, too. His last sunset has come and gone. His last party, too. His last evening with friends. And now his last . . . time.

His hands are shaking again. He doesn't fault himself for this like he did before, though, because, well, this is pretty intense. When Blair said what she said out by the pool, he knew right away that she wasn't kidding. He knew just as quickly that he didn't want to do it—that it wouldn't be right to do it. But then Robbie looked at Cat, and Cat was looking at him.

Is this what she wants? he wondered.

He's afraid for Cat to see him without his T-shirt on. He's been strategic with all those hoodies and sweatshirts. Those long-sleeved sun shirts and draped towels. They've been keeping him warm, but they've also been hiding what he looks like now. Hiding the fact that he's shrinking away. He doesn't want that to be how she remembers him: her old friend, nearly gone now.

If this is what she wants, though, he'll do it. After all, this is Cat, and Robbie loves Cat.

He can hear her brushing her teeth in the bathroom. In a minute she'll be done, and the door will open, and when it does, Robbie will ask, *Cat, is this really what you want?* And if she says yes, he'll hold out his hand to her and hope that she takes it.

But then he thinks of Casey Green.

A year or so ago, when Robbie had lunch with Cat in L.A., he encouraged her to talk to their waitress. She was pretty and shy-seeming, and when she'd come to their table Robbie could've sworn the young woman had looked at Cat in a way he'd never noticed another woman look at her before. It'd been such a small moment—like a little tremor there in the bustling restaurant—but it had been powerful enough to cause Robbie to briefly imagine them together, Cat and the waitress.

Now, to Robbie's surprise, he's imagining Cat with Casey.

He can see them in his imagination—as clear as a vivid

memory—holding hands and smiling together. He laughs to himself, because that *definitely* wasn't part of the plan. Somehow, though, it's perfect.

Cat doesn't belong with Robbie, even if just for a few moments in a room overlooking the beach on the last night of his life. Maybe she doesn't belong with Casey Green either, for that matter. But, in Robbie's mind at least, she looks happy and loved.

When the bathroom door finally opens, Cat steps tentatively into the bedroom and smiles. She says "Robbie," just as he says "Cat." She tells him to go first.

"We can't do this," he says.

The smile stays, but her eyes go damp. "I know," Cat says. "But can I lay with you for a while?"

"Of course," says Robbie. And then he holds out his hand.

Monday

Chapter 52

Wade is experiencing that feeling you get when you wake up in a place that clearly isn't yours, like you've been kidnapped and drugged by warlords.

Is this my apartment? Where am I? Did I have a dream about Paul McCartney and Ringo Starr? Did I have sex last night?

A few seconds pass; his head clears. It's Monday morning, and he's on Fenwick Island. And, yes, he *did* have sex last night.

Wade hasn't been living a life of celibacy. He's cycled through the dating apps, like everyone. His sexual experiences, though, particularly the memorable, meaningful kind, have been sporadic enough to be categorized as rare, like the Winter Olympics, and he sighs a sleepy, swoony sigh as he thinks of how radiant Jane's face looked last night when she laughed at him. He'd nearly tripped getting out of his pants in this very bedroom, and she thought it was hilarious.

"Are you okay?" she'd whispered. Despite being consenting adults in a private room with a rock concert going on outside, they whispered back and forth like teenagers, like they could be busted at any second.

"I think I pulled a hammy," he told her.

"Come here, I'll check it out for you."

He gets out of bed now. He grabs a half-full bottle of water from the nightstand and steps out onto his balcony. It's a hot, sunny morning, and the banner planes are already out. A particularly sputtery one cruises by, reminding everyone to wear sunscreen. Wade notices that Robbie's Range Rover is gone. The LeBaron, which Dash rescued from Bethany Beach, sits in the driveway next to Blair and Martin's minivan.

Back in his room, he sees his iPhone. He picks it up like he always does first thing in the morning, but notes to himself that it's nice not to be hoping for a message from his agent. He does have a text, though. To his unabashed delight, it's from Jane.

How far did you say it is from Fenwick to Baltimore?

2.5 hour drive, give or take, he writes. Then he adds, Faster in a private jet.

Relationships get more complex as they go—awkward conversations and miscommunication and misunderstandings and arguments and difficult decisions. This part, though? This is the easy part, and Wade decides he's going to let himself enjoy it.

Chapter 53

One room over, Blair is the only member of her family awake, which is nothing short of a miracle. Kids—hers included—don't sleep in. It's as if they're born with alarm clocks in their heads that've been set for the break of dawn.

Not today, though. Michelle and Kenny are dead to the world. Beside her, Martin is, too. She analyzes the tricky, jagged shape of his bed head against the glow of the morning sun. She imagines a different room and a different man. She returns to the fantasy of the last few months: Mr. McGee in bed beside her. The image is putrid now, like a bitter taste in her mouth.

Blair sits up, but she doesn't get up—not yet. Through the window, she can see the Odyssey. She can also see Imaginary Taylor Swift, who has somehow gotten ahold of an imaginary golf club, which she's using now to smash the headlights and front bumper.

Fuck this thing, Blair! Fuck this goddamn minivan!

Blair and Martin had sex in their bathroom last night. They would have done it in bed like civilized married people, but the twins, despite some low-level begging from Martin, insisted on sleeping in the room with their parents. So, when Michelle and Kenny were finally asleep between them, Blair nodded to the bathroom door on the other side of the room. Communication hasn't been their strong suit lately, but Martin knew what she meant.

They tiptoed into the bathroom and shut the door. Blair put the dimmers up halfway, and they kissed in romantic semidarkness.

"That bikini," he whispered.

Blair thought he was just speaking in erotic generalities, but he was being literal. She'd hung her new swimsuit on the shower rod to dry, and there it was, skimpy and dangling.

"Maybe you could put it on," he said.

"Really?"

He smiled, blushing. "I really think you should."

She made him turn around. The fabric was damp and chilly against her skin. "Okay," she said, vulnerable suddenly. She knew how good she looked wearing it, but being in a swimsuit out of context brought on a rush of self-consciousness.

He held her by the hips and moved his eyes up and down her body. "Damn," he said.

"Everyone looks at me, you know," she said. "Except you. When did that stop? You used to call me Beautiful Blair."

Marriage is often full of accusations and denials. About little things, mostly, but big things sometimes, too. Martin has a particular look, maybe all husbands do, when he knows he's wrong. That's how he looked last night: ashamed and sorry. "I don't know," he said. "I think I let myself forget. But you are beautiful."

She lifted herself up and sat down on the counter, next to the sink. She understood what he meant, because maybe she'd let herself forget a few things, too. She looked at his hands on her hips, so smooth and strong. She took a fistful of his T-shirt and pulled him toward her. "Don't forget again, okay?"

She looks at the red bikini, which is now lying on the floor beside the bed. It's Young Blair's swimsuit, for sure, but apparently Adult Blair can pull it off, too. She can be who she is *now*: a wife and a mom. But she can hold on to bits of what she used to be, too. Isn't that what aging is—just you, tweaked and reshaped along the way? She thinks of the slideshow from last night. All four of them through the years: Blair, Cat, Robbie, and Wade. They've grown up, taken slightly different forms, but they're basically the same people that they've always been.

"Do you think they did it?" It's Martin, awake now.

"What?" she whispers.

He checks to make sure the kids are still asleep. "Cat and Robbie," he says. "You know."

She'd somehow forgotten all about that. It was her idea, but, sober now in the light of day, she realizes that she was wrong to think it was something they should do. "I don't know," she says. "I hope not."

Martin reaches for her and runs his hand through her hair. "I'm glad I came back."

"Me too," she says.

There's a sound from out in the hallway. It must be Dash, because no normal-size person could make that much noise just walking.

Blair rolls over and faces Martin. The twins are between them, but they've scooted low in the big bed, so she has a clear look into his eyes. A few weeks after they got engaged, Martin asked her something that she's never quite forgotten. The engagement ring he gave her when he proposed was expensive and stunning, but it was hastily purchased, and the band was slightly too big. One Wednesday night after work, Martin picked it back up from the jeweler, who'd switched out the band. They were leaning on the kitchen island in his condo; she hadn't fully moved in yet. Martin made a little show of re-proposing—of dropping to one knee. His expression changed when he looked up at her, like he'd just been struck by some dark thought. He touched her stomach, in which minuscule versions of their children floated. "Would you have said yes if it was just us?" he asked.

She told him yes then, and she stands by it now. Because Wade was right. Two adorable kids. A husband who loves her. Could be worse, right?

Chapter 54

Cat reaches for him. It's a reflex upon waking next to another person: friend, lover, or otherwise. Robbie's not there, though. He must've gone back to his room—or he's downstairs making coffee, which sounds fantastic. She doesn't remember saying good night. They were lying together, talking. He'd started shivering, so they got under the covers.

"The odds," Robbie said. He rubbed his arms, trying to warm himself. "It would've been a long shot anyway."

"Oh good," she said, "I was hoping we could talk about math."

He smiled. "What I mean is, nothing's changed. I'll help you. The doctors—the expense of it all. I can help you get a baby. Even if I'm gone. That's what you want, right?"

Beneath the comforter, she slid closer, hoping to make him warmer, and then she looked up at the clean, perfectly white ceiling. "I don't know," she said. "What if it isn't?"

She must've fallen asleep a few minutes later.

Goodbye, Cat.

There are footsteps in the hallway, loud and heavy.

She's flying back to L.A. this evening on Robbie's plane. She won't be there long, though, because Blair was right: Cat belongs on this side of the country. She'll lean in to being alone, own it the way she owns being short. Besides, East Coast lonely is easier than West Coast lonely, probably because the weather is shittier. Maybe she'll get a dog. Buster was pretty cute. She could become a corgi lady.

Now, though, coffee.

Robbie isn't downstairs in the kitchen, but the Keurig is. She pops a pod in and starts pushing buttons. She's not exactly sure what she's doing, but it works. She adds cream and sugar and then leans back against the counter, content with the quiet as she looks past the deck at the ocean. It's such a gentle, lovely morning that it barely registers as odd that Casey Green is sitting on a deck chair outside. Cat smiles into her coffee.

Casey's clunky sandals are off, set side by side on the deck, and her feet are up. There's a little notebook in her lap. She runs a hand through her red hair and looks down on the beach, clearly enjoying this peaceful moment on the deck of a rogue capitalist's ill-begotten mansion.

That stuff before, her pep talk to herself about short-legged dogs and owning loneliness? It all still applies. Cat is committed to needing others less. But there's no harm in going outside and saying hello, right?

She makes another cup in the Keurig, lucking out again with random button-pushing. She slides the door open and clears her throat. "I called the police. You have thirty seconds to vacate the premises."

Casey sits up. "They'll never catch me," she says.

Cat hands Casey the mug. "Pod coffee. I took a guess and added cream."

"Thanks. You guessed right."

Cat sits. A banner plane passes hauling an ad for a local dermatologist. "So, what's up?" she asks. "You just stop over for some free coffee?"

Casey sips. "He texted me, actually."

"Who?"

"Robbie. An hour ago. Bright and early. A text from Robbie Malcolm. He called me Miss Green. I took a screenshot of it for my records."

When you find a girl sitting on a deck waiting, it's nice to think that she might be waiting for you. "Oh," she says. "Well, what'd he say?"

"He said I should come over this morning. He said every good story needs an ending."

"Well, I haven't seen him," she says. "I haven't seen anyone, actually. It's just me."

Casey sets her coffee down. "I'm glad he texted."

"You are?"

"It gave me an excuse to see you again."

Cat doesn't let herself smile. Instead, she waits.

"I need to . . . well, a couple of things." Casey opens a small handbag and digs around. She finds an iPhone and holds it out, and Cat is confused, because, *Did this chick buy me an iPhone?* But then Cat realizes that it's hers. "I stopped by the minigolf course on the way here to look for it. I thought you'd want it back."

The screen is cracked, like it's taken a bullet. "How did you—?"

"I was tailing you."

"Tailing me?"

"All of you. At the course. You threw that really far, by the way. I was impressed."

Cat hits the Home button, and her wrecked phone comes to life. Two things strike her immediately: 1 percent of her battery remains, and she has a text message. It's from Gabrielle. Just two words: I'm sorry.

"You can get it repaired," says Casey. "They fix iPhone screens now."

She's been waiting for a message from Gabrielle all weekend, and now that one has arrived, all Cat can think about is Casey Green searching a go-cart track for her lost phone.

"I also wanted to say I'm sorry," says Casey. "For how I acted yesterday when you asked me out. You took me by surprise."

Cat wishes now that maybe she'd gotten dressed instead of just stumbling out here in her jammies like a stoned high school kid.

"The journalist source thing," says Casey, "that's real. It can be messy, too, depending on where you work. And this is an important story for me."

"Okay," Cat says.

Casey Green laughs, flustered. "But when I was researching you—you know, planning my beach ambush—I basically stalked you on social media. I already told you how funny you are on Twitter, right? But I looked at all your pictures on Instagram, too. A lot."

Cat smiles now. She can't help it. "You did?"

"I told myself I was just gathering details. But then, there I was, looking at a picture of you pretending to kiss a lobster from a year ago, and I was like, Do I have a crush on this girl?"

Cat laughs. Casey laughs. The banner plane makes another pass with its sunscreen ad. "Well?" Cat says. "Do you?"

"I think I might," says Casey. "I like that you're short like me, and that you can chuck a phone. And I've been thinking about you in your running outfit for, like, two days. And when you told me that your best friend was sick, I wanted to hold your hand. And when you told me about the Rejects, I wanted to hug you. I wanted to hug all of you. Even fucking Robbie Malcolm. I didn't have friends like that when I came out. You were lucky."

Cat feels sickeningly gooey, like her insides have turned into candy and kitten gifs. "You could have, you know. Held my hand. Or hugged me. Either."

"There's kind of a statute of limitations on the journalist source thing. It's doesn't last forever."

"Well, I'm pretty patient," Cat says. "I mean, actually, no, I'm terrible at being patient. But maybe I could try."

Casey takes a deep breath and says, "But."

There's always a but. Adulthood is just a string of buts, like an iron fence between you and all of the things you want in the world. "What?"

"You live in L.A., Cat. I've tried long-distance. It doesn't work. L.A. might as well be Mars. Also, my therapist, she says I need to like myself before I can expect someone else to like me."

"Well, you should fire her," Cat says.

"You think?"

"Yeah. I absolutely hate myself, and chicks fall in love with me all the time."

Casey twists the silver spiral of her notebook. Blushing has revealed a whole new set of freckles on her forehead and neck. Cat looks down at her phone again. It isn't Gabrielle's most recent text that catches her eye now. Instead, it's the one before. Cat reads it in full just before her phone dies in her hand.

Then you should go out and find her.

"What if I didn't live on Mars, though?" Cat asks. "What if I was closer?"

Casey looks like she has questions, and Cat is ready to answer them. But then Dash bursts out onto the deck, startling both of them. "Is Robbie out here?" he asks.

"Um," says Cat, "I don't think so."

"Shit," he says. "Goddammit." He's holding a sheet of paper, which flutters in a gust from the shore.

"Dash," she says. "What's that?"

"It's a note from Robbie."

The way Dash says that word: *note*.

"What's it say?" asks Cat.

Wade is at the open door now, along with Blair and Martin. Everyone's in their pajamas. The twins are behind them, pouring cereal in the kitchen. "What's going on?" says Wade.

"We really, really need to get to the Delaware Coastal Airport," says Dash.

"What's at the Delaware Coastal Airport?" asks Blair.

"It's where Robbie keeps his plane."

"The jet?" says Cat.

"No," says Dash. "The other one. The little one." His eyes skim the letter. "I think Robbie's about to do something really stupid."

Chapter 55

Rick Light is in charge of all aircraft coming in and out of Delaware Coastal Airport. This mostly means the banner planes. He's a big guy with a silver shag of hair and matching mustache. He's sixty-five years old. The top two buttons of his work shirt are open, and there's a pack of Marlboros in his chest pocket.

"Finally gonna fly this beauty, huh?" Rick asks. His voice echoes in the tin hangar.

"That's my plan," says Robbie. "Seems like a good day for it. Nice and clear."

"I folded your banner up for you." Rick toes a vinyl pile just to the side of the landing gear. It's the banner from Thursday: CAT, BLAIR, WADE, MARTIN, MICHELLE & KENNY: WELCOME TO THE BEACH! Only two letters are visible now: WE—. "Hope your pals enjoyed it."

"They did," says Robbie. "Thanks for the flyover. I appreciate it."

Rick nods and runs his hand along the propeller. "She's all ready for you. Gassed up and thoroughly gone through. Gave her a good wash, too, after I passed over your place on Friday."

If Robbie had another go at life, he thinks he might choose to do it like this: be a guy in charge of cool airplanes at a sleepy beach airport. "Thanks again, Rick," he says.

"You should give a run by Assateague Island," says Rick. "The horses are out sometimes in the morning. Fun to see them from the air."

"Maybe I'll do that."

"Come on by when you're back. We should have some donuts left. I'll heat up some coffee for you."

Robbie stands back and watches as Rick and one of the mechanics tow the plane onto the open pavement outside the hangar, and then Rick gives him a little wave, like a salute. It's a Piper PA-18 Super Cub, bright white with a red stripe. It's a tiny plane, about the size of an old Jeep with wings. Robbie climbs in, and it starts with a sputtering whirl.

It's been a while since Robbie has flown it. He learned a few years ago. At the time, it seemed like something he'd do more, and now, as he accelerates down the runway—the little engine shoving him back in his seat—he wishes he had.

He wanted to say goodbye to each of his friends last night. That would've been nice. Not *goodbye* goodbye, because he couldn't tell them what he was going to do. Just a hug would've been enough, though, a goodbye disguised as a "good night." But then Blair said what she said, and the night took a turn.

He did get to say goodbye to Cat, though, earlier. She wasn't quite awake, but it counted. She was lying next to him, rolled onto her side. Before easing out of bed and dressing in silence, he watched her. As softly as he could, Robbie moved the hair off her face and whispered, "Goodbye, Cat." And then, "Sorry about this," because he knew she'd take this the hardest.

For the others, he had to settle for stopping by their closed doors. He pressed his ear up to the wood of each. Silence across the board.

Stupidly, he didn't think through the logistics of actually getting to the airport, though. His plan had been to take the LeBaron. He'd keep the top down and smell all those smells of his youth, let his hair blow back, and then he'd park it behind the hangar for his friends or whomever to collect later. But then he couldn't find the keys. They were probably somewhere in Dash's room. Consequently, Robbie was forced to accept that the last car ride of his life wouldn't be in a cool little convertible but in his Range Rover—his office on wheels.

There's a lightness now, a feeling like weightlessness, as he's up in the air, aloft over sleepy Delaware. He veers hard, and the Piper responds, sending him toward the beach. There's a voice in Robbie's ear now—Rick's, from his headset. "Smooth sailing, Robbie. Enjoy yourself."

He's not alone up here. Robbie can see some floating dots in the distance along the horizon, each hauling a fluttering banner. He ignores them, though, like cars on a lonely highway. His ears fill and then pop, and as he notes the endless blue of the sky ahead, he considers how he feels. Sick, of course, but less so today than yesterday. Dr. Osborne told him that would happen, that it'd be like his sickness faded in and out. One day you're totally dying. The next day you're still dying, but dying a little less, it seems.

But the sky. *It's beautiful,* he thinks. Then he says it aloud. "It's beautiful."

Robbie angles the Piper, dipping the wing downward a few degrees for a better look at the approaching coastline. That's when he sees the LeBaron. There aren't many vehicles on the roads—mostly beer delivery trucks and buses—so it's tough to miss the flash of turquoise and the five little heads: a driver, a passenger, and three people crammed in back. Robbie can't tell who's driving, but they're going very fast.

Chapter 56

"Faster, Dash. Hit it, man!"

"What do you mean, hit it?" says Dash. "I *am* hitting it! This isn't a Ferrari, Wade! It's a thirty-year-old Chrysler!"

The car shimmies, like it might break apart beneath them.

"Well, shit! We have to get there!"

"We will!" says Dash. "We almost are! See?"

Wade looks at his phone. He's holding it open to Waze so Dash can see where they're going. Speeding desperately toward something while tracking yourself on a nav system is infuriating. How could they be two minutes away? They were four minutes away like ten minutes ago, and they're practically flying.

Wade shouts into the windy space between them. "How did you let this happen? Aren't you supposed to keep track of him? You're his bodyguard!"

"Don't be a dick, Wade!" Cat calls from the back. She's between Blair and the redheaded reporter. He suddenly can't remember her name. "This isn't his fault! He couldn't have anticipated this! *We* didn't! Just let him drive!"

Dash looks at Wade and then the road. The big man's face is all worry and pain.

"You're right!" says Wade. "Shit! I'm sorry. I just . . . I just can't believe this! Turn left up here!"

Dash barely brakes, and the LeBaron skids onto an access road. The reporter shouts and clutches the side of the car; her hair blows wildly, like fire.

"What if this is better, Wade?"

He looks back. It's Blair, holding her hair at the side of her neck.

"What?"

"This is clearly what he wants!" she says. "He planned it, right? He planned everything! Who are we to—"

"No!" says Wade.

"No?" she replies.

"Yeah, no! This isn't how it's going to be!"

"Why, though?" she asks. "Who says we get to be in charge of this?"

Wade is too desperate and heartsick to consider whether or not Blair is right. He thinks of him and Robbie playing videogames together in their basements, when it was just the two of them. Wade thinks of baseball games and beers and friendship and love and Paul McCartney and Ringo Starr and one painful tattoo, and he wants more of all of it.

Dash veers right, and the airfield is visible now. Little planes are scattered about.

"There's his car!" says Cat. "See!"

Robbie's Range Rover is parked next to a station wagon in a small lot beside a simple square building. Wade is up and out of the car before Dash fully stops, and now he's running toward the front door.

Chapter 51

"I just . . . I just push this thing here, right? This? Then I talk?"

It's Wade's voice in his headset. Robbie closes his eyes. "God-dammit, Wade," he whispers.

He can picture them so clearly, his friends, gathered around Rick's radio. He wonders if they've even gotten dressed. Rick probably offered them donuts.

"Robbie? Robbie, come in," says Wade. "Can you hear me? Robbie, come in."

He's some four thousand feet in the air now. "Hi, Wade," he says. "You don't have to say 'come in.' This isn't World War II. It's basi-cally just like a phone." A small burst of static crackles in his ears.

"Oh, okay," says Wade. "Well, what the hell are you doing up there, man?"

Robbie squints at the sun. "Did Dash show you the note I left?"

"Yeah."

"That pretty clearly lays out what I'm doing up here."

"You can't," says Wade. "Not like this. This isn't right."

Robbie can't help but take exception. Because *this* is perfect. He'll float above the shoreline for a while. Then, he'll turn out toward the ocean. He'll watch the fuel gauge. He'll fly and fly until the red warning light glows and the engine sputters and stalls. He'll just drift away. He won't feel a thing.

"Robbie?" says Wade. "Are you there?"

"How would you prefer I do it, Wade?"

"I'd prefer you *didn't* do it."

"I've run the numbers," Robbie says. "Months of pain. Wasting away. Dying in some bed." Another crackle. "I think I'd rather cut my losses."

"Robbie, are you okay?" It's Cat's voice.

"Yeah, Cat, I'm fine. This is . . . this is fine. Don't worry about me, okay? I've thought this through."

"Dude," she says. Just "Dude," though, nothing else. He's pretty sure she's crying. Some birds fly below the Piper, another V shape, like back in Dr. Osborne's office, and he thinks of letting them lead him to wherever they're going.

"You're just scared, Robbie," says Wade.

"Of course I'm scared. It's scary, Wade."

"I get it," he says. "But you've got *us*. We can be scared together. We can be scared *with* you. This weekend. It was great, right?"

"It was," says Robbie. "I had a nice time."

"We did, too. I got a fucking tattoo, Robbie. Do you know how much that hurt? It's all pink and swollen."

Robbie looks down at his own arm, puffy still at the edges of each black letter. "It was worth it, though," he says. "Right?"

"Fuck yeah, it was," says Wade. "That's what I'm saying. It doesn't have to be the end. We can have *more* weekends. More music. More rides in that shitty car you bought us. More *days*, Robbie. There's more we can do. We can . . . we can live."

"But you're all busy, Wade. You aren't going to just—"

"Busy? What do you mean *busy*? Cat and I don't even have jobs. Blair works at home. We can be with you. Every day. Come back to Baltimore with me. You can hang out at my parents' place. They'd love to see you. You can tell my mom all about how you know Natalie Portman. My dad has a Peloton. Cat's coming back, too. She's done with California."

"It's true, Robbie," says Cat. "I'm coming back. Soon. Like, right away, I think."

"And Blair's just down in D.C. That's nothing. Forty-five minutes away."

"Hi, Robbie." It's Blair's voice now. "I'm here, too. And I love you."

Robbie breathes in.

"We all love you, Robbie," says Wade. "Even Dash, I think."

"Yeah, boss," Dash says. "I'm kind of pissed at you for sneaking out on me. You know you're not supposed to do that. But I *do* love you. As your head of security, I'm forbidding you from doing this."

Some chop in the air shakes the Piper; Robbie's hands vibrate on the yoke. He noses down, briefly testing the sensation of what it'd feel like to fall from the sky.

"My point is," says Wade, "I know you invited us here so you could say goodbye. But you gave us a fresh start, too. We're back. All of us. You managed to fix us, you rich dickhead. We're friends again. *Real* friends. I talked to Blair. I've been avoiding her for like six years, but I'm good now. I don't love her anymore. Well, I mean, I *do,* but not in a creepy, life-ruining way. And I really think I like Jane. I met her because of you, because of this weekend. And I want you to be here to see where that goes. And you should see Cat and this redhead girl. They're vibing like crazy. I think we *all* want to see where that goes."

"Um, my name is Casey, by the way," says Casey.

"Right," says Wade. "Sorry. Hi, Casey. I don't want to be awkward, but you and Cat are really cute together."

"Jesus, Wade," says Cat.

Robbie listens to them chatter at one another, his idiot friends. "Hello, Miss Green," he says. "Glad you could join us."

"Hi, Robbie," Casey replies. Her voice is even—a bit cold—because she still thinks people like him are as bad as war criminals, but it's nice that she's there. "I got your text. Not for nothing, but I really think I can write a better ending than this. Honestly, this is a little melodramatic."

Robbie is quiet, and so are they. There's just the hum of the

Piper. He pulls back on the yoke and feels himself lift again, up over the horizon line. No clouds, just blue. It's been lonely to live the way that he's lived: driven but aimless, rich but wanting. And now, sick. He's not alone, though. That's clear. These people— these voices in his ear. He loves them, and they love him. "But I'm gonna die, Wade," Robbie says. "There's nothing we can do about it."

"I know you are," Wade says. "But not today."

And Wade's right. He isn't. Still, though, Wade keeps talking. "This is your sad song, man," he says. "You just . . . you just gotta make it better."

Static. The propeller spins almost invisibly in front of him. Wind and passing pockets of gentle turbulence. His own pulse beats in his ears. "Wade?" says Robbie.

"Yeah?"

"Did you just quote 'Hey Jude' over an airplane radio to try to get me to not kill myself?"

"I guess I did," he says. "I'm bros with Paul McCartney now, so I'm probably gonna be doing things like that a lot."

"Okay. Now I'm *definitely* crashing this thing into the ocean. Goodbye, everyone."

Wade laughs gently in Robbie's ears. It sounds like he might be crying, but Robbie can't tell for sure. "You're not ready yet, Robbie," he says. "Well, maybe *you* are. I don't know. But this isn't just about you. It's about us. And *we* aren't ready. Not even close. So, please. Seriously. Can you come back?"

January

Living with your parents when you're in your thirties isn't ideal. At minimum, it means something has gone wrong. A plan awry. Expectations, realistic or otherwise, unmet. While this is certainly the case for Wade, he has to admit, the last few months have actually been really nice.

At his parents' place in northern Baltimore, he's eaten better than he has in years. Salads. Fresh fruit. Legitimate meals, with silverware and sides, set out on the table each night around six-thirty. He's sleeping normal, adult hours, too, and he's working out regularly for the first time since college. It's not like he's over at the CrossFit gym on Key Highway flipping tractor tires and screaming at cement walls like a lunatic, but he's splitting time with his dad on the Peloton, doing some push-ups, and running a few times a week. Cat helped him pick out a pair of running shoes, and she introduced him to all the breathable running gear people wear now, like air-conditioned silk.

"Do you think this shirt's too nipply, though?" he asked her before a 5K in September down in D.C. That's where Cat lives now. She'd signed him up for the race without telling him, along with Casey Green, who was visiting Cat from New York. Cat and Casey stood there in their matching ponytails assessing Wade's nipples.

"The running community is a pretty nipply bunch," Cat said. "Some dudes put Band-Aids over theirs. I don't know. Maybe try that."

"Wait, what?" he asked. "God, runners are weird."

Cat and Casey are so adorable together that you pretty much want to punch them right in their faces. Aesthetically speaking, their dual shortness works nicely, like they were designed to be together, but their personalities mesh well, too. There's a subtlety to their new, tentative pre-couplehood that Wade appreciates. That's what Cat calls them; they're a pre-couple, which means they're lying low for some indeterminate amount of time and pretending not to be crazy about each other. Occasionally, Wade will catch some small show of affection—interlocked pinkies beneath the table or a gentle hand across a lower back—and he'll seize on it like an obnoxious big brother. "Get a room, you two. Jeez."

"We're still figuring it out," she told Wade a few weeks ago.

Cat wasn't specific about the "it" in that sentence. Maybe she was talking about the distance—all those Amtrak bills piling up. Or maybe it was the job thing. Casey is still at *HypeReport,* and Cat is working for National Geographic in D.C. Robbie didn't get her the job. Nobody did. Turns out she's a wonderful producer and an absolute ninja in interviews.

"Where do I see myself in five years? Hmm, probably two promotions in by then, honestly."

By not crashing himself into the Atlantic Ocean last summer, Robbie was able to continue offering his help to Blair, Cat, and Wade. For Cat, this included assistance with IVF treatments. She politely declined, though. "For now, I'm just gonna live," she said. "My uterus isn't going anywhere."

FOR THE RECORD, ALTHOUGH WADE is living at home and using his dad's Internet exercise bike and eating wonderful organic food, he isn't being a total freeloader. Wade is proudly contributing to the family in many ways. He mowed the lawn all summer, raked leaves in the fall, and he drags the recycling buckets down to the curb every Wednesday night for Thursday-morning pickup. These are all things Wade also did when he was thirteen years old, so it's not exactly a sign of great personal growth, but still, it's important to help out.

He watches Orioles and Ravens games with his dad, and they listen to music together. A lot of it. Wade hooked his dad up with a SiriusXM account, which gives him twenty-four-hour access to The Beatles Channel. It's not vinyl, of course, but it'll do.

"Did you know Ringo wasn't the original drummer?"

"Yeah, Dad, I know."

Wade goes to the grocery store and runs errands for his mom, and he's joined her book club. He's the only person under sixty, and the only guy. He pays his parents a thousand dollars a month in rent, which is reasonable for a home in the Baltimore suburbs with no visible water stains on the bathroom ceilings. He helped his mom light the oven's pilot light last week and managed not to blow himself up.

As far as money goes, Wade has been working full-time at a bookstore–slash–coffee shop near Johns Hopkins called Bird in Hand. His experience as a onetime novelist and a former barista and a current hipster and an overall nerd makes him ideal for the job. Additionally, if all goes well, some more money might be coming in soon.

Next week, Brandon Ross, Wade's agent, will begin shopping a new Wade Stephens manuscript. This one is a little different from his others. It's a children's book, the first of what Wade hopes will be a series. It's called "Uptown Squirrel," written by Wade Stephens and illustrated by Blair Harden. Along with the completed first book, Brandon will include a proposal for several follow-ups: "American Squirrel," "Big Squirrels Don't Cry," "Where My Squirrels At," "Fat Bottomed Squirrels," and "Squirrel, You'll Be a Woman Soon."

"I mean, holy shit, these things practically write themselves!"

Brandon shouted that last week when Wade and Blair spoke with him on a conference call. "You have any idea how many pop songs have the word *girl* in the title? You two are freaking geniuses!"

"Well, I wouldn't say *geniuses*," said Blair. She's not used to industry hyperbole yet. As a veteran in the field, Wade knows enough to know that you should enjoy praise while it lasts, because it often doesn't last for long.

"I'm serious," said Brandon. "We'll be going to auction for sure. Kids' books are gold mines. I showed Duncan the manuscript, and he about shit his little pants. He loved it—especially the pictures, Blair. I definitely want to get one of the movie agents on this. And we could do an album, too—easily. Like Kidz Bop, but with squirrels. Maybe we could consider other rodents, too. Maybe a whole band! Cute animals playing music and singing and shit!"

Wade didn't have the heart to tell Brandon that he was dangerously close to turning their little squirrel pun project into Alvin and the Chipmunks. Whatever happens, though, Wade is writing again, and Blair is making art. It's not the kind of writing or art they imagined for themselves, but here they are, and work is work.

"Should I be nervous that your new business partner happens to be one of the most beautiful women I've ever met?"

Jane asked him this recently. He and Blair had just finished a brainstorming session over FaceTime. Some of Blair's "Uptown Squirrel" sketches were scattered on the couch. "Nah," he replied. "We're just old friends."

Unlike Cat and Casey, Wade and Jane aren't *figuring out* anything, nor are they *pre*-coupling. They *have* figured it out, and they're all in, both of them. They take turns visiting each other whenever they can. When she's in Baltimore, Jane and Wade hang out with Wade's dad in the den and listen to the Beatles. She likes to say things like "I think Paul did his best work with Wings," just to annoy them. Wade's dad helped Jane get the brakes on her Hyundai fixed, so it doesn't sound like a vampire being murdered every time she stops now.

"You should try not to screw this up. She's a good one."

"Yeah, Dad, I know."

This upcoming spring, Wade will be moving to Fenwick Island officially. Jane will keep running Viking Golf, of course, because she enjoys it, and last summer was the business's best in decades. Wade still needs to decide how he's going to fill his time once he gets there, though. There's no hurry, of course, because Robbie left him five million dollars.

ALONG WITH CO-OWNERSHIP OF VIKING Golf and the house on Fenwick Island, that's how much Robbie left the Rejects: five million dollars each. "It's a good number," he told them. He actually said that, *a good number.* "Just enough to not *completely* ruin your lives."

Wade could feel guilty about so much unearned good fortune. They all could. Or they could just accept it and someday try to do something worthwhile with it. If they do well, maybe they really can do good. As far as his owning 33 percent of Viking Golf, though, Jane has made it very clear that she will not be calling Wade "boss" anytime soon.

ROBBIE PASSED AWAY LAST WEEK.

Even when you see it coming, when it announces itself well in advance, death is like a sudden explosion, leaving you shell-shocked and dazed in its aftermath. It hits him now, that grief, as he leans heavily on the pew in front of him.

None of them really consider themselves Catholic anymore, but Robbie's mom does, and she wanted his funeral here, at the Baltimore Basilica, a church downtown. Wade looks up at the stained glass and thinks of playing horse with Robbie in Wade's driveway. Their games lasted for hours, because they were both awful. He thinks of helping Robbie learn to drive and listening to him talk about math. Math, math, math.

They're all in a pew together, three rows from the front: Jane and Wade, Dash, Cat and Casey, and Blair and Martin with the twins. As far as funerals go, it's the most surreal Wade has ever attended. He's sad, of course; they all are, standing silently together; but it's hard to focus on sadness, because every time he turns his head he notices a different famous person wearing black.

That's the thing about rich people: apparently they all know one another.

He recognizes some of them from the news, like financial reporters and anchors. A few politicians stand with grim-faced security details. Natalie Portman is here with her startlingly handsome husband. Wade's mom, who's a few rows back, keeps staring at her. Michael Bloomberg showed up, and he somehow looks even shorter than he did when Wade and Robbie saw him at Yankee Stadium. Bono is short, too, it turns out—surprisingly so—but cool-looking. The rock star removed his sunglasses when the ceremony started, which is something.

Some fellow CEOs and hedge fund monsters lurk about, too. Wade doesn't know who they are, but he can just tell they're somebody, the way rich people exude being rich. Bill and Melinda Gates sit with Bill Clinton, sans Hillary. Robbie's ex-girlfriends are here, settled far away from one another. All in all, not a bad showing. Wade keeps craning his neck, looking for Paul or Ringo, but neither seems to be here, which is just as well. For Wade, crying in front of the Beatles once is plenty for a lifetime.

Jane is on Wade's left; Blair is on his right. "You're way prettier than Natalie Portman, by the way," he whispers into his friend's ear.

"*Shhh,*" Blair tells him. But then she mouths, "Thank you."

Blair and Martin gave Wade and Jane a ride here in Blair's new Chevy Tahoe. The minivan, thank God, is long gone. The twins have brought their squirrel pictures. Michelle is holding hers to her chest, and Kenny keeps looking up at the closed coffin in front of the altar.

BACK ON FENWICK ISLAND LAST May, in Cat's room after she threw up, Robbie told them all what he feared would happen if he had a normal wake. He described a dismal version of the group going out together and then never seeing one another again. He was right about a few things. Last night, after the visitation, the Rejects and their entourage *did* in fact go to the Mt. Washington Tavern, like he'd predicted. It wasn't dismal at all, though, and certainly not the last time they'd see one another. They drank and laughed. They talked about the future—their individual futures and their collective future as friends. They planned to meet annually in Fenwick Island, every Memorial Day weekend. A new tradition forged.

Blair and Martin talked about taking a trip to Europe. They looked happy—Blair especially. Martin had his arm around her most of the evening. They spoke in the royal we, the way couples do. We're doing Pilates together, if you can believe it. We're trying to get Kenny to stop calling his penis his ding-dong. That kind of thing.

When the dust settled after the living wake, Blair stopped short of ruining Mr. McGee's life and career. She did, however, make things very awkward for him by telling the other mothers from school what was going on. She knew each of them well enough to invite them to coffee. Blair told Wade how sad each of the women was. This made Blair sad, too, but also grateful. Like her, they'd pinned their hopes on something that was simply never going to happen.

"I thought he was my do-over," Blair told Wade. "Turns out I had to make my own do-over."

After an initial few drinks at the Mt. Washington Tavern, Cat bet Dash that he couldn't bench-press her, so he did just that, right there atop a damp table. The entire bar cheered as the giant lifted Cat ten times, with no visible effort. Later, Cat and Casey were nestled on barstools, leaning into each other. When Casey got up to go to the restroom, Wade squeezed in next to Cat.

"You know what?" he said. "I like you two together. Even if you're just pre-together."

"I guess she's not so bad," said Cat. She was wearing a big black sweater. "It's nice to be with someone who wants to be with me. It's a refreshing change of pace."

Casey's article about Robbie came out earlier this week: "The Rise, Death, and Redemption of Robbie Malcolm." It was all-encompassing. The origins of the Baltimore Prep Rejects. The ugly viatical settlements that paved the way to billions. The charitable donations he made and the causes he spearheaded in an attempt to repent. His friends from high school who talked him down from his own airplane over the ocean. Casey also reported that Robbie tracked down as many of the families involved in the settlements as he could before he died. He reimbursed each of them, with considerable interest, and he set up numerous educational trusts and healthcare funds for their descendants. To judge by the reaction to Casey's article in the Twitterverse, some feel it's too little too late. For others, though, it just further feeds Robbie's legend. Good guys and bad guys, heroes and villains. It's all a matter of perspective.

Wade had to raise his voice to be heard over the Tavern's music system. "She's better than *not so bad,* and you know it."

He and Cat both looked over at the ladies' room, from which Casey had just exited. She waved at the group and asked if they wanted another round, which, of course, they did.

"Okay, yeah, she's pretty great," said Cat. "It's the hair, right?"

"I think she thinks you're pretty great, too," said Wade.

"Of course she does," said Cat. "What girl wouldn't wanna be with me?" It was typical Cat, talking shit to deflect a compliment, but her eyes teared up. Wade wasn't sure why; maybe she was thinking of Robbie. Whatever it was, Wade took advantage of her vulnerability to shove her off her barstool and steal what was left of her beer, because Wade really is her obnoxious big brother, and he will be for the rest of their lives.

AFTER THE FUNERAL, THE REJECTS go the cemetery. It's cold and sad, and everyone huddles together as best they can. The priest doesn't know Robbie, which is to be expected, so he continues leaning heavily on things he's clearly googled. Robbie's parents, long divorced, stand side by side.

And then, when it's over, like a party breaking up, attendees scatter, walking slowly back to their cars. Wade hugs Blair and then Cat; he can feel them both shivering under their coats. The twins are obviously freezing their littles asses off, but they're being good sports about it.

"I was wondering if the three of you might want to take a ride," says Dash. He's talking to Blair, Cat, and Wade.

"Um, to where?" says Cat.

"I'd rather not say just yet." Dash rubs his gloved hands together. "And if it's okay, maybe it's just the four of us?"

A moment passes in which logistics are contemplated.

"Casey, Jane, you two wanna come with me and the twins?" asks Martin. "Donuts, maybe? Plenty of room in the new car."

Moments later, Dash and the remaining Rejects are heading north, in yet another Cadillac Escalade. Wade sits up front, Blair and Cat in the back. The interior is warm, the seats are soft, and everyone is mildly hungover from last night and tired from being sad, so no one speaks for a while. Outside the closed windows, the view goes from urban to suburban to rural.

It's hillier out in the country than it is in Baltimore. After maybe twenty minutes of driving, the road crests high, giving them a view of surprisingly vast winter farmland. Dash hits the turn signal at the beginning of a white picket fence. A sign welcomes them to Free State Stables. "And here we go," says Dash.

"Where are we?" Blair whispers, more to herself than to them.

"One last little surprise from Robbie," says Dash.

He parks the Escalade in the grass next to a blue pickup and points to a long single-story barn. "We're going in there." A few horses wearing thick blankets watch from a penned-in meadow. Blair and Cat are holding hands, two shivering friends.

Inside, it's about as deluxe as a barn can be, clean and heated. Two beautiful horses stick their heads out from bays. Their enormous eyes are calm but focused.

"Hey, everyone," says Dash, talking to the horses. "Where's my girl at?"

He leads them to the last bay, at the back of the barn. Blair, Cat, and Wade look over a low-slung door and discover a small brown cow standing next to a pile of hay. The animal sniffs the air. A few straws of hay stick from her mouth as her nostrils flare.

"There she is," says Dash.

"Oh," says Blair. "She's pretty."

"Everyone, meet Helen." Dash makes a kissy noise and the cow takes a tentative step forward. "Come on, sweetie. Don't worry, they're friends." Helen takes a few more steps and eases her head over the door. Blair and Cat pet between her brown eyes.

"Hello, you," whispers Cat. "You're little for a cow."

"She is, right?" says Dash. "This is what cows look like when they aren't being fattened up."

Helen nudges Blair's hand, leaning in for more love.

"She likes you," says Dash.

"Who does she belong to?" Cat asks.

His friends haven't caught on yet, but Wade has, and he knows that he's about to cry. It's Helen, the escaped cow from Iowa, safe and sound now in a big, warm barn in Maryland. "I don't believe it," he says.

Dash laughs. "She belongs to *you*. All three of you, actually."

"Oh, Robbie," says Blair.

Dash scratches Helen's big ear. "She's a lucky girl."

Acknowledgments

Every time I write one of these lists there are more and more people to thank. There's a lesson in that, I suppose. What often seems like such a solitary activity is actually anything but.

Ryan Effgen has been a wise early reader of all my novels, and he was particularly helpful this time. So, too, were my good friends at the Fiction Writers Co-op.

Randy McAlpine and my wife, Kate Norman, had the misfortune of having to try to help me understand how the financial industry works. I called Randy a couple of years ago and asked him, "What's something a rich person could do that's legal but really, really shady?" He didn't disappoint. Dave Dundas helped me build a fictional art studio, and Amanda Ozarowski offered some much-needed assurance when my confidence was at its shakiest.

Jesseca Salky continues to be a wonderful agent and friend. Her guidance through so much turbulence this past year has been a lifesaver. And thanks to the rest of the team at SLM, especially Rachel Altemose.

I simply couldn't ask for a better publisher than Ballantine Books. Thanks to Jennifer Hershey, Kara Welsh, and Kim Hovey for their support. To Luke Epplin, Diane Hobbing, Melissa Sanford, Colleen Nuccio, and Jesse Shuman for working so hard on my behalf. To Mimi Lipson for her copyediting skills. To Jessie Bright for her fantastic cover design. And, of course, to my editor,

Anne Speyer. This is the first time I've had an editor on board from the initial idea to the final draft, and it was such a great experience. Anne's talent and intelligence are all over this book.

I'd also like to thank Peter Asher, Chris Carter, and Geoff Lloyd, all of whom have utterly delightful programs on The Beatles Channel on SiriusXM. Their knowledge, anecdotes, and love for the Beatles were a constant source of inspiration as I wrote this.

To everyone listed above, as Ringo would say, peace and love.

About the Author

MATTHEW NORMAN lives in Baltimore, Maryland, with his wife and two children and holds an MFA from George Mason University. His previous novels include *Last Couple Standing*, *We're All Damaged*, and *Domestic Violets*.

thenormannation.com
Twitter: @TheNormanNation
Instagram: @thenormannation
Find Matthew Norman on Facebook

About the Type

THIS BOOK was set in Bembo, a typeface based on an old-style Roman face that was used for Cardinal Pietro Bembo's tract *De Aetna* in 1495. Bembo was cut by Francesco Griffo (1450–1518) in the early sixteenth century for Italian Renaissance printer and publisher Aldus Manutius (1449–1515). The Lanston Monotype Company of Philadelphia brought the well-proportioned letterforms of Bembo to the United States in the 1930s.